Heroe Don't Cry

Denise Buckley

Strategic Book Publishing and Rights Co.

Strategic Book Publishing and Rights Co.
12620 FM 1960, Suite A4-507
Houston, TX 77065
www.sbpra.com

ISBN: 978-1-62516-419-3

Typography and page composition by J. K. Eckert & Company

I dedicate this book to my children,

Kevin, Gregory, Caron, and Deborah,

and their families,

with all my love.

About the Author

Denise Buckley was born near Manchester and now lives in the English Lake District. She has been writing for a number of years, but only started writing her first novel in 2011, published in 2012: *Yesterday's Tomorrows: The Dark Secret*. This novel, *Heroes Don't Cry*, is the sequel. The author is married and has four children, seven grandchildren, and two great-grandchildren.

Preface

Growing up in World War II near Manchester was an experience. Everyone helped each other, and things were never thrown away, just passed on to someone else or recycled. My parents both worked in the cotton mill, and I had two older sisters. I knew all my neighbours and had respect for my elders. We were taught right from wrong and our playground was the street. Although money was short, I can never remember feeling that I missed anything, as everyone was the same, but we appreciated everything we had. I had a happy childhood with a close family.

Acknowledgments

A big thank-you to Peggy Savage, my friend and fellow author, who has been a big influence in my life. Also to Maggie Norton, who is always there for help and advice.

Chapter 1

The sound of enemy planes overhead sent a chill down Ruth's spine. Every time she heard them, she felt the same. *Would they get it this time?* The Anderson shelter was cold and damp, and the paraffin heater didn't give them much warmth for a cold December night. They didn't have much protection, either, if they had a direct hit, but it was their best bet. She looked at her son Jonathon. He was eighteen and waiting for his call-up papers to join the war. It was frightening.

"Do you want the last drop, Jonathon?" Ruth shook the flask she held in her hand.

"No thanks. You have it, Mam. I think Dad's asleep." As if to prove him right, a gentle snore could be heard from Alfred.

Ruth tried to act as normal as she could and keep calm, but it wasn't how she felt. Time passes so quickly, and it didn't seem that long ago when Jonathon was off to school for the first time in his little short pants. He was a lovely child with his blond, curly hair and angelic looks. His temperament was not like his father's…not yet, anyway, and she hoped that would continue. She looked at both girls asleep in the cot they shared. Poor Shirley was ten years old, with her knees up under her chin. There would have to be some changes made for her in this shelter, as she would be unable to sleep like that soon. Then there was Jessie. Little Jessie was two years old, happy and contented, and didn't know what the war meant. If they had known the war was imminent, then maybe Jessie would never have been born, but that would have been sad. Last of all was Alfred, her husband—second husband—father of her two girls who now shared her life.

They sat in silence for a while except for the activity going on not far away. They heard the enemy planes going over, and it sounded as if there were many of them. It was a threat in their daily life that she could do without. This war was going on too long; they'd all had enough now. After taking a quick peek outside, she could see the skies looking red with fire. Ruth sipped the last of the tea from her cup. She kept her thoughts deep inside as she listened for the all-clear siren. When it eventually came, Ruth sighed with relief. They had been spared for another day, but who could know for how long. She gathered everything she could together.

"Alfred, wake up." Ruth nudged him awake. "The all-clear's gone. Come and help me with the children."

Alfred got to his feet and, going over to the cot, lifted Shirley.

"Come on, sleepy head. It's time we went back inside."

Shirley moaned, but stayed asleep as Alfred carried her up the garden path to the back door.

Jonathon picked up Jessie from the cot and followed his dad into the house, while Ruth carried the basket with the flask.

"I'll come back for the bedding, Mam. Just leave it there."

"It'll wait until morning, son. Let's all get to bed."

Ruth dumped everything in the kitchen. The fire had died down, and there was only a glow left in the grate. It felt cold now in the usually cosy kitchen. The holly they had collected the previous day seemed to mock her as she placed her flask and basket on the table covered in a chenille cloth. Ruth looked around the room. It didn't seem right with the Christmas decorations, poor as they were. The paper chains that hung across the room, made so carefully by Shirley and Jessie, made her smile when she thought of the mess they made, but it did make them happy doing it. How could the enemy come on a bombing trip now? They didn't seem to care that there were children who were going to die—and at Christmas. No, it wasn't right. Hitler had a lot to answer for. This war was tiring, too. If they weren't bombed in their home, they were going to die of exhaustion. Locking the back door, she made her way upstairs again. Ruth tucked the children up in bed, but found it difficult to go back to sleep when she, at last, lay down. She couldn't help but think about the poor people who were bombed that night and would be without their dear ones and a home, and she tossed and turned until fatigue took over.

They all got up later the following morning...not too late, but late enough to make Alfred rush around to open up the business next door for the workers. It was Christmas Eve, and there was much to do. Ruth hurried the breakfast and rushed the girls so she could take them with her to do the shopping for the things they would need over the Christmas holiday.

"This Hitler has a lot to answer for," Shirley muttered as she quickly washed and dressed.

Ruth smiled to herself, as she realised her daughter had picked up something she often said.

Ruth's thoughts returned to the last war. She was courting Billy then. Dear Billy, he was a lovely man and husband. It seemed a lifetime ago, and so much had happened since. There was a time when she never thought she would become a mother, but now she was a mother of three.

Alfred and Jonathon went to the other half of their property, the printing business, and started work. Ruth dressed Jessie in her warm coat and hat, checked that Shirley was wrapped up well, and then, placing Jessie in her trolley, she picked up her basket and pushed the trolley to Mary's shop, with Shirley tagging along. She hadn't seen her sister Mary for a while, so if she could possibly join her, it would be nice to have a chat over a cup of tea before she picked up the shopping.

Barbara, her niece, was helping her mother in the shop, so Mary took a well-earned break. They'd been busy, and Mary looked tired.

"Are you okay, Mary? Did you get much sleep last night?"

"Not really. How are you managing with this war?" Mary pushed a plate of biscuits towards Ruth. "It's frightening, isn't it? And I'm worn out." Ruth declined the biscuits, but the children both took one and sat crunching them.

"It's the children I'm afraid for. At least we've had some life."

"And hopefully we'll have much more. We're not too bad here, Ruth. Now, Manchester…"

"I know. I feel sorry for them."

"I think they got hit badly last night. From what I hear, it was blitzed. Have you heard anything?" Mary asked.

"It looked bad. The sky was red. There must have been a lot of fire. You never know what's going to happen from one day to the next."

Mary gave a sigh of relief. "I'm just glad we don't live near the wagon works anymore in Dukinfield. They're always trying to hit that."

"They haven't managed it yet."

"It doesn't mean they won't."

"It's freezing in the shelter, isn't it? Or is yours warm? I know ours isn't." Ruth shivered at the thought.

"It doesn't matter how cosy it is. It's not like being in your own bed, Ruth."

"That's true."

"Are you still coming over tonight? I was thinking of making a potato pie."

"That's tempting, Mary, but I don't think so. It's a bit dangerous just now to be away from home after last night. We just don't know what Adolf has in mind. Besides that, there are things to sort out." Ruth gave the children a sly look. "You know what I mean? Father Christmas will be coming, so I'll need to be prepared."

"I know what you mean. Never mind, we'll postpone it until New Year. It may have quietened down by that time."

"And I won't be so busy. You come over to us, Mary, and I'll make a rabbit pie."

"Good, that'll do it. I like your rabbit pie, and we haven't had one for a while. We'll see how things go."

Ruth took the girls to Arcadia, the co-op. Father Christmas was there in his grotto, and Ruth asked the girls if they wanted to go to see him. Shirley declined; she said she was too old, but Jessie was excited and couldn't wait for her turn. She was given a game and looked forward to getting home to play with it.

That night the family awoke to the sirens.

"Not again," Jonathon muttered under his breath. It was a chilling sound—wails that would penetrate any dream and make you jump awake. He could hear the sound of his mam in the kitchen and dad waking up the girls. Dad, whom he always called Dad because he was the only one he'd ever known, was going through the routine. They always went through it step by step, in a quick panic, but thoroughly, even though they were always in the shelter when the enemy planes came over. After, he could hear his mam making a flask of tea and dad preparing to take his half-sisters to the Anderson shelter in the back garden.

"Jonathon, are you awake?" Ruth called.

"Coming," he answered in return.

Jonathon swung his legs out of bed, slipped on his coat and shoes, and went to help with his younger sisters. He went into the kitchen and found his mam checking the list on the cupboard door...again.

BEFORE I GO TO BED

1. Turn off the gas at the main.
2. Leave some water in the bath.
3. Fill a bucket and leave it handy with a bucket of sand or fine earth.
4. Leave additional clothing with a friend, as a further precaution.
5. Put a pair of outdoor shoes and warm coat by my bed for sudden emergencies. Keep a bag packed with necessities I may need and have my gas mask ready.

His mam knew what the paper said; she'd looked at it often enough. The list was issued by The Ministry of Information, and although it was a necessity, it drove Jonathon mad. His mam swore by it, though, and they had to check the directions whenever they heard the sirens.

Jonathon picked up the bag that contained the bedding for the cot, and they silently left the house, carrying their necessities, and walked up the garden path. It was dark, and they daren't shine a light. They could use a torch, but when the enemy were imminent, they preferred not to. Jumping down into the shelter, he gave a helping hand to Shirley and Mam, while his dad held Jessie in his arms. Jonathon watched as his dad carefully climbed down to join them. They put down the bags and emptied the bedding into the cot and quickly prepared it.

"Good thing I've aired them today," Mam said as his dad placed Jessie in the cot and Shirley got in at the opposite end and lay with her knees bent. The sirens stopped, and they listened intently. The adults sat on hard-back kitchen chairs as there wasn't much room in the shelter, and Dad lit the paraffin stove that stood in the corner.

"Let's hope we're not in here for long," whispered Dad. "I'm already missing my bed."

There were a few minutes of snatched sleep, and then the droning sound of enemy aircraft was heard overhead. The planes seemed as if they were passing over, but they knew to wait for the all clear before they moved. They listened to the whining sounds of the bombs dropping and the explosions that followed. They didn't know where they were being released, and the girls slept through it all. Dad put his head through the doorway of the shelter.

"Somebody's getting it," Dad whispered, "I can see the red sky again."

"Come in, Alfred, and thank goodness it isn't us. The children are far too young," Mam sighed with relief.

"Not this time we're getting it, but it could be us next," Jonathon answered. "But I bet Manchester is suffering again."

"Jonathon, don't talk like that. I don't need it, dear."

"We shouldn't get complacent, though, Mam."

"I know, Jonathon, but I don't want reminding."

After they emptied the flask of tea, they heard the sirens again for the all clear.

"C'mon, children, let's get you inside."

Shirley woke as her dad carried Jessie back into the house, so the rest of them followed him up the garden path. The sky had the same red glow as the night before, and they all climbed thankfully back into bed.

"Merry Christmas!" Alfred called to them.

"Some Christmas," Jonathon called back.

§§§§§

The evening paper on Christmas Eve had the headline "The Christmas Blitz: Heavy bombing in the city of Manchester." The article read: "The heaviest bombing raids have killed an estimated 684 people and injured 2,364. Manchester Cathedral, the Royal Exchange, and the Free Trade Hall were among the large buildings damaged. Two hundred and seventy aircraft dropped 272 tons of high explosive and 1,032 incendiary bombs; on the second night, 171 aircraft dropped another 195 tons of high explosive and 893 incendiaries. After the bombings, Nazi propaganda is declaring that the entire city had been burned to the ground."

It was a frightening thought and made them all realise how lucky they were—this time. Ruth worried about Jonathon; she worried about all of them surviving this war. It was much worse than the last. They didn't suffer the bombs like this before. The Germans were making their mark, but Ruth decided that if this were going to be their last Christmas, then they were going to enjoy it.

They all slept a little later Christmas morning, and when Ruth got up, she prepared the breakfast while Alfred lit the fire. The girls opened their presents that Alfred had left at the side of their bed, and as soon as the room warmed, Ruth shouted for them to come down. Jonathon chose to stay in bed a while longer.

"What would you like for your breakfast, girls? Would you like a boiled egg this morning?" Eggs were rationed, but this was a special morning.

"Please, can I have mine not too soft, Mam?" Shirley asked.

Ruth placed the eggs in a small pan and buttered the bread for the children, while they took down the socks that had been left on the string and were now full of little things like sweets, nuts, a tangerine, and a little chocolate, too. Ruth told them that under no circumstances were they to eat any of it until after breakfast, but after they pleaded, she allowed them one sweet each.

Alfred prepared the vegetables, while Ruth placed the chicken that was already plucked and cleaned in the roasting tin. Placing it in the oven in the fireplace along with a few potatoes, she asked Alfred to stoke up the fire to make sure they cooked. The black-leaded metal of the fireplace shone. It had been freshly painted that week and cleaned inside, ready for Christmas. Even the string under the mantelpiece that had their stockings pegged to it had been renewed. Ruth and Alfred allowed the girls to open the rest of their presents, and as soon as Jonathon came downstairs, they all opened theirs. Ruth knew this would probably be the last Christmas that Jonathon would spend with them for a while and tried to make it one to remember.

Alfred went to the local club with Jonathon for his Christmas pint, a family tradition, while Ruth and the girls prepared dinner. The vegetables were in the pan and placed on the shelf above the oven to cook, and the plates were warming at the other side of the shelf. The kettle was filled and placed back on its trivet over the fire, while the girls set the table and looked forward to the day. The smell from the cooking began to make them all hungry, and they waited patiently for the men to return for their Christmas dinner.

Ruth enjoyed staying at home with the girls, playing their new games and discussing their presents. Their order book for printing wasn't too bad, not as good as it was before the war, but it kept them going. Alan, who once worked for them through his apprenticeship, was now a sergeant in the army and fighting somewhere abroad. Alfred's brother Robert, his wife Beryl, and Marian, a young woman who lived nearby, also worked with them in their business. Jonathon hadn't been to grammar school as they would have liked, plus he had missed out on university. He seemed keen to become a doctor, but then changed his mind. Ruth never knew why for sure, but she was very disappointed. He said it was because he now preferred to go into business with his dad. Both Ruth and Alfred always had the rule that they would allow the children to make up their own minds, so they didn't persuade him otherwise. Ruth was sure that Jonathon chose the business because they didn't have another son to follow in Alfred's footsteps, but Jonathon insisted that was not the reason.

Jonathon worried about leaving. He worked hard in his dad's business and hoped they would manage without him, but his dad insisted they would be fine.

Chapter 2

On the following Saturday afternoon, Jonathon decided to go to the market to see if there was anyone around that he knew, to go to the pub for a drink. His friends would be in there, so he was sure of a laugh. He turned into a side street as a shortcut. The thump in the middle of his back made Jonathon stumble against the wall of the house he was passing. He turned around with his temper flaring.

"What was that for?" he gasped.

A man with dilated pupils and a nasty look disfiguring his face stood facing him. "Leave my wife alone."

Jonathon stood up to his full height and stared straight back at him. The man was angry, there was no disputing that, and Jonathon began to think…which of his conquests was this character's wife? He didn't know, and there were many women who threw themselves into his arms.

"I don't know what you're talking about,' he answered truthfully.

"Oh, don't give me that. You were seen kissing, with your arms around each other." The man spat out the words, and Jonathon breathed a sigh of relief. If that was all . . .

"That means nothing. A kiss can be a sign of friendship. Haven't you ever kissed a woman like that? If you haven't, then you've missed something in your life." The man made a grab for him, but Jonathon dodged his hand easily. This wasn't the first time he'd been accused of something like this, and he knew it wouldn't be the last. "For goodness' sake, man, stop showing yourself up."

This time the man hesitated, a little unsure of himself, thought Jonathon.

"If you're lying, then I'll be back…and I'll kill you." He walked off determinedly without a backward glance.

Jonathon watched him for a while to make sure he didn't change his mind and return for another punch. He must be more careful. Women! Hell, but they were a problem. He could see curtains twitching and knew the residents had heard the argument. He was embarrassed.

No sooner had the man disappeared, then three girls came round the corner and called to him. The threat forgotten for the moment, he stood and talked to them for a while. One of them flirted outrageously with him, but he decided to ignore it. He'd had enough of women for a while; they caused too many problems, and besides, he would be going to join up soon. After that, he decided to go back home.

Later in the evening after the family meal with his Mam, Dad, and sisters, he met a few friends and went into town. On Saturday evening, there were a number of people about. Although life could be difficult with a war going on, people got on with their lives, blackout or no blackout. They knew where the air-raid shelters were, and they were always aware that at any time, there could be a warning siren. Jonathon always kept a small torch in his jacket pocket for emergencies. Sometimes, people wondered if the shelters the government provided were as safe as they were made out to be. Because of this, some were quite willing to shelter in shop doorways or anything with a roof. Under the stairs of their homes was popular or in a cellar, if they had one.

One of the lads, Brian, suggested they go dancing at the local Palais, so they all made their way to the dance hall. There was no bar, so they sat on the balcony for a while and watched the dancers below. One of the girls stood out from the rest, and for a while, Jonathon watched her. Brian goaded him to go and ask her for a dance, but he declined. No women! He'd had enough. A little later, they went downstairs and had a few dances with a variety of girls, but the conversation was always the same.

"What's your name? Where do you work?" Jonathon felt bored with it all.

Jonathon's eyes turned back to the girl he watched earlier. She was dancing with a coloured man. His skin wasn't absolutely black, but he was very dark-skinned. He had seen the young man a few weeks before, obviously attractive to women, as he always had a bevy of girls hanging around him. Maybe he had friends or relatives close by, as Jonathon was sure he didn't live locally or he would have seen the man over the years. Jonathon didn't like the attention the man was giving this girl, so when the last waltz started, Jonathon couldn't resist the temptation any longer. He walked over to her before the other man had a chance.

"Can I have this dance, please?"

She nodded, and he led her on to the dance floor. The lights were dimmed, and he slid his hand around her waist as they began to waltz. She was as light as a feather and danced beautifully.

"Do you live near here?" *Here we go again,* he thought, *I'm asking the usual stupid questions,* although this time he found himself really listening for her answers.

"Dukinfield."

"Oh, good! My mother comes from Dukinfield. What's your name? She may know you."

"Ann Meredith," she answered.

Jonathon held her as closely as he dare. She smelled good, and they chatted. She was easy to talk to and had a husky sensual voice. He was enjoying the dance, but then the music stopped and she turned to walk away.

"Can I walk you home?" he asked.

"No.'

He was stunned. "Why?"

"I don't think I need to answer that, but I'm going home with friends."

"Why not me?" he asked again. This girl was a challenge, and she was a challenge worth taking on.

"Because—I don't want to," she said flippantly and walked away to join her friends again.

This didn't happen. Jonathon knew he was good-looking. Come to think of it, he didn't know why, as he'd seen a picture of his real dad, who drowned before he was born. He didn't look anything like him or Mam. His mother always wore a locket around her neck on a gold chain with his dad's worn-out photograph inside. She would often show it to him when he was a young lad, and he didn't look anything like him from what he remembered, not that he'd seen it for a while. Who wouldn't remember their dad's photograph? When he thought about it, he supposed he looked more like his mam's half-sister, Aunty Mary, than anyone else. Silly, really, but oh well! Jonathon watched the girl whom he now knew as Ann. There was something about her. She wasn't painted with the bright red lipstick and pink rouged cheeks, like a lot of girls. Ann had very little lipstick on. She didn't need it. Her smile was enough. It was wide and sincere. She had lovely teeth, too. Her hair was fair, nothing spectacular, but shiny and healthy looking. You couldn't call her a stunner like a few he had already dated, so why did she hold so much attraction for him—and why had she refused his offer to walk her home, he wondered?

The lads made fun of him when he told them he'd been refused. "Now you know what it feels like," Brian laughed.

All the way home, his thoughts were on Ann. Had she heard of his reputation? If people only knew that his reputation was mostly false. Sure, he liked girls and he was no goody-goody, but he wasn't a heartbreaker like they seemed to think.

He was met by his dad when he arrived back home.

"Manchester got it last night. There were a lot of people killed. I suppose we should count our blessings, but it's a shame for them in Manchester."

"How do you know?"

"It was on the wireless."

Jonathon thanked his lucky stars they lived in Ashton.

Going to sleep that night was difficult for Jonathon. He found it hard to accept that Ann didn't want him. What was the matter with him that she didn't like? Who the hell did she think she was anyway, Rita Hayworth?

§ § § § §

It was New Year's Eve, and Aunty Mary and Uncle Peter were coming to spend the evening with Ruth and Alfred and have a few drinks. Jonathon went out to meet his friends for the night at the Palais and left his sisters to join the adults when they brought out the playing cards.

Jonathon's friends were all waiting for him in the local pub. "Have you all got your tickets?" Jonathon asked, and they all nodded their heads.

"I know who you'll be looking for," Brian said with a wink.

Jonathon smiled. Brian was right; he did hope to see Ann again, and maybe she would allow him to walk her home tonight. He didn't like to be refused. He didn't like it at all.

Ann wasn't there, and Jonathon felt miserable. The others were dancing and having fun, while Jonathon sat quietly upstairs and watched everyone else. At times, he was joined by some girl or other, but he didn't feel very sociable, so they soon gave up on him. The ladies excuse me waltz started, and a girl came and asked him to dance, but he refused that one, too.

"Guess what, Jons?" Brian joined him and sat in the next chair.

"What?" Jonathon replied in a bored voice.

"I know where Ann is...you know, that girl you were fancying last week."

"Where?" Brian had his full interest.

"She's going away."

"When?" Jonathon asked.

"She's going on Thursday."

"Where's she going?"

"I don't know. Go and ask her friend yourself."

Jonathon watched the girl in question, but couldn't see the point of asking about Ann. After all, he was waiting for his call-up papers anytime. It was one of those things. Fate, they called it. Mam and Dad had told him about that often enough, but in his book, it was nothing other than the war and bloody Hitler.

Midnight came along when the lights went low and the counting began, and Jonathon slipped out of the Palais and went home. He couldn't face watching everyone kissing and having fun. He felt miserable. Whether it was because he'd missed out on Ann or because he knew he would be called up soon, he didn't know and didn't care. All he wanted was to get home.

He arrived home much earlier than his usual New Year's Eve night out, and the family was eating rabbit pie. They left their plates and wished him a happy new year, and then Jonathon helped himself to some pie before going upstairs to bed. The family went back to their game of Newmarket, and Jonathon could hear them enjoying themselves. *Marvellous,* he thought. *My kid sisters are having a better time than I.*

It was Jessie's third birthday on the second of January, so they all had a little party with the remains of the Christmas food. Jonathon knew in his heart that it could be a long time before he would be around for another birthday party, so he felt a little sad. He watched his family and hoped that one day he would be here to see all this again, as you couldn't count on anything in a war.

It was three weeks later that Jonathon heard the man who punched him was looking for him again because his wife was pregnant. The man knew that he himself wasn't the father, as he was a sailor and was at sea when she became pregnant, so he was out for the kill. Jonathon did see them both out together once, but avoided them. He knew he wasn't the father, so goodness knows where her husband had got that idea. He dreaded the confrontation that was in the cards. He didn't like to accuse the man's wife of telling lies, and would he be believed anyway?

Jonathon was relieved when he returned home and found his call-up papers had arrived. Now it was settled; he would join the Air Force. More than anything, he wanted to be a pilot, so he was keeping his fingers crossed. He had studied aircraft since the war began and had learned a lot from books, so with that knowledge, he hoped it would stand him in good stead.

It had been snowing, so he wrapped himself up and walked to his Aunty Mary's house. She had the day off from their shop, and she made him a cup of tea.

"So you're going to go to war just like your dad? I bet your mam is worried to death."

"I'm not going in the Army like my dad. I'm joining the Air Force."

"I believe so."

"Can you tell me anything about my dad, Auntie Mary?"

"Like what, Jonathon?"

"Why did he drown himself, and especially just before I was born?"

"Why don't you ask your mam?"

"I've tried, but she changes the subject."

"She loved your dad, so I suppose she still finds it painful."

"So why did he commit suicide?"

"There's really only your dad who could tell you that. I know he loved your mam."

"So why, I wonder?"

"I think his war wounds bothered him a lot, as sometimes, in fact quite often, he used a cane. He had a permanent limp, you know. He couldn't stand for long, and he found it very difficult finding a job."

"Do you think that's what it was?

"I suppose he would think he was a burden at times with your mam being the main bread winner, but I don't think for a minute that it bothered your mam. Who knows what goes through a man's mind to make him do something like that. All I know is that it almost killed your mam, and of course, that would have been the end of you, too."

"My mam says that you saved my life."

"We all helped each other. We had to, as times were hard."

Jonathon felt glad that he'd spoken to his Aunty Mary about his dad. It cleared up a lot of things, but he still wished he knew what made his father commit suicide. He couldn't understand him not wanting to see his only child. There must be more to it, and he hoped that one day, he would really get to know the reason.

Jonathon stopped in the shop on the way home to see Uncle Peter and his cousin Barbara, who helped in the shop after school. They had always been close, and sometimes he would take Barbara out if she had no one else to go with, and then make sure she arrived home safely. The shop was busy with customers, so he waited until they had a spare moment. Uncle Peter shook his hand.

"Make mincemeat of them Germans, Jonathon, and come home all in one piece."

When he hugged Barbara, she cried. "Take care, Jonathon. I'd hate anything to happen to you."

"Don't worry, Barbara, I won't let it. We'll have a real party when it's all over and I'm home again."

Barbara smiled. "Make sure of that."

"I will." Jonathon kissed her on the cheek and had another hug before he left. He waved his hand as he went through the door and noticed she was crying again.

Saying good-bye to his parents and sisters wasn't easy. An underlying thought was in all the adults' minds. They were aware that life was a big fat question mark. Not only could he be killed, but with the air raids, and only the Anderson shelter for protection in the back garden, they all knew they could get it anytime, too. They weren't foolproof; it could happen to anyone.

Going into the printer shop next door, he took a last look around. He would miss this place and those cups of tea his mother would bring through. There wouldn't be any of that where he was going. Hitler had a lot to answer for, but he would do his best to protect his country, whatever that entailed.

When he left to join the RAF, he hugged his mam, and when his dad offered his hand, Jonathon ignored it and hugged him, too. He gave Shirley a kiss on her cheek, and they laughed as she wiped it off. Jonathon picked up Jessie and kissed her on her cheek, too, but this time it wasn't wiped off, so he gave her an extra hug. She just looked at him with her big, blue, innocent eyes, and it was hard for him not to cry as he buried his head into her blonde curls. There were tears shed and not only by his mother, but his dad, too. Jonathon kept a brave face and wouldn't allow tears to show. As soon as he left the house, he released the tears and allowed them to run down his face. He wiped them away. He was a man—a bomber pilot, or so he hoped to be. He was going to help save his country…and heroes don't cry.

Chapter 3

Jonathon began his training. After tests and a medical exam, which he came through easily, he was enlisted as a pilot under training and placed on the reserve. It was something he had always dreamed about, and he couldn't believe his luck. He was sent to Babbacombe and soon found that there was a lot to learn before he became a pilot. As he wrote home later, with all the physical training, he felt fit and strong. Finally, he was proud to become a leading aircraftman. Only then was he allowed home on leave.

His mother cried and hugged him when she saw him in his uniform. "Oh, Jonathon, you look so smart. You've become a man, and I never even noticed before."

"Thank you very much!" Jonathon answered with a frown.

"Up, up." Jessie stood with her arms held high.

Jonathon picked her up and lifted her so that she could touch the ceiling, as she seemed to have a fascination for that. After, he was awarded with a big hug. His dad also gave him a hug, patting his back as he did it.

"Glad to see you, son. How has it gone?"

By the time he had brought them up to date, Shirley was home from school, and she threw herself into his arms.

"I've missed you, Jonathon. Will you take me to the pictures while you're home? There's a cowboy film on at the Roxy. Will you take me, please?"

"What do you want to go to the pictures with me for?" Jonathon asked.

Ruth smiled. "She wants to show you off to her friends. Shirley's proud of her big brother, especially now that he's wearing a uniform."

Jonathon wrapped his arm around her. "Is that right, Shirl?" Shirley nodded. "Okay, then," Jonathon agreed, and Shirley beamed back at him.

It felt good to be back in his very own bed, and Jonathon slept like a baby.

15

The following day, he went out with his friends. The company of his friends was something he'd missed, but two days later, Jonathon received a telegram to report to Wilmslow.

"That was a short visit, Mam. Let's hope the next one will be a bit longer."

Mam cried as she scolded him. "Take care, Jonathon, please. We want you home safely."

It was sad to be saying good-bye again, and so soon. There wasn't time to do the things he wanted to do, no time to see the people he'd like to.

Shirley was very disappointed when she learned that Jonathon had to go, as she hadn't had a chance to show him off to her friends, and that was important to Shirley, plus she never did get to see the cowboy film.

Jonathon almost always brought Shirley something back when he came home, but if only he'd bring her a banana, that's what she wanted more than anything—a banana, a nice big yellow fat banana. Once, a girl brought a banana into school, and Shirley was so envious. Secretly, she hoped that one day Jonathon would bring one home for her, and then she could be the centre of attention at school like the other girl had been. Bananas were a fruit she couldn't ever remember seeing, except for pictures, until she saw the one at school. *What did they taste like?* she wondered. Every night she ended her prayers with, "And please, God, bring me a banana."

Selected for flying training in America, Jonathon felt really pleased with himself. When he heard the news, he felt as if he was getting there at last. First, he must go to Scotland to embark on a ship for his journey. It was a pity he didn't see more of Scotland, as he had never been before. The ship was one of many, but theirs soon left the convoy and proceeded to Newfoundland. They had a boat drill wearing lifebelts to prepare for whatever fate threw at them. After Newfoundland, they were sent to Toronto, but only to pick up grey suits. The plan was for them to travel to the United States as civilian aeronautical students. It was a little awe-inspiring.

Georgia was the next stop, but it was a long journey. The best bit was having a few stops and being given fruit and cookies. It was a relief for them all when they arrived at the civilian flying school that was taken over by the U.S. Army Air Corps. Now they could wear khaki shirts and slacks and were treated like U.S. cadets from West Point. When on excursions into town, they wore their civilian clothes.

Jonathon was amazed at the food, as the Americans weren't involved with the war. Food was in short supply at home, but Jonathon soon learned to appreciate the American southern fried chicken, French fries, and pecan and pumpkin pies, but the iced tea was nothing like his mother made. He learned to eat with a fork and wore flying goggles around his neck. Goggles were no longer worn once they had flown solo.

He enjoyed the turkey and cranberry sauce with all the trimmings in November for Thanksgiving Day. It was a new experience, and the dance in the evening was enjoyable. For the first time, he was introduced to the jitterbug, and he had to admit that the English way of dancing was boring compared to the American jitterbug. They had a rugby match, and the locals that watched were surprised, as the participants wore no protective clothing.

Jonathon didn't feel happy at his attempts to fly, and his instructor must have felt the same. He didn't feel confident at all, but the flight commander still believed in Jonathon. He knew he was keen, so he returned him for further instruction. This turned out to be the right decision, as he passed the flight commander twenty-hour and forty-hour—and also the army sixty-hour—checks with no further problems. Jonathon was on his way.

Only 45 percent of them came through that rigorous course. They left there to start the next stage of training. It was exciting, but at the same time, they felt sorry to leave, as they had learned so much and been made really welcome.

Two days after dual flying, Jonathon went solo. Formation flying took place at night and through the day. On one daytime formation flight, the engine cut, and Jonathon had to use the hand pump to keep the aircraft flying. After their intensive training, it made them realise how important it had all been.

§ § § § §

Jonathon graduated and received his American wings and became honorary Second Lieutenant in the United States Army Air Corps.

"December 8, 1941—Japan at War: Honolulu and Pearl Harbor bombed by Japanese planes," the headlines screamed. Now there was a change in attitude. They were given a different uniform, and the Americans were now in the war. It was sad for them, but the English lads knew in their own mind that they had a better chance of winning the war with their involvement, plus it could end sooner.

Most of the lads declined an RAF Commission, so they were soon back in England for Christmas and sent to Bournemouth before they were allowed home. That's where he met Ann again, in a bar while on a night out with his friend Roger.

Fascinating, unreachable, and untouchable Ann, the girl who had really turned his head in Ashton, was here. He wanted to immediately take her in his arms, but he didn't want the embarrassment of her refusing him in front of the others. He just stood and looked at her with grateful pleasure, and the surprise must have shown in his face.

"Hello, friend, you're a long way from Ashton," and then she smiled as she moved closer.

"What are you doing here?" he asked.

"Duty called. I'm a wireless operator when I'm working, but at this moment, I'm enjoying time off."

"You gave me quite a surprise."

"Did I? I hope it was a pleasant one. When did you get the call up?"

"Not long after seeing you," Jonathon answered.

"I joined ten days after I saw you at the Palais, Now you know why I didn't want to get involved with you by allowing you to walk me home."

Roger chipped in. "Oh, you know each other?"

Ann smiled at him, "Oh, yes…we're old friends," she added. "It was funny. I joined the WRAF and reported in. You should have seen us, Jonathon. We were all there with our gas masks on our shoulders in their little cardboard boxes and trying to march carrying our cases. We hadn't had any training, so that was a laugh. We were out of step and not even in a straight line. What a sight we must have looked."

"Raw recruits. I'd have loved to see you."

"I'm glad you didn't. From there, I was sent to Wiltshire to train. I enjoyed that. Then it was various other camps, but how about you?"

Jonathon explained where he'd been and what he'd got up to. It felt good to find someone who came from home. Roger retreated elsewhere, so he and Ann spent the rest of the evening together, and then he walked her back. They stood and talked for a while, and after kissing her goodnight, he asked her if she would see him again, and she agreed. He felt elated.

When he was preparing for his date with Ann the following evening, he could feel the butterflies in the pit of his stomach. It was a new experience for him to be nervous. He wanted so much to make an impression.

They went to the pictures to see *All Quiet on the Western Front* with Lew Ayres. Jonathon sneaked his arm around Ann's shoulders when they found seats at the back of the cinema, and she didn't stop him. It was an old film about the First World War and sad, but it brought home to them what the war was all about. When they came out of the cinema, Jonathon walked her back to the place where she was billeted, shining his torch for her to see where she was going. They stood at the corner of the street and talked for a while.

Her lips were warm and responsive when he found the nerve to kiss her, but then the warning sirens took them by surprise. They ran for the nearest shelter and met many others who were doing the same. When they sat down, someone produced an accordion and began to play it. Everyone joined in the war songs that were given an airing. "It's a Long Way to Tipperary" never sounded better, and "Run Rabbit Run" was sung more than once with great gusto. Unfortunately, it didn't drown out the noise of the explosions, as the incendiary bombs dropped around them. One of the bombs hit the entrance of the shelter and made them all jump. Some of the women screamed. Jonathon could see Ann shaking, so he put his arm around her and cuddled her. Her hair smelled good, and her skin felt soft against his.

"Thank you," she whispered.

"You're very welcome," he answered and felt grateful for the chance to hold her close.

They stayed there until after the all clear and then went outside.

There were people wandering the streets with blood on their clothes and devastation everywhere. They could see the fire brigade working flat out to control the fires that were burning and another explosion could be heard above the voices that were shouting. They heard one of the firemen shout to someone.

"Get away, you thieving bugger." Jonathon and Ann watched him chase a young lad away.

The fireman turned to them. "They take anything they can from these bombed houses. They're heathens!"

Jonathon and Ann hurried back to their quarters to see if there was anything they could do. They were immediately given fresh orders to return to the devastation to help the civilians, and Jonathon joined his company. Jonathon learned something that day: Take life with a pinch of salt and grab your pleasures while you can, because tomorrow is a long black void.

Jonathon hoped that he would be home for Christmas, as it wasn't the same away from home, but at least he had Ann. He took her to a small hotel where they spent the weekend leave together, and they signed in as man and wife. Ann agreed with Jonathon that, when there was a war, you had to grab at any happiness you could, and they did.

They lay in bed in each other's arms. It wasn't the most comfortable bed, but they didn't care.

"I never thought I would go out with a pilot," Ann said.

"Why ever not?"

"When I was at Devon, it was frightening. It was mostly Australian and Canadian crew on coastal command. I would get upset when I got to know the lads and they didn't come back. I've even seen an aircraft blow up before they even had a chance to get in and fly off the station. I was glad to leave there."

"I must admit, Ann, I never realized what love was about until I met you." Jonathon snuggled her neck.

"Is it really love, Jons, or is it the situation we're in? After all, we've only been together ten days."

Jonathon sat up and looked down at her. "It doesn't seem like ten days. I feel as if I've known you forever."

"I know what you mean, but it *is* only a few days. Are you certain of your feelings?"

"What do you mean? You don't think you're in love with me? How insincere. You certainly had me fooled."

"Do you think you're in love with me, really?" she queried.

"Very much…but I see I'm wasting my time."

"Are you sure it's not just the war?" she asked as Jonathon jumped out of bed. "What are you doing?"

He kneeled at the side of the bed. "I'm proposing, you idiot. Will you marry me…please?" he begged.

"Oh, you silly sod," she laughed.

"No, I mean it, Ann. I want you to be my wife just as soon as it can be arranged, if you're willing."

"Jonathon." Ann was quiet, and he worried about her answer. "On one condition."

"What's that?"

"As long as you promise to buy me a more comfortable bed than this one."

Jonathon shouted with excitement. "Come here, you." He jumped back into bed and wrapped his arms around her. "Hello, wife," he whispered in her ear.

When they left the hotel, they went into the first jeweller shop they came across and inspected the rings.

"You don't need to buy me a ring yet, Jonathon."

"Oh, yes, I do," Jonathon replied. "I don't want you being picked up by someone else."

"Picked up! How dare you, Lieutenant. I'm not that kind of girl," Ann laughed.

As money was short, and Ann's birthday made her a Capricorn, they settled for an unusual silver ring with a garnet stone.

"It's the only one in existence, as each one is styled individually by a local man," the salesman told them.

Jonathon paid for the ring and when they reached their room, he scratched "J.A." on the flank of the ring with a small knife he always kept in his pocket

"Now it is definitely an individual. There'll be nobody else with one like this."

"No one may want one like that, either. Your engraving leaves a lot to be desired," Ann laughed. "But I love it."

"And I promise I'll buy you a proper gold ring as soon as I can, and next time, it will be a diamond instead of a garnet," Jonathon promised.

"I love this one, and I promise I'll never take it off."

§§§§§§

The night they returned to base, there was another raid. It didn't last very long, but it was too close for comfort. As they left the shelter, he caught his hand on a sharp piece of metal, and it began to bleed. Ann wrapped her clean handkerchief around it.

"There you are. Now we must get back and get some shut eye, or we'll be fit for nothing."

Taking her in his arms, he kissed her passionately, and just before she left him, she whispered in his ear, "*Je t'aime.*"

"What does that mean?"

Ann smiled. "Goodnight, Jonathon. See you soon."

When he arrived back, the sirens began to blare again and things moved quickly, until, exhausted, he went to bed. He slept well until it was time to leave his "pit." The following morning, they had new orders to go help to remove the debris from the bombing of the previous night. When he arrived, it was only then that he realized it was the place where Ann was billeted, and there was nothing left of the hotel but rubble. He called to one of the firemen who were on duty.

"Are there any survivors from this place?"

The answer came back, "No."

"None at all?"

"Not a one," the man answered. "They're all dead."

Jonathon was numb. He couldn't believe Ann was gone.

"Bloody Germans!" he swore. He wanted to cry, but his heart was breaking and he couldn't find a tear. Putting his hands into his pocket for a cigarette, he felt the handkerchief from the previous evening. He took it out and sat looking at Ann's handkerchief. It still carried her perfume. He hadn't noticed before, but there was an "A" in one of the corners. This was all he had of her—a bloody handkerchief, thanks to the Gerries!

"*Je t'aime.*" That's what she whispered before she walked out of his life...forever! "Oh, Ann,' he sighed. And what the hell did she mean with those foreign words?

It was good to go home for his Christmas leave, and after buying some very green bananas when he was in America, which were now almost ripe, it gave him great pleasure to place them on the table for the family. Breaking two off, he gave them to Shirley. Shirley's face was a picture when he gave them to her. Her eyes were like saucers. Separating them, she struggled, as her fingers couldn't open one of the bananas quickly enough, as she didn't know how.

"They're not fully ripe yet, Shirl. Are you sure you want to eat one now?"

"Please, Jonathon. I can't wait to eat it."

"Okay, if that's all right with Mam."

Ruth nodded, and Jonathon showed Shirley how to peel it. Shirley didn't need any help to eat it, but she kept the other for school. It was the answer to all her prayers.

"It's the best Christmas present of all, Jonathon. Thank you." Shirley flung her arms around his neck, and he gave her a hug.

"I must admit, Christmas wouldn't be the same without you, son." Ruth smiled, but he could see the tears in her eyes.

"I'll be here for Jessie's birthday, too," Jonathon went closer and whispered in Ruth's ear, "plus I think she'll be happy with the doll I bought her."

"I'm sure she will be," said Ruth, smiling.

Jonathon felt as if it had been a lifetime since he had seen his family, but nothing was changed at home. He was hugged and kissed and cried over. He took Shirley to the pictures, after he'd promised to take her to whichever movie she wished. The American way of speech had integrated into his own without him even realizing, and Ruth pulled him up on that.

"Jonathon, you're speaking like an American, or Yank, as everyone seems to call them. You're English, so please speak English."

Christmas was soon over and his leave came to an end, so it was back to the barracks. Every time they said their good-byes, it was sad, as they knew it could be for the last time.

Chapter 4

Ruth was up early. The raid from the night before had been a little too close and frightening. She worried about Jonathon and what he was doing. Alfred had gone to work, Shirley to school, and Jessie had no idea what a cruel world she was living in.

Ruth took the dirty dishes off the table and tidied the white cloth away, replacing it with the brown chenille cover. Stoking the fire, she then made herself a cup of tea from the used tea leaves, as she had to be careful with the ration. The socks she had washed and placed above the fire were now dry, so she put them away. Relaxing back into her armchair, she sipped her tea as she enjoyed the peace and quiet. Ruth thought about putting on the radio, but then changed her mind. Did she really want to listen to the news and get depressed all over again? No! She would enjoy the peace, while Jessie was playing with a cardboard box, dried butter beans, and a big spoon, bless her! As she drank her tea, her thoughts returned to Jonathon, and she checked the time. It was news time, so she couldn't resist turning on the wireless after all to see if there was any news about him.

The poor Jews were really suffering. The Germans were putting them through it. There were tales of them having to wear stars to show they were Jews and being robbed of their freedom. They were taking them away to goodness knows where. It was bad. Ruth hoped the Germans would never take over England. With lots of luck, the forces would protect them and keep them all safe. The air raids were bad enough. Ruth looked through the kitchen window at the snowstorm that was raging. It was cold and the snow was drifting. It covered the errors in the garden. The trees now took on new clothes of white, like a new bride. Snow was so beautiful, but unfortunately, it was cold, too. The outlook for everyone was grey, but it still rained, and the snow still fell to help to make sense of it all. She felt glad that Jonathon was already at camp and not travelling in this weather or she would have been more worried than she already was. Jonathon's state of health worried her more than anything. He had seemed a little withdrawn when he was home. It wasn't like him. Ever since the day she accepted him after he was born, following her rape by her stepsister's Uncle George, there was a bond. It was a dark secret that only she and Billy, her late husband, knew about. Billy's suicide because of the rape only made the bond between mother and son stronger. Since then, there had only been Jonathon and her—until Alfred…and he didn't know her secret and never would. Her stepsister Mary never guessed anything was wrong, and Ruth herself would never tell. Jonathon was special, but he would never know why. She always thought that if she told the truth about his birth, he wouldn't be loved by the family, and it wasn't his fault. How could she tell him that besides raping her, his father was a bully and had committed murder, too? He was hanged for that, and it would stay a well-kept secret that Uncle George was his father, and she would keep that secret until the day she died.

She thought back to when she began to see Alfred on a serious, regular basis. Dear, dear Alfred. He was special too with the way he wouldn't take no for an answer when he proposed. How considerate he was; when it was icy underfoot, he would allow her to link his arm and keep a firm grip of it to stop her falling onto the ground. Her only experience of relations with a man before had been the rape, as Billy, her husband, had the wounds of war that prevented them having relations. Remembering her fear of the unknown when Alfred proposed made her smile. He had been so patient and so loving, and now they had the girls. There was so much to thank him for. A faint flush coloured her cheeks at the thought. Dear, dear Alfred.

As soon as Jessie went to bed for her afternoon nap, Ruth went outside to clean out the Anderson shelter and prepare it for the next visit. She hoped it wouldn't be too soon. It was cold in there in the best of weathers, so they didn't look forward to sleeping there on such cold nights in winter. Somehow, she couldn't see how the airplanes could see to fly with the snow, but you never know, and they had to be ready. Ruth swept the floor and removed the spiderwebs that had already found a home there. Jessie didn't like spiders and would scream if she saw one. Returning to the house, she tried to use her old footsteps in the snow, as it was getting deep. Going back inside, Ruth stoked the fire for the hot water.

Soon Jessie called her, so Ruth went upstairs and brought her down, giving her beans, a spoon, and her scales to play with, as she liked them best, and then jumped at the sound of a door opening.

"Ruthie, get the kettle on. I'm ready for a cuppa. Are you?" Alfred walked into the house from the printing business next door as Ruth began to light the gas ring. "Are you joining me, sweetheart?" he asked.

"Of course," Ruth answered. Going over to the kettle, she began to fill it.

"Jessie's looking busy with those beans again," he grinned. "Typical, isn't it? You could spend a fortune on presents, and kids prefer to play with the box they came in. Would you believe it?"

"That's what children do. I remember my Grandma giving me the same things to play with when I was little."

"It's not a bad thing while the war's on. Let's face it. You can't get things like toys nowadays."

"She's a contented child, bless her!" Ruth dried the cups and saucers and set them out while Alfred prepared the teapot.

"Have we any biscuits?" Alfred asked.

"Don't you like my cake anymore?" Ruth pretended to be hurt.

"You've made a cake? That's good. You know I love your homemade cake. How do you manage with the rations?"

"You know me, Alfred. I'm just careful." Ruth went to the pantry and took out the cake. Placing it on the table, she cut him a good-sized piece.

"Poor Jonathon, I bet he wished he were here to share it with me." Alfred took a large bite.

"He hasn't written to me for a while. I'm due a letter, but I'll write to him tonight. I just hope it reaches him okay."

"I bet he's met a girl. That's what courting does for you. You forget your poor family." Alfred took another bite of the cake.

"Jonathon's not like that. If he is courting, it wouldn't stop him from writing."

After that, they didn't mention his name again, both worrying about Jonathon's silence on their own.

§ § § § §

Five months later, after Alfred returned to his work after his tea break, there was a knock on the door. Ruth opened it to find a young woman standing there, carrying a suitcase and obviously heavily pregnant. "Could I speak to you in private, please?" the young woman asked.

Ruth opened the door wider and allowed the young woman to enter.

"Would you like to come through and sit down?" Ruth felt curious.

"I'm Nora Bennett," the young woman said, "and my husband has thrown me out because I'm expecting your son's baby."

Ruth couldn't believe it. "Jonathon's baby? Are you sure? He never mentioned anything about it."

Nora Bennett was indignant in her reply. "Of course I am."

Ruth didn't know what to say. She was surprised—even shocked—to say the least, but at the same time grateful. She would have a part of Jonathon if anything happened to him, but that thought worried her, too. Ruth felt sorry for the girl, if indeed she was expecting Jonathon's baby. She couldn't take this in.

"I have no sisters or brothers to live with, and I'm an orphan, so I have nowhere else to go. Can I stay here, as I don't know what else to do?" She began to cry.

"Oh, dear! I shall need to speak to my husband. If you can wait a minute, I'll go and find him." Ruth hurried next door.

Seeing Alfred, she dragged him to one side. "I have a Nora Bennett next door saying she's expecting Jonathon's baby, and she wants to come and live with us. I suppose she could use Jonathon's room. What do you think?"

"I think I'd better come and meet her."

Alfred immediately finished what he was doing and followed Ruth inside the house. "Now then, young lady, what's all this about?"

"I'm expecting your son's baby, and I have nowhere to live."

"Really."

"My husband is in the Navy and is away from home a lot. I got lonely."

"So you had an affair with our son? Is that it?"

"Yes!"

"And you have nowhere else to go?" asked Alfred.

"I have no family I can turn to. I'm an orphan."

"Yes, I believe so. Well then, Ruth, you'd better find her somewhere to sleep."

Alfred looked at Ruth in bewilderment, shrugged his shoulders, and then left her to it and returned to his work.

"Would you like a cup of tea first while you tell me all about it? Then I'll take you upstairs and show you your bedroom."

Nora picked up her suitcase again, so Ruth assumed that she didn't want a cup of tea and a chat. Ruth led her upstairs and into Jonathon's bedroom. Taking her son's clothes and belongings away, she turned to Nora. "You can unpack and use the wardrobe and tall boy. Just make yourself comfortable. I'll bring some sheets and pillowcases and make the bed later."

Ruth took Jonathon's things into the bedroom she shared with Alfred and put them away in suitcases. Going downstairs, Ruth put the kettle on the fire, prepared the teapot, and set out cups and saucers. After a while, Nora joined her.

"How far are you with the baby?"

"Seven months."

"So when exactly are you due?"

"Fourteenth of August."

"But your husband has only just found out about the baby?" Ruth asked.

"Well, yes. When he came home on leave, at first I told him I'd slept with Jonathon. He was angry, and he told me that if I became pregnant with another man's child while he was away, then he'd kill the man and I wasn't to be there when he returned. He only returned yesterday and threw me out this morning. Where else could I go?" Ruth shivered and felt glad that Jonathon wasn't around at the same time as Nora's husband.

"Would you like a cup of tea now?" Nora nodded.

They drank their tea, without Nora revealing much, and Ruth began to make a meal. Deciding what to make for meals was always a problem. This shortage of food gave Ruth a headache, as she couldn't always find enough ingredients. One cake and one pie a week was all they could manage, owing to the shortage of lard and sugar. Rhubarb grew in the garden, but it used up too much sugar and Ruth didn't like to use saccharin; it had a taste. They could obtain black market eggs, and they ate a few of them through the week. Imagination played a big part in their meals, and luckily, Ruth used hers. Maybe Nora could contribute a few rations to help things along, too.

§ § § § §

When the sound of the siren drill was heard throughout the school, Shirley and the rest of her class all lined up at the front of the classroom. When the teacher gave the order, they made their way to the shelter outside.

"It's only a drill. It's not real," one child said to another.

"They're just making sure that we all know what we're doing in case the Germans come and start dropping bombs," said another child.

"Be quiet. We don't want any of that talk," the teacher shouted. "Take no notice, children. There's no need to be afraid. Keep in line there and don't forget your gas masks. Keep them with you at all times."

It was very orderly, and the teacher beamed her satisfaction. By the time they were all seated inside the shelter on the wooden slat benches all facing each other, the sound of the children's noisy chattering could be heard. After a short time, the teacher gave the order, and they all lined up again and made their way back to the classroom.

"Whose gas mask is this?" The teacher held up the box containing the mask. No one answered, so she took out the mask and held it up. "It's a Mickey Mouse gas mask. Now who owns one of these?"

Shirley could feel the heat rising as she watched the teacher with her gas mask on full view. Everyone turned and looked at her, but no one spoke. Looking straight at Shirley, the teacher barked. "It's yours, isn't it, girl?'

"Yes, miss," Shirley answered as she squirmed in her seat.

"Come and collect it then. You seem to misplace it far too many times for my liking."

Shirley left her seat and walked to the front. Her cheeks burned with embarrassment as she took the mask from her teacher. Carrying it back to her seat, she was aware of all the tittering among the other children.

Jean, Shirley's friend, whispered, "Why don't you ask your mam and dad for a new one. Then you can be like the rest of us."

Shirley nodded and smiled. She couldn't ask her parents for a new one. They really thought this mask was the best for her, but she hated it. So many times she tried to lose it, but it always came back. Everyone else had a black one, but hers was a silly pink Mickey Mouse with a big floppy nose. It was an embarrassment.

Shirley sat on the back row on the extreme right from the teacher. This was the top seat. They changed it every week after their Friday morning arithmetic test. Shirley tried her best to get to the top as the boy she liked best, Peter, was clever and was always in the top few. Funnily enough, though, they never seemed to share a desk because if one made it to the top desk, then the other didn't. Shirley was aware that Peter didn't share the same feelings. Sometimes, she would sit and look at him without him knowing. He had lovely fair, wavy hair. It was unfair; she would have loved to have hair like that, but hers was a mousy brown, so her mam said, and straight. She now sneaked a look at Peter. She could see the length of his eyelashes. He had lovely eyes with long lashes that were dark, like his eyebrows, so they stood out more. Why couldn't she have long lashes like that? She did once try to improve hers by trimming them and coating them with Vaseline. Someone once told her that her eyelashes would grow longer and thicker after doing that. They were wrong.

Some of the children weren't good at arithmetic, so Shirley would often help them out. It was something she enjoyed doing, and the other children sought her out. Reading was the same. Maybe it was because she did a lot of it at home. Sometimes, her dad would ask her to proofread for him.

Shirley was introduced to Nora as soon as she arrived home and found her in the kitchen reading. Nora hardly spoke to her.

After school on Friday, Shirley asked her mother a favour.

"It's my birthday tomorrow, Mam, so do you think that I can sleep over with Jean Burton. Her mam says I can if it's all right with you." Shirley didn't like Nora very much, even though she was going to make her an auntie. Home didn't feel the same with her around.

"Okay, on one condition."

"What?"

"That you promise to be good and do what you're told."

"I promise."

"Then you can, and tomorrow night, we'll take you to the pictures."

That evening, Jean's Auntie Maggie was going out on a date. Maggie lived with the Burtons, as her parents were killed when they lived in Manchester, so her sister offered her a home. Maggie was much younger than Jean's mother, and the younger girls watched in fascination as Maggie prepared her leg tanning makeup and painted her legs. Jean was called to help by picking up the special pencil and drawing a line down the back of Maggie's legs to make it look as if she wore stockings.

"Get the line straight, Jean. Don't give it any wavy lines."

"I won't," and Jean turned to Shirley and pulled a face.

When it came to Maggie's makeup, Shirley was amazed to see her use the soot from the chimney on her eyes. Makeup was something that was in short supply, so girls had to improvise. A touch of lipstick on her cheeks for rouge, then the bright red lipstick on her lips, and she was done.

"I can't wait to grow up and wear makeup," Shirley told Jean. Her mind drifted off to the imaginary future when she would wear makeup and go dancing. She would be like Cinderella and be the belle of the ball, and the boys would all want to dance with her…especially Peter.

"You haven't long to wait, only another five years." Maggie spoke with a little sarcasm in her voice.

"No, only four now. It's my birthday tomorrow, and I'm eleven, and my mam says I can wear makeup when I'm fifteen.'

"Let's play Ludo when she's gone out." Jean brought her back to the present.

"All right then," Shirley agreed.

When they finished their game, Jean's dad switched on the radio. They all listened to *Sincerely Yours* with Vera Lynne. After she sang "We'll Meet Again," she read out messages from the men who were fighting in the war. Shirley hoped to hear from Jonathon, but he wasn't mentioned.

Shirley and Jean went to bed that night and talked and giggled for a long time until they heard Maggie come home. They could hear her talking downstairs to a young man, so Jean put her finger over her mouth.

"Shh! Aunty Maggie's brought a boy home. I'm creeping downstairs to see what they're doing."

"What if she sees you?" but Jean had already left the bedroom.

After a while, she heard Maggie shout, "Jean, get to bed."

Jean came back into the bedroom as her mother called, "What's the matter?"

"I just went for a drink of water, Mam," Jean answered.

Shirley and Jean giggled quietly, but didn't dare talk to each other after that, and they soon went to sleep.

The sirens began to wail not long after. They both put on their shoes and coats over their pyjamas. Jean's parents herded them all together at the bottom of the stairs, including Aunty Maggie and her boyfriend, and they all made their way to the pantry in the kitchen under the stairs. Jean's family didn't possess an Anderson shelter because they had no garden and her parents thought that this was the next safest place to be; at least they could help themselves to food and drink. Inside the pantry, they had a little stove so that they could boil a kettle, too. It was made out with a small single bed that Shirley and her friend both shared. It was a squeeze, but cosy. The adults sat on kitchen chairs that they only just managed to get in. It wasn't long before Mr. Burton was sound asleep, and Shirley was fascinated, wondering how he managed to stay on the chair without falling off.

Shirley couldn't settle. She worried about her family. Throwing the covers back, she sprang to her feet and put on her shoes. "I'm going home."

"You can't. The Germans are coming," Jean sleepily murmured.

Mrs. Burton attempted to stop her. "Sit down, love," she grabbed at her arm. "Someone stop her, she could get killed. Stop her-r-r."

Shirley burst through the pantry door, ran through the kitchen, opened the front door, and ran up the street as quickly as she could to get home. No one was going to stop her. Going home was a feeling of necessity. She could hear the enemy planes coming. There was the faint hum that got louder, and she tried to run faster, but she couldn't see too well in the dark. Looking up into the sky, she could see the planes silhouetted against the moonlit sky not too far away. Her legs wouldn't or daren't go any quicker for fear of falling or tripping. Then the explosions started as the Germans began to drop their incendiary bombs. Shirley was very, very afraid. An arm came round her waist, and she was lifted off her feet. It was a man—Auntie Maggie's boyfriend—and he was running back again to the house they had just left. The explosions were close, and they could see the fires. There was another explosion as they neared the house, and that one knocked them to the ground. There was dust and shattered glass. Shirley heard him shout, and she thought he'd been hit, but then she realised it was Jean's house that had been bombed. Shirley screamed. Both she and the young man got to their feet, and he put his arms around her as they watched in disbelief at the sight before them. They both checked over each other to make sure they were okay and dusted themselves off.

"They can't survive that, none of them," the young man muttered. "They didn't get a chance. If it hadn't been for you…you've saved my life and yours. What's your name?"

"Shirley," she said between sobs, "and you saved my life too, mister...er..."

"Call me Jimmy. I suppose you could say that we're even. Both life savers, eh!"

"I bet you're really upset about Jean's Auntie Maggie, aren't you?"

"I'm upset for all of them—they seemed a nice family—but men don't cry, Shirley, and besides, I didn't know her that well. It's terribly sad all the same." Shirley then noticed his cheeks; they were glistening as if he had shed a few tears. The firemen soon arrived and worked on the fire. Although Shirley and Jimmy stood for a while and watched them work, they knew there wasn't a hope.

"Come on, Shirley, we'd better get you home. It's no good standing here any longer. It's morning now, so we'd better let your family know you're okay." Jimmy took her hand, and they walked slowly back to Shirley's home.

Shirley felt sorry for Jimmy, not being allowed to cry. She was sobbing and couldn't stop. He was so brave. When they got close to her house, they met her mam, who was on the way to see if she was okay.

"That was a bad raid. I was worried to death. Are you all right, love?"

Shirley sobbed. "Jean's dead, Mam, and so is her mam and dad, and her Auntie Maggie."

Ruth frowned, and it was a while before she spoke. "I don't understand. What do you mean they're dead...and who's this then?"

"I'm Jimmy, pleased to meet you." Jimmy offered his hand to Ruth, who shook it. "Your daughter saved my life, but unfortunately the family, who were all in the house, has been killed. It was a direct hit. They wouldn't know what hit them."

"Oh, my God!' Ruth looked horrified. "So how did Shirley escape, and where do you fit in?"

"I took Maggie home last night. I believe it's Shirley's friend's auntie, and I stayed because of the sirens. Come to think about it, I could do with getting home to check on Gran and Sue."

"Who are Gran and Sue?" asked Shirley, but Jimmy shrugged it off.

"You'd better come home with us, while you tell us how you managed to escape. You can join us for breakfast before you go home."

When Ruth and Alfred listened to the full story, they were horrified, but more than grateful to Jimmy and thankful that Shirley had survived.

"What made you decide to come home?" Ruth asked.

"I don't know, Mam. I was worried and just made my mind up, and that was it. I left my clothes there, so I only have my pyjamas and shoes. Sorry! I suppose I've lost them now."

Ruth shook her head. "I'm counting my blessings, dear."

After breakfast, Jimmy made a move to go home. Shirley walked him to the front door, and they both hugged each other.

"I'll never forget you, Shirley."

"And I'll never forget you, Jimmy."

"We have a special bond, girl. I shall pop round and see you again before long. You're special. I could take you to the pictures next week if you like."

"I'd like that, but I think we'd better ask my mam first if it's okay."

They returned inside. "Is it all right if I take Shirley to the pictures next week?" Jimmy asked.

Her mam looked surprised. "She saved my life, and I'm eternally grateful to her." He used those words again. "She's special, and I thought it would be nice to reward her."

"Do you know it's her eleventh birthday today? I don't think she'll be forgetting it in a hurry."

"Neither will I…ever."

Shirley's mam agreed to allow her to go to the pictures with Jimmy, so they decided to go the following Wednesday. He said he'd call for her. Shirley walked him to the front door again, went outside, and watched him walk down the street before going back inside the house.

Who would have guessed that she would be going to the pictures with Auntie Maggie's boyfriend next week? What would Maggie say? Then it all came back to her as if she'd pushed it to the back of her mind. Her friend Jean and her family were dead. She would miss Jean and poor Maggie, too—and the family. Jean had been her best friend. Shirley felt empty. War wasn't nice.

Chapter 5

Jonathon, who had now been made a sergeant, and Roger were posted to a Polish squadron immediately. They felt more confident with each other for company and were glad they were together when they had their first flight test, as it wouldn't have been the same with anyone else. Their orders were to bomb and disrupt enemy transports in France. Most flights were at night, and after they were given necessary details, Jonathon and Roger planned their route and studied a topographical map, noting any high ground and major obstructions plus any known flak areas.

They would all take off singly and fly behind enemy lines, patrolling for about an hour, and then another mosquito would take their place. During the patrol, they searched out movements on the ground. If they spotted something, they went lower to investigate. If the movement proved to be a train, lorries, tanks, or barges, they would then attack from low level with bombs, machine guns, or cannons. Jonathon sometimes felt a little apprehensive, as there was always a danger of going too low. Most losses were due to hitting the ground or obstructions like power lines or trees. If Roger thought they were too low, he would shout "Up!" and Jonathon never argued, but immediately pulled back the stick to gain height as quickly as possible.

One night, Jonathon and Roger took off and needed to carry extra fuel in wing tanks. Jonathon had an air of apprehension about this attack, but didn't tell Roger. He'd never had this feeling before, but it was there in the depths of his belly. While patrolling, they saw some movement. They circled round and dropped flares on what was an enemy transport. They attacked them, and the transport stopped and appeared damaged, but then the flares went out. Cruising lower, they were unexpectedly attacked by a night fighter. They fired in return, and there was a long battle. The enemy fired a long burst of cannon fire, and although they immediately took action, the port engine caught fire.

They didn't know where they were. Everything was going wrong, and they had lost their bearings. Roger operated the fire extinguisher and Jonathon "feathered" the propeller. A further burst of gunfire caused the starboard engine to catch fire. Jonathon throttled back and operated the fire extinguisher, but as the fire did not go out, he ordered Roger to bail out. Roger refused at first, but eventually realized there was nothing to be done, so he pushed himself through and out. While this was happening, the aircraft lost height rapidly. Jonathon struggled out of his seat and dived through the opening, pulling the ripcord as soon as he was clear of the aircraft. Feeling the pull as the parachute opened, he wondered where on earth he was. He could be in France, Belgium, or wherever the hell! Looking down, he realized he was too low. His time was up, and he didn't stand a chance. Feeling certain that he would be killed when he hit the ground, he waited for the inevitable. With a swoosh of broken twigs and falling leaves, he landed in a large bush that broke his fall. He prayed and thanked his lucky stars he was still alive. Was he hurt? He didn't think so. Gosh, he was lucky!

Where was Roger? Jonathon lay in a heap among the branches for a few seconds, while he sorted out his thoughts. Scrambling out of the bush, he stared up at the sky. How had he managed to survive that? He must have a guardian angel looking after him. After gathering his parachute together, he stuffed it into the bush to hide it and ran. He saw the glow from the plane when it crashed a distance away. Luckily, he had fallen in a wooded area close to a road, and there were vehicles moving along it; he could see them through the trees. Then again, if he could see them, maybe they could have seen him. He thought he'd better hide in case he was spotted, so he dropped into a hollow in the ground and covered himself with a branch from a bush close by. It wasn't the best of camouflage, but it was the best he could do at the moment. There was no way he could watch the activity without revealing himself too much, so he kept hidden as best he could and waited.

As soon as everything went quiet, Jonathon climbed out of the hollow and began to run as fast as he could again. The weather was warm, and he felt clammy, even at this time of the day. Some of the German soldiers from the vehicles must have been chasing him, as he could hear them crashing through the woods, and the bullets they were shooting were only just missing him. He looked around for somewhere to hide. There was a fallen log covered in moss with tall weeds behind, so he hid among the weeds, hoping, but doubting, it would give him enough cover and waited for what seemed a lifetime. He was sure to be caught; there were too many of them. He knew his chance of survival wasn't good.

Voices were coming closer, too close for comfort, and Jonathon stayed still and quiet, hoping they would pass by. After what seemed an eternity, a few German soldiers came close. Jonathon could hear their feet crunching the bracken underfoot, and he broke into a cold sweat. Did they know he was here? How close were they? He didn't know. Sure they would hear him, he tried holding his breath, but he couldn't. He could hear them talking and wished he knew what they were saying. Why the heck didn't he learn to speak German at school? Maybe he should have gone to university. They stopped talking. It was dark, so Jonathon couldn't guess as to what was going on. His heart beat so fast, he felt as if it was going to burst through his chest. He could feel something crawling on his neck; it itched, but he was too petrified to scratch in case they could hear him. He found himself holding his breath again. He had to breathe. He eventually took a breath and waited, hoping their hearing wasn't too good. To him it sounded loud, but maybe not. Then Jonathon heard the sound of running water.

Dirty bastard! he thought when he realized the German soldier was relieving himself. A little more to the right, and Jonathon would have gotten the lot.

Jonathon kept still. He could feel the sweat running down his face and the same desire to relieve himself was getting desperate, but he daren't. If he made the slightest noise, the German soldiers would find him.

The soldiers were talking and laughing at something, so he dared to change his position to watch them. How he wished he knew what they were saying, but he didn't, and then he saw the small flame, which gave way to the glow of a cigarette. *So they must be having a rest,* he thought, and it was just his luck for them to choose here to do it.

When the soldiers eventually left, Jonathon waited as long as he could before he emptied his bladder, and oh boy, that felt good. He didn't dare move from his hiding place, so he settled down for a while. Exhaustion took over, and he soon fell asleep. Suddenly, something woke him. He listened to try to distinguish the noise, but put it down to some kind of animal…or it could be soldiers. It was still dark, but light enough to see where he was going, so when he was sure there was no one around, he crawled forward. There was still no sound, so he stood up and started walking quickly, his ears and eyes forever searching and listening for any sound of soldiers, making sure there was no one behind or around him. He had no idea where he was or where he was going, and where was Roger, for goodness' sake? He had to find somewhere safe and soon, so he broke into a run, but exhaustion made him stop and sit on a large stone to get his breath. He couldn't believe he'd been so lucky, but what now? Was he safe for the moment, or were there still soldiers in the vicinity?

It was quiet and eerily still, but maybe it felt that way because he was almost caught earlier. He wasn't injured, except for a few scratches from his fall and maybe a few splinters. There was a bit of blood—he could feel it on his face—but that was nothing compared to a broken leg or arm. At least a few scratches wouldn't stop him. It was a blessing, as it was going to be difficult enough moving about without a broken leg. Luck was on his side up to now, but for how long? He kept his ears open, listening for any little noise, but there didn't seem to be any danger, so he pressed on.

There was something going on. He could hear shouts, and there were shots. Maybe it was Roger. Had they found him? Not knowing was dreadful, and he only wished he had the wings of a bird so that he could view from above. It was too dangerous to climb a tree, so he kept on moving forward.

Jonathon walked for a way before he heard someone cough. Could it by some miracle be Roger? He worried about him and hoped he was okay. Could it be him? He stopped in his tracks and waited. Hiding as best he could, he kept quiet, waiting to see whom it was and if the person came close. It was a group of soldiers; he could hear them talking now, and Jonathon thanked his lucky stars they didn't come too close. Again he'd been lucky. Was it the same group of soldiers that was looking for him before? Were they still looking for him? It could be crawling with soldiers around here, he wouldn't know, but he had to go on.

Jonathon waited a while longer before he started to walk again. Where was Roger? He could be close and he wouldn't even know it; they could even pass each other. The trees and bushes grew thick, which was a blessing in one way, but not if he wanted to find Roger. Sleep was trying to take him over, which could be dangerous, he thought, as it could affect his responses. He must find somewhere to get his head down, somewhere safe, but where? His thoughts turned to his bed at home and how he wished he were curled up there at this very minute.

He stumbled, walked, and then ran when he heard a noise, until he came to the edge of the wood. Jonathon could see a field to his left, and there appeared to be a farmhouse on the other side of the pasture with a large barn attached. It looked badly in need of repair, but at least it had a roof of some kind. He stood for a while, watching, listening until he felt it was safe to run across the field. Looking at his watch, he realized that it was still very early in the day, and with a bit of luck, no one would be up and about. He ran a short distance, and then threw himself down and waited. There was no response, so he ran the rest of the way until he reached the barn and carefully opened the door. It creaked, and he hesitated, listening, but he could see only cows in there. They looked at him curiously and then looked away again, indifferent. The stench of fresh manure overpowered his senses, and looking down at the floor made him falter. He stood a while, but there was no stirring from the farmhouse so he hesitantly entered the barn. There was a ladder leaning on the hayloft above, so Jonathon squelched forward and climbed it. Finding some fresh hay stacked there, he made himself a bed. From there, he could watch for any unexpected visitors, like German soldiers, but still keep well hidden.

Jonathon muttered to himself, "I don't know where you are, Roger, but I hope you're having as much luck as I am."

Looking down at his boots, he realized that he'd brought much of the cow dung with him, and it didn't smell very sweet. The hay rustled close by, and Jonathon could hear rats squealing, so he decided to keep his socks on. He'd heard stories of rats eating people's toes before, and he needed all his.

His thoughts turned to his family. He wondered what they were doing now. Picturing the scene, he imagined there would be a fire burning for the hot water and they would all be at the table eating breakfast, drinking tea, and talking to each other. How he wished he could be with them this minute, instead of lying in a rat-filled stinking barn with a leaking roof and no home comforts.

"Oh, well, they say muck for luck," he muttered to himself as he took his boots off. "If it's true, then I'm going to be the luckiest man of all." Jonathon lay down and took a deep breath, filling his nostrils with the smell of fresh hay. It was definitely cosier than the woods, and he soon fell fast asleep.

Chapter 6

Jimmy collected Shirley from her home the following Wednesday to take her to the pictures. She had been standing at the window, all ready, looking down the street for him for the past hour. Shirley couldn't hide her excitement, and Ruth felt relief when Jimmy knocked at the door.

"At last!" Ruth muttered under her breath.

Putting down her darning, Ruth walked down the hall and opened the door to Jimmy, while Shirley put on her cardigan, and then met Jimmy at the door.

"Don't get cold. Are you sure you'll be warm enough with that?" Ruth scolded.

"Yes, Mam, it's hot."

"Now don't forget, if the sirens go, Shirley, then follow Jimmy and don't lose him. There'll be a warning on the screen if there is a raid. Don't, whatever you do, try to get home after the sirens go. You must go for cover in a shelter."

"Don't worry, Mrs. Turner, I'll look after her." Turning to Shirley, Jimmy added, "Come on, trouble."

Shirley giggled and followed him outside, and Ruth watched them walk up the street. Ruth noticed that Shirley had chosen to wear her best frock and polish her shoes. It was obvious she liked Jimmy. He seemed a nice boy, but it seemed odd watching her eleven-year-old daughter walking out with a young man, and she hoped it wouldn't happen too often.

Nora was on her way in and saw Jimmy at the door. "Who the hell was that? He was a bit of all right," she said when they walked away.

"It's Shirley's new friend."

"Friend! She knows how to pick 'em."

Ruth could find Nora irritating at times, and this was one of them. "There's nothing in it. They're just friends."

"If you say so, but I've heard of men like that. You know there are those who like little girls."

"I believe so."

Not wanting to get into a conversation on those lines, she turned and went back into the kitchen while Nora closed the front door behind her. Ruth thought a lot about what Nora said, though, but eventually dismissed it from her mind. Jimmy seemed okay, but Ruth decided to keep a closer eye on Shirley from then on.

Jimmy took Shirley to the corner shop for some sweets with his coupons, and she didn't hesitate in her choice.

"Can I have two ounces of pear drops, please?" Shirley asked.

"You can have more of anything you want," he answered, "as long as I have enough coupons."

"Pear drops are okay."

"Wouldn't you like some chocolate?"

"I like pear drops."

"Okay then, pear drops it is." Jimmy paid for them, and they left the shop.

"Why don't you like chocolate?"

"I do."

"Then why didn't you have some when I asked?"

"I didn't like to take advantage."

"You are an unusual young lady, Shirley." He smiled and tucked her arm in his.

As they walked down the street, they passed Peter. He gave Shirley a quizzical look when he saw her linking Jimmy.

It was a good cowboy film of her choice, *Robin Hood of the Pecos* with Roy Rogers and George "Gabby" Hayes, and they both enjoyed it. Walking home after, he again made her link his arm, which she did, and they chatted as if they'd known each other all their lives.

"I like Gabby Hayes, don't you?" asked Shirley.

"Don't you like Roy Rogers?" asked Jimmy. "The girls usually like him."

"I do like Roy Rogers, but I like his horse Trigger more. I think he's funny."

Shirley didn't feel shy at all with Jimmy, and she linked him, while he shone his torch ahead of her so that she wouldn't trip and fall.

"My brother is in the RAF, and he's a pilot. He's going to bomb the Germans," Shirley told Jimmy. "Have you any brothers and sisters?' "

"No, there's only me."

"Who do you live with then?"

"Gran. There's just me and Gran."

"Does she work?"

"No, she's too old."

"Where's your mam and dad?"

Jimmy laughed. "Gran and Sue, her friend, more than compensate for parents."

As he didn't explain any more, Shirley stopped asking questions.

Jimmy loved cowboy films, so taking Shirley to watch one was a pleasure. Also he liked the girl's company. If someone told him a while ago that he would be taking an eleven-year-old girl to the pictures and would enjoy it, he would have never believed them, but this girl was special.

Shirley loved her visit to the pictures with Jimmy and hoped he would take her again. He was invited into the house for a cup of tea and a toast. As he left, after giving Shirley a hug, he casually mentioned that he was joining the Army a few days later. He asked Shirley if she would write to him, and she said she would. When he left, Shirley ran upstairs and cried herself to sleep.

§ § § § § §

A few weeks later on Saturday night, Shirley awoke to the call of alarm from her mam.

"Shirley, Shirley, get up, they're here, the sirens, go to the shelter. Nora, are you awake? Come to the shelter."

"No, leave me here. I'm too tired," replied Nora.

"No, come to the shelter before the planes come," Ruth called in a panic.

Alfred was annoyed. "Come on, Ruth. She's a big girl. She can decide for herself. We have our own children to consider."

Shirley moved automatically, as she got out of bed, putting on her shoes and coat over her pyjamas and going downstairs to the sound of the warning sirens. Why did the Germans have to do their bombing in the middle of the night? She knew why, really, as it had been explained to her, but they were a nuisance. Her dad was collecting Jessie from her cot and taking her to the Anderson shelter in the back garden. It wasn't very pleasant in there, and it wasn't a place that anyone looked forward to going to, but it had to be done for safety's sake. Shirley imagined her bed now lying empty. It was snug and comfortable in there, but here they were on the way to the shelter again, the cold, cold shelter where it smelled and was damp. At least she had somewhere to lie down, which was more than her mam and dad had. Nora was an idiot! After that last episode with her friend and Jimmy, Shirley was more than eager to go. Her mam was now filling the flask with tea, and she helped her carry everything up the garden path to the shelter, amid the threatening drone of enemy aircraft in the distance.

Ruth was reluctant to leave the house with Nora in bed. What if something happened? It was her future grandchild, and she knew she would never forgive herself if anything did happen. They hurriedly stepped down into the shelter. Alfred lit the paraffin stove that stood in the corner and gave out a weird glow. It was now beginning to smell, too, and Jessie was already in the cot, so Shirley climbed in and tried to find a comfortable position. Before her mam and dad sat down, her mam fussed over the girls as she tucked them in, and her dad set out the cups.

"Everything will be okay. We'll wake you up again when we can go back inside the house. Now go to sleep and don't you worry." Ruth kissed them both.

Alfred eventually sat in his chair.

"Pour the tea, Alfred. I'm just going back into the house to see if I can tempt Nora to join us."

"You can't. They're coming over now. You could get killed."

"That's why I must go back for Nora. I'd never forgive myself."

Hurrying down the garden path, she thought about this girl who was expecting Jonathon's child. If she was honest with herself, she didn't like her very much. Nora was lazy, hardly ever getting out of bed before noon; she was sarcastic and made much more work for Ruth. There was no gratitude in her, and she seemed to think Ruth was her personal slave. No, she didn't like her very much, and she gathered Alfred wasn't too keen, either. She couldn't understand what Jonathon was thinking about when he went with her. Ruth decided that she would insist that Nora apply for a council house as soon as possible. Opening the kitchen door, she went to the bottom of the stairs.

"Nora, Nora, can you hear me? Nora, the bombers are coming over the house now. Hurry up and come down." Ruth had no response, so she gave up and returned to the shelter. She had her family to think about, and the children still needed a mother.

Shirley worried about her mam after she left the shelter. She couldn't stand it if she got killed. What would she do without her mother? She'd have her dad, but she couldn't manage without her mam. Shirley's memories were still vivid in her mind of what happened to her friend and her family, so she lay quiet and apprehensively waited for her mother to return.

"It's only me, and I'm on my own. Nora's still asleep." Ruth climbed down into the shelter.

"Lazy gi—"

"Shh!" Ruth cut in as she sat on a chair.

Alfred pushed a cup of tea in her hand. "W-e-e-ell, she is."

Shirley snuggled down and felt safe now that her mam was back with them.

"Are you happy now?" Alfred looked disgusted at Ruth. "You could have been killed through that...through that . . ."

Ruth stopped him. "The children, Alfred."

"I think we need to discuss this."

Ruth felt as if her body should still be in bed. She felt exhausted and was only just coming round to the land of the living. Alfred gratefully accepted the second cup of tea that was thrust into his hand, and he curled his fingers around it for the warmth. He took his first sip and heard the explosions from the bombs that were dropping not too far away. Each night the sirens were heard, it ended like this, and there was always the worry of "Will it be us tonight?" and then the relief when the all-clear sounded. As yet, they had fared well, but they had to play safe.

Alfred began to shut his eyes again after he'd finished his cup of tea, and soon he was gently snoring. When he almost fell off the chair, he woke up. It was light outside, and there was no noise except for the gentle patter of rain on the privet hedge at the back of the garden. When he looked at the rest of the family, they were still sleeping. He pushed his head outside and listened. A distant sound of children playing and a dog barking made him realise they had slept too long, so he gently shook Ruth.

"Ruth." He raised his voice. "Ruth...Ruth...it's gone quiet. I think it's over."

Ruth opened her eyes. "Has the all-clear gone?"

"I didn't hear it, love."

"I can't hear any planes."

Alfred got up from the chair and began to collect the things together, but Ruth put her head outside and shouted to the next-door neighbour.

"Clara, are you there?" There was no answer. "What time is it?"

Alfred looked at his watch. "It's nine-thirty. Crikey, we've slept in."

Ruth guessed they'd slept a while, as her neck hurt from sitting in a bad position, but the girls were still asleep. They wakened them, and then they all moved back into the house.

"Those goldenrod are opening up in the garden. I think I'll cut a few. It'll brighten the house up, if nothing else."

Alfred hurried to open the business and found the staff waiting outside.

His brother said, "Where have you been? We've been standing here for ages. I tried knocking on the door, but you didn't hear." They all continued to pull Alfred's leg, so he left them to it to have his breakfast next door.

Nora sat at the kitchen table, eating her breakfast cereal and having a cup of tea. Obviously, she had missed Ruth taking her a cup of tea in bed that morning and Alfred's brother must have disturbed her enough for her to get up. Ruth had put the kettle on to make another pot of tea and noticed there was no milk left for them. Nora must have used the lot. Ruth felt bitter. Nora was uncaring and greedy. When she bought sweets, she never shared them, but would sit in front of the children and eat them all. Even her ration book was something Ruth had to beg for, and she was sure that Nora was selling some of her coupons. Alfred noticed Ruth was angry, and he could feel his temper rising, too.

Ruth tried to control herself for the sake of Jonathon's unborn child. Shirley ran to the nearby shop for some cereal, as Nora had emptied the box, while Ruth waited to hear the clip-clop of the milkman's horse to take out the jug for a quart of milk. Alfred prepared for work, while Ruth started on the breakfast. He checked through the shop and walked outside, looking up the street and then down. Looking up to the roof to confirm there was no damage, he caught the sign above the shop: Turner & Son, Printers and Bookbinders. It still gave him a thrill when he saw his name there on show for all to see. The sign was placed there many years before by his father. It was taken down when he died five years earlier, but now Alfred had placed it back in position again since Jonathon joined him. Everything was in order. After all, except for his blood, Jonathon was his son.

"Okay, Dad?" Shirley had been to the shop, come home, and deposited the cereal in the kitchen, and then came out of the house without him even seeing her.

"Seem to be." They both went back inside and into the kitchen for their breakfast.

"Everything okay?" Ruth asked as she sat at the table.

"Yes, but somebody got it," Alfred said, "I heard the bombs dropping."

"Do you think there'll be some shrapnel in the street, Dad?" Shirley asked. "A girl at school picked up a lot the last time we were bombed."

"Kids! They'll always find something to play with from any situation." Alfred laughed.

After they finished breakfast, Ruth washed the pots at the sink and looked over the garden. She must take advantage of those flowers and bring some in. As soon as she finished, she picked up the scissors, tucked them in her overall pocket, and went outside. Walking down the garden path, she looked around. She loved the garden, even though it was looking in a sorry state. She must do something with it, as there were many people who wished they owned a garden, but didn't. As soon as she had some free time, she would sort it out, but meanwhile…taking out the scissors from her overall pocket, she began to cut the flowers.

§§§§§

A few days later, a postcard arrived for Shirley. She became very excited and couldn't wait to read it. It was from Jimmy, and after reading it, she left it on the table propped up by the vase of goldenrod. If her mam wanted to read it, she could. She did feel special that Jimmy had written to her. It was a short letter, telling her that he was now a soldier preparing to fight the Germans. Maybe he would see her brother. When she wrote back, she would write to say that if he saw Jonathon to tell him that she missed him a lot.

Ruth gave Shirley a writing pad and envelopes so that she could write to Jimmy, and Shirley wrote to him very quickly in answer. Watching for the postman every morning became monotonous, but it wasn't long before she received a letter.

Dear Shirley,

Thank you for your very welcome letter, as life isn't pleasant here, but we're getting on with it. I'm being told what to do and when to do it. It's called discipline, a necessity in the forces, especially in the middle of a war.

Enjoy yourself with whatever you're doing and be thankful that you're at home, as it's where I long to be.

I often think of the night I took you to the pictures. You were a great comfort to me and held a good conversation. What's more, I shall never forget how you saved my life.

How's school?

Your friend, Jimmy

"How's Jimmy?" asked Ruth.

"He says it's not pleasant there and he's missing home."

"Poor man." Ruth's thoughts immediately went to Jonathon. Where is he and what is he doing? There had been no letter or any communication of any kind and she worried. If anything had happened, she consoled herself with the thought that she would have been notified…wouldn't she? Ruth frowned.

Chapter 7

Jonathon lay with his eyes closed and thought about his family. He hadn't written to his mam for a while and was sure that she would be worried, but there was nothing he could do about it now. Ann had taken all his thoughts and time he had to spare while he was in Bournemouth, poor Ann. Listening to the birds from outside and the swallows flying in and out of the barn through the broken window, he became aware that he could hear voices. He opened his eyes and listened. The stench from the cows, mixed with the hay, made him realize where he was. The smell was strong, but Jonathon didn't move, he just listened as the farmer began to milk and talk to the animals. The voice he could hear sounded French. He didn't know what the man was saying, as he didn't understand much of the language and couldn't remember his French lessons from school, but now he wished he'd paid more attention. So that's where he must be, somewhere in France…but where? He kept still and silent until the farmer went and all was quiet again. Why didn't he try to milk a cow last night? He could have enjoyed the fresh milk. His stomach began to rumble. At least the milk would have been something inside him. He must be careful if someone came close or they would hear his tummy grumbling.

When the farmer left, Jonathon stayed where he was and tried to go back to sleep. He decided to wait a while before he moved. If it were France, then everyone would be taking a nap later, so he would wait for that. Before he had the chance, he heard cars driving up to the house. Jonathon got up and moved to the small round window in the loft and looked out. There were two Jeeps full of German soldiers. His heart began to beat faster. Did they know he was here? Had he been seen? Some hero he was; he was terrified. There were no weapons around, and he only had a small gun. He watched quietly and waited for the inevitable.

They disappeared into the farmhouse, and then Jonathon heard a scream. A woman was dragged away from the house. She managed to break away and run, but she didn't run very far before she was grabbed and dragged again, and then pushed into the Jeep. He couldn't do a thing to help. There were too many of them, and he hardly had anything to fight with. All he could do was watch. His eyes were blurred with the tears that had sprung to his eyes. How could they do that to a defenceless woman? She didn't stand a chance. Then he thought about Ann again. Those Germans had a lot to answer for. He bit his bottom lip. Just wait until he could get back into his ship. He'd show them.

Next, they appeared again with a man. He looked like the farmer who had milked the cows earlier; he was struggling, but they hit him with the butt of a gun and then threw him into the Jeep.

After the soldiers left, Jonathon listened, put his boots back on, finally went back down the ladder, and with trepidation, ventured outside. There was no sign of the German soldiers, plus no way of knowing they had even been there. He went inside the house. There was a chair lying on its back, and the table still held a half-eaten breakfast the French couple had been forced to abandon, so after standing the chair back on its legs, he sat to finish the meal. He was very hungry, and although sad, it was a shame not to eat it when he was in need. Jonathon wondered where they had taken the couple and what their fate would be. Nothing would surprise him as to the outcome of whether they lived or died. He began to eat. He knew he would need to move on soon, as the German soldiers could return, and it would be obvious to them that there was someone else around. But first, he would fill his belly. As he sat eating, the door opened and a young woman entered. He hadn't seen her coming. Where did she come from?

She wore pants and a jacket. Her hair was short and in a bob. She was slim and very attractive. Speaking in French, she looked angry, and he guessed she was asking for the couple, but Jonathon didn't answer. Then she must have noticed his uniform, which, by now, was looking a little grubby. She spoke in English.

"You are English?" she asked, and her face looked friendlier.

"Er...yes," Jonathon answered hesitantly.

"Are you trying to escape from the Germans?"

Jonathon was still dubious.

"Please don't be afraid. I can help you."

"Yes, I am hiding, or trying to. I'm obviously not very good at it,' Jonathon answered as he got to his feet from the table. He knew he had to trust someone sooner or later, so why not this young woman?

"My name is Michèle.' She offered her hand. "Please don't be afraid. I'll help you.'

I'm Jonathon and I'm very pleased to meet you,' Jonathon shook Michèle's hand.

"Where are my parents?" she asked.

Jonathon swallowed. Would she be as friendly towards him when he told her that he watched the soldiers take them away without helping them? "The soldiers came. They took them away."

Michèle broke down and whatever she said was in French, and she had a lot to say.

Jonathon felt dreadful. He walked outside and left her to grieve. Finding a container outside with a continual stream of water that obviously came from a well, he washed his hands and face. Michèle eventually joined him. She looked terrible. Her eyes were puffy, and her face looked tear-stained.

"Where were you when it happened?" she asked.

He stood and turned towards her. "I was in the barn. They didn't know…no one knew. I'm sorry I couldn't help them. There were too many."

"You watched it happen?"

"Yes, unfortunately. It was over very quickly. They just dragged them out and into their Jeep, and then drove away."

Michèle looked into the distance and spoke as if she were talking to someone. "I will avenge…I promise." Then she turned towards Jonathon. "Did they rape my mother?'

"No. I don't think so."

"It would not surprise me. Filthy Germans, their brains are in the sewers." Jonathon looked at this slip of a girl and wanted to put his arm around her shoulders and hold her, as he could feel her pain, but he kept away so it wouldn't be misinterpreted.

"Do you know why they took them away?" Jonathon asked.

"More than likely because someone informed them that I was in the French resistance."

"Are you?"

Michèle nodded. "Come, we must find you some clothes to change into before we go. We must be quick before they return."

Jonathon waited while Michèle went inside the house to find the clothes. It was lovely here with the open fields and landscape…and dangerous. He wished he had visited France before the war. It was sad that so much violence was happening now. Eventually, Michèle came outside and gave him some trousers and a shirt.

"Here, try those on."

"Are these your father's?"

"Yes, but he doesn't need them anymore. If the Germans return, they will more than likely take them, so you may as well have them."

Jonathon stripped off his outer clothes.

"You have splinters. Would you like me to remove them?"

"Have we the time?"

"It won't take a minute." Michèle found a needle and began to dig into the base of his back. "Where did you get these?"

"My parachute dropped me into a bush."

Michèle made an undecipherable comment. "Here, that's the best I can do at this time. Now try the clothes on." She looked up to his face. "You are hurt?"

"I'm okay."

"You have blood on your head."

"It's only a scratch, I think."

"I will bathe it for you."

Michèle went back inside the house and came out with a cloth. "Bend down while I bathe it, please."

Jonathon bent down and could feel her gently wash the graze on his head. She had a lovely touch, gentle but…lovely. He liked it.

"That will do. At least it's clean now."

Jonathon dressed himself, and the clothes didn't fit him too badly. As he wrapped up his uniform, he began to transfer things into the pants Michèle had given him, but found it difficult to find everything, so he rummaged through his pockets.

Michèle looked confused. "What are you doing?"

"I'm just looking for something before I wrap it up. Ah! There it is," and Michèle watched as he took a handkerchief from the top pocket of his uniform and pushed it into the pocket of the pants.

"A handkerchief? We do have those, also."

"I'm sorry, but this one is special."

"We must bury your uniform somewhere. Maybe hide it in the garden."

"No, I'll take the risk and carry it with me. At least if I'm caught wearing it, they may treat me a little better."

"The Germans have no rules," Michèle said with a frown, so Jonathon took it outside and buried it. "We must hide it well, because if the soldiers find it, they will know straight away that there has been an English pilot here, and there will be retributions."

Michèle walked towards the nearby wood, and Jonathon followed. A slip of a girl she may be, but she was stronger than she looked. What these people had to endure with the Nazis, Jonathon could only guess after what he'd seen, and he didn't like it.

"You speak good English. Where did you learn?"

"My aunt married an Englishman, and they live in England. When I was born, my mother was very ill, so for the first seven years, I lived with them."

"In England?"

"Yes, in Datchet near London."

"Were you happy there?"

"Oh, yes. It seemed strange when I came home and everyone spoke French. I am fond of my aunt and uncle, and they would pay for my flights to visit them every year."

"Do you still go and visit them, or should I say, did you go and visit until the war?"

"Yes, I did. Hitler is a bad man. He is splitting up families and murdering so many people and children."

"I suppose you miss them?"

"Yes, but working with the Maqui makes me feel as if I am shortening the war."

"How long have you been a member of the resistance?"

"Six months ago, I started as a sympathizer and then eventually joined them, and that is why I can help you."

"I'm glad you joined the resistance."

Michèle turned to him and half-smiled. "I would be, if it wasn't for what has happened to my parents," she answered.

"Of course." Jonathon noticed a signpost. "Where are we going?"

Michèle pointed. "There is a man I want you to meet here." Jonathon read "Le Bourg d'Hem."

"Why? Will he help me?"

"Of course! Why else would I want you to meet him?"

Jonathon walked for a while with Michèle until they came to a farm. She ushered him into the farmhouse. When they stepped into the kitchen, they surprised the couple sitting at the table.

"Michèle!" They all began to speak in French, so Jonathon stood silently by.

Michèle turned and looked at Jonathon, and then she turned back to the man. "This is Didier, and Didier, this is Jonathon, an English pilot." Didier sprung to his feet and held out his hand. He spoke in French, but Jonathon didn't understand what he was saying, so Michèle explained.

"Please speak in English. Jonathon can't speak French."

"Pardon, monsieur, I asked if you were shot down."

"Yes, I was," answered Jonathon.

"When did it happen?"

"Yesterday, early in the morning."

"I saw your plane crash. We came looking for you, but you were nowhere to be found. All we found were the Germans, and they shot at us."

"I heard the shots, but thought they were shooting at me, so I hid, and that is why you couldn't find me, but thank you anyway."

"We are in the French resistance, so we can help you. Please, *monsieur*, sit and eat. I will pour you a drink."

Both Michèle and Jonathon joined them at the table and discussed their plans.

"What about the animals at the farm?" Michèle was concerned.

"Don't worry. They will be looked after until maybe you can take over, if that is what you wish."

After hiding in the village for a few days, they were given bicycles. Didier gave Jonathon a knife. "Using a gun is noisy and brings more soldiers your way, but this is quiet."

Michèle and Jonathon rode their bicycles to a farm a few miles away, and the farmer's wife gave them both a meal. They took him down into the cellar and showed him the secret room where Jonathon could go if there was any danger. It looked like a brick wall, but behind some shelving, there was a doorway, and through there was a room with a bed, a well with good clear water, crockery, cutlery, and tins with an opener. He could manage for a time, and Jonathon hoped he would never need it, or if he did, not need it for long.

"The well has good water," Michèle explained, as the farmer and his wife couldn't speak English. "And the bucket," Michèle pointed to a tin bucket in the corner of the room, "is for sanitary purposes. I'm afraid there is no toilet. Even they don't have a toilet."

"That's fine." Jonathon looked around the room and noticed a couple of airbricks on the outside wall. He would need to keep quiet if there were any soldiers around, but at least the air wouldn't get too stale.

"I wouldn't even use a torch when the soldiers are around if I were you. Do you think you will manage if the worst happens?"

"I will. Tell them thank you, please, Michèle. I really appreciate this."

"They know. Come, we can go back upstairs for now."

They sat and talked to the farmer and his wife, and Michèle told Jonathon their names were Yves and Véronique. Jonathon didn't do much talking, as he didn't understand what they were saying, but he listened and attempted to pick up an odd word.

Later, Michèle told Jonathon she was leaving, but she would pop in the following day to see how he was getting along. He walked her outside, and she kissed him on both cheeks. As she pulled away, he pulled her close and gave her a fleeting kiss on the lips.

"We've done it your way, and that was mine."

Michèle stretched up and gave him a quick kiss on the lips. "I like your way best."

Jonathon watched her walk away. He liked her. A lot.

Chapter 8

While Ruth, Alfred, and Jessie were having a quiet breakfast, after Shirley had left for school, they were disturbed by a loud knocking on the door. Ruth answered the door, and the dreaded telegraph boy stood there. Everyone knew that when a soldier was killed, the boy would come and visit his family, riding a motorcycle with a telegram. It was a living nightmare, and everyone would watch him as soon as he entered the street to see where he stopped. Now it was her turn to receive one. Ruth felt as if her heart was being ripped out of her body as she shakily tore it open and read that Jonathon was missing. The words were all too familiar after the First World War when it happened to Billy, her first husband. She told Alfred. They both left Jessie eating her breakfast, as they couldn't eat anymore.

Alfred hugged Ruth. "It doesn't say he's dead, Ruth, just missing in action. It's like history repeating itself. Didn't his dad go missing, too?" Ruth nodded. "If you remember, he didn't get killed. He came home. Wounded maybe, but he came home."

"I know."

Ruth thought about Billy and how Alfred would never know the effect of Billy's wounds and how the war had ruined their lives forever. He didn't know how those wounds stopped them from having a normal marriage with children and how Billy was wounded as much inside as out. Ruth promised Billy she would never tell anyone, and she never had. If it hadn't been for Mary's Uncle George and the rape, there would never have been a Jonathon. Was history repeating itself? Would Jonathon return? Or would he return, but be wounded?

"Well, then, Jonathon will come home, too. You see if I'm not right."

Alfred worried about Ruth, but wouldn't let her see it. He had to stay strong for her sake. He knew there was always a special bond between her and Jonathon. Maybe it was because he was the firstborn, or maybe because she only had the one son, but even so, Alfred knew it would hit Ruth hard, but now he should leave her and go to work.

"Will you be all right if I leave?"

"Yes, Alfred, I'll be fine." Alfred kissed her on the cheek and reluctantly went to work.

When Nora finally came down for her breakfast, Ruth told her about Jonathon. Nora didn't cry, she showed no emotion at all, and she wasn't even put off her food. In fact, she seemed to eat more than usual.

Ruth watched Nora eating her breakfast and felt choked. Poor Jonathon could have crashed and gone up in flames; Nora obviously didn't care, and in that moment, Ruth found herself hating the girl. *Stop it!* Ruth scolded herself. He could be safe, but then again he could be captured and tortured. Her mind worked overtime, and she ran upstairs. Entering her bedroom, she flung herself on the bed and sobbed quietly. The thought of her son being tortured was too much to bear. Where is Jonathon? What is he doing? And more importantly, is he safe?

Ruth lay on her back for a while, staring into space, and thought back to when Jonathon was conceived. It seemed a lifetime ago when it happened, on that night on the side of the canal. If only she had known at the time that it was her stepfather's brother, but it was too dark to see. Could she have done something to stop him? She thought back to his character and consoled herself that no one could have stopped him. He was bent on raping her, and he was a vicious man. Thinking back to her injuries after the attack made her realize just how nasty he was. My poor Billy, she thought. Unable to give her a child, and then finding her pregnant with another man's baby—how many humiliations could the man take? Poor, poor Billy. She could understand more now as to why he drowned himself. Ruth wiped her tears and made her way back down the stairs.

Going into the garden, she began to pull a few weeds and made a compost heap behind the Anderson shelter. She had to do something, and she didn't feel like housework. Venting her anger, she pulled up the weeds, and that made her feel better.

When Shirley came home, Ruth told her that Jonathon was missing, and she cried—they both did—but Ruth attempted to console Shirley like Alfred had with her.

"It doesn't mean he's gone forever, Shirley, but he's missing, and they don't know where he is."

"How is he missing, Mam?"

"His plane didn't return, so they guess it came down. No one knows where. He could be trying to get home at this very minute. We just don't know, but we must be brave and trust in Jonathon to come home."

Shirley wiped away her tears immediately and looked serene. "He will come home, Mam. I feel that he will come home…and safely."

Ruth shivered, and then smiled at Shirley and wished that she could be so positive. Shirley didn't really understand what death was or all the dangers a pilot could endure when he was on the run in a war. Later, Ruth answered the door again after hearing a quiet knock and was confronted by a lady from the church whom she knew slightly.

"I wondered if you would mind taking an evacuee, Mrs. Turner."

"I haven't thought about it. Come in, and I'll just see my husband for his opinion."

An evacuee had never entered her mind. They didn't have a spare bedroom, and they already had Nora, who was a handful on her own, but an evacuee, a child…Ruth didn't think she could cope with such a problem. Still, those poor children had been taken from their homes and families and placed with strangers, so when she thought about it, why not? At least they could give a child a happy and comfortable home.

Ruth led her into the kitchen and the lady sat in the nearest chair.

"I won't be a minute." Ruth disappeared into the workshop.

"Someone from the church has called…"

"What now?" Alfred sounded weary.

Ruth and Alfred had a quick discussion about the possibility and responsibility of taking on an evacuee.

"I wouldn't mind, you know that, but it'll be difficult for you, Ruth. How can you manage it with the business and Nora? Plus, you have your own children, and there isn't a spare bedroom."

"I'll manage somehow, as long as you don't mind."

Alfred watched her turn away and leave the room, and his admiration for her never waned. Maybe it could be a blessing in disguise, as it would keep Ruth occupied and keep her mind off Jonathon. It could be a good decision to accept the child. Ruth joined the lady again.

"I don't mind as long as the child is a girl and isn't too young, as with the business and everything, I don't think I could cope."

"That's fine, Mrs. Turner. I shall try and find someone suitable for you."

It was two weeks before Ruth opened the door to find the woman holding the hand of a child, a pretty girl, but she looked unkempt. Ruth felt relieved it was a girl, as it would have been impossible otherwise.

"This is Nancy Howarth. Nancy is ten years old and from London. She is an only child, but I thought she would get on well with your girls."

Ruth looked at Nancy, really looked at her; she looked much younger than Shirley, even though there wasn't much difference in their years. Nancy was smaller, undernourished at a guess, and her eyes were dark and sunken. Her coat looked as if it had seen better days, and her shoes were well worn. She wasn't wearing socks, and she had a small parcel wrapped in brown paper that, Ruth gathered, held what clothes she possessed. Her gas mask hung around her neck, and she had a label.

"I think we'll cut that label off first. What do you say, Nancy?"

"Yes, missus." Ruth went to get the scissors, while Nancy stood and waited until Ruth cut the label off. She felt as if she was liberating the poor child.

"Has she both parents at home?" Ruth asked the lady who accompanied her.

"No. There's just her and her mother. Her father died, and her mam is finding it difficult to look after her, as their home was bombed. She really needs someone to care for her, and I know I can count on you to do that. Anyway, I'll leave her with you. I'm sure you'll all get on fine."

Ruth showed the woman to the door, and then returned to Nancy.

"Have you eaten?" Ruth smiled at Nancy in the hope of making her feel welcome.

Nancy's answer was a whisper. "Yes, thank you, missus. I had some sandwiches."

Ruth began to take off her gas mask. "Do you know any of the other evacuees around here?"

"No, missus."

Ruth felt sympathy for Nancy. "You're all alone, then? Never mind, you can play with Jessie until Shirley comes home from school. Is that all right?"

"Yes, missus."

"Shirley isn't much older than you, so that's okay, isn't it?"

"Yes, missus."

"I don't like you calling me 'missus.' What would you like to call me, Mrs. Turner or Auntie Ruth? I think Auntie Ruth would be nicer, don't you?"

"Yes, mi—, Auntie Ruth," Nancy answered

Ruth gave a little laugh. "It doesn't matter if you forget what to call me. Just give me a name you feel comfortable with, dear." Ruth looked at the girl and noticed her hair needed washing and brushing, as it was a little matted. "How would you like a bath, Nancy? I can run it for you and you can bathe yourself, but I'll have to wash your hair. Okay?"

"Yes." Her eyes showed no emotion.

"You'll feel refreshed when all that travel dust is washed away."

"Yes."

"You'll enjoy a nice bath."

"But you're going to wash my hair?"

"Yes. Is that okay?"

"Yes."

Ruth took her and Jessie upstairs to the bathroom. She gave Jessie something to play with, and realized that it wasn't going to be easy with Nancy. There was a lot she didn't know about this young stranger, and she hoped there would be no complications.

Jonathon's bedroom was being used for Nora, so Nancy would have to share with Shirley, and she hoped they would both get on okay, as they would need to share a double bed. After Ruth had washed the girl's back and shoulders, she asked Nancy if she would like to finish off herself and left her to it, and then went back and washed Nancy's hair. Wrapping a large towel around her, Ruth took her downstairs and gave her biscuits, and they both had a cup of tea while Jessie drank some milk.

Ruth picked up the Snowfire ointment from the cupboard that she kept for when the children's hands became chapped and warmed it in front of the fire. When it started to melt, she gently rubbed it on the back of Nancy's hands.

"Am I hurting you, dear?" Ruth asked.

"No, but what does it do?"

"It will help to heal your hands. I'll put this on each day until your hands feel better. They look ever so sore, dear." Nancy nodded.

After they had their cup of tea, Ruth went upstairs and came down with something of Shirley's for Nancy to wear and began to wash the clothes that Nancy discarded. Then they waited for Shirley to come home.

When Shirley arrived home, she was so excited to have a girl to share her bedroom that Ruth thanked her lucky stars. Ruth found Shirley so patient with Nancy and generous with her things, it brought tears to her eyes. Games were found, and her daughter offered Nancy her books to read, but Ruth suspected the girl couldn't read very well, as she didn't show much enthusiasm. She decided to have a word in her daughter's ear and maybe get Shirley to help with her reading.

Alfred came through, and she introduced him. "This is Uncle Alfred, and this is our Nancy."

Ruth noticed there were tears in Nancy's eyes. Maybe this was too much.

Nora came home and was introduced to Nancy, but she didn't look very pleased to see the girl. "Another kid! As long as she doesn't make too much noise and keep me awake."

Ruth could have said a lot to Nora, but she bit her bottom lip. She gave them all sausage and mash for their tea, but Nancy ate too much.

"Is everything all right, Nancy?" Ruth asked.

"I feel sick," Nancy replied.

Ruth laughed. "I'm not surprised with what you've eaten."

"We don't have that much at home."

"I'm sorry, Nancy. You must tell me what you usually eat, and then I won't overfeed you."

"My mam can't afford much."

"That's sad, but don't think you have to eat enough to last you in case you don't get anything else for a while. You'll have food on a regular basis now, dear."

"I'm sorry, Aunty Ruth."

"I'll treat your hair tonight, Nancy, and yours, too, Shirley." Ruth told Shirley that Nancy had head lice, but not to say anything to her. She didn't tell Nancy, as she didn't want to cause her any stress.

As she rubbed vinegar into their hair, Nora understood why she was doing it.

"Ugh! Don't come near me if you have nits. I don't want them."

"Nora, I don't think that was called for. It's only a precaution," Ruth lied, and Nancy looked upset.

Before Ruth took Shirley and Nancy up to bed, she wrapped a towel around their heads and tucked them in like a turban, telling them to sleep with them on. Nancy didn't object. Ruth felt that she had to treat Shirley the same as Nancy, just so that she wouldn't feel as if she was being picked on, and Shirley was so good to go along with it. When they did go upstairs to bed, Nancy was amazed when she found that she was to share a bedroom with Shirley…and no one else.

"Is it all ours?" she asked wide-eyed.

"Yes, dear," Ruth answered with a smile.

"Aren't we sharing the room with anybody else?"

"No, dear. Jessie stays in mine and Uncle Alfred's bedroom. It's just yours and Shirley's. Is that okay?"

Nancy didn't say anything else, but dived into bed with Shirley, and they both pulled the covers up to their necks. Bending over, Ruth kissed them both on their foreheads.

"Good night, girls. Hope you sleep well."

"Good night," Nancy and Shirley answered in unison. Ruth returned downstairs to the sound of both girls giggling, and that made her feel good.

Ruth made a list of the things Nancy needed. The child didn't come with much, so it was a long list. She scratched her head a lot and would need that nipped in the bud, and Ruth made a note of that. She must search for her fine-tooth comb, and then she could keep a check on their hair. Last thing she wanted was for her to pass them on to her girls, so she must keep on top of it and maybe give her girls the same treatment just to make sure. It was a good thing that the school holidays were coming up. Nancy was very thin and undernourished and would need building up before she really started school.

Everyone was suffering from a shortage of vitamins, but Nancy more so. Her hands were sore with dry skin and so was her face, and that meant she would need more Snowfire to rub on her hands, and maybe a bit of something on her face, too. There wasn't much left in the cupboard, so she would need more both for Nancy and her girls. Maybe another jar of malt and cod liver oil to help to build her up wouldn't go amiss, either. In case Nancy developed a cough, she would get some more Fennings Lung Healers and Scott's Emulsion. The thought of fever cure went through her mind, but she was sure that Nancy would think she was poisoning her if she gave her that. Ruth would first need to build her confidence and show her lots of love.

The following morning after Alfred had returned to work, and Shirley had gone to school, Ruth went upstairs with a cup of tea for Nora and found Nancy sitting up in bed.

"Can I get up?" the girl asked.

"Of course, dear. Just get up when you're ready, and I'll give you some breakfast."

"Have I got some breakfast?"

"I'll make you some when you're ready."

"Just for me?"

"Yes, of course, dear."

Nancy ate cereal, and when Ruth offered her toast, she ate that, too.

"What do you normally eat for your breakfast, Nancy?"

"We don't usually have any."

"Don't you, dear?"

"My mam never had any money for breakfast."

Ruth felt as if someone had stabbed at her heart. Poor things! They must be really poor. Ruth remembered what that was like from when she was a child. The hunger pains and…no, it was a time she would rather forget and look forward.

After Nancy finished her breakfast, Ruth found more clothes of Shirley's. "You can have these, Nancy. They were Shirley's, but I don't think she'll mind if I give them to you. Is that all right?"

Nancy's face beamed. Shirley didn't have that many clothes; it was the coupons mainly that made everyone struggle, but she had to give Nancy some of them, as the girl hardly had a thing to wear. Some clothes were getting too small for Shirley anyway, but they would fit the girl fine. After Nancy put them all away in the drawer that Ruth had allocated for her, they went shopping and called on Mary.

Mary was glad to see her and made a fuss of Nancy. They stayed for a cup of tea while they caught up with the news, and then they did the shopping. Nancy was so excited when Ruth bought her two new dresses. Ruth had to watch how much she spent. Luckily, she had been saving up her clothes coupons, but just one pair of shoes, pyjamas, and underclothes used all the coupons. Alfred could last a little longer without a new shirt, and she could manage for a while with her old shoes. There were other necessities bought for the girl that didn't need coupons. It was expensive, though, taking on an evacuee.

That evening, she treated Nancy's hair again before tucking her into bed. She was a lovely child and showed her appreciation for everything Ruth did. Things Shirley took for granted were making Nancy very happy.

Shirley was still discovering Nancy's past home life. Ruth came into the kitchen where she and Nancy were playing a game at the table, and Ruth went over to the sink to wash the pots. Shirley left Nancy to help Ruth and whispered to her mam while she was drying them.

"Nancy lost some of her friends in London, Mam."

"Really."

"Yes, she told me they were killed by the bombs."

Ruth shuddered and thought how awful it must have been for the child.

"She says that they would play in the rubble after the bombs, and they had secret dens. They would go through the bricks and stuff and sometimes find a chair or a piece of mirror and take it to their den. Nancy said it was exciting because they never knew what they would find."

"That's terrible."

"I don't think Nancy had a home, Mam."

"What do you mean, dear?"

"She told me they were bombed out of their home and lived with someone else. They only had one room to live in with one bed they both shared."

"Living in London isn't very good. They appear to have more than their fair share of bombs."

"I'm glad we don't live in London. Thanks, Mam!"

"What for?"

"For not making us live in London." Ruth laughed.

Nancy called for Shirley to come and finish their game, so Shirley left Ruth to finish off. *Those poor children in London,* Ruth thought, *they must have a rough life...and the poor people who lost their home, too.*

Ruth took Nancy to school to enroll her before they all broke up for the main holidays, and she started the following week. Shirley took her under her wing and introduced her to all her friends, but she had to go into a different class, so the girl soon made her own friends. At first, Ruth took her to school, but she watched Nancy as she joined other girls. The girl was doing fine. Her hair looked healthy now, and Ruth plaited it and put it in ribbons. Her clothes were freshly washed and ironed, and she looked a different girl than the one who was delivered to her door with her little parcel, gas mask, and label with her name written on it. Yes, she had made a difference.

§ § § § §

Ruth made sure that Nancy wrote to her mam on a regular basis. There did seem a lot of love between them, and she knew that Nancy missed her. Ruth once wrote on the bottom of the girl's letter, telling her mam that she could speak to Nancy on the business phone. If she rang between the girls' finishing at school time and before Alfred finished work, then that would be the best time.

The phone call came a few days later, and Shirley answered it. While Shirley went to tell Nancy, Ruth took over the phone. "Hello, Mrs. Howarth, I'm Ruth. I'm looking after your daughter and thought it would be nice to speak to you myself, if only to assure you that she is fine and well."

"Please call me Hilda," she answered.

"Thank you. You know you are free to visit Nancy any time you like, You'll be very welcome. The children are now on their school holidays, so Nancy would be free to spend time with you. You can stay as long as you want."

Hilda burst into tears. "I'm so grateful to you, and I'm sorry I can't send you any money, but things are hard just now. I'll try and make it up to you as soon as I can."

"Don't worry about that. I'll meet you off the train if you tell me when you're coming."

"That will be wonderful."

Nancy took over the phone, and Ruth left them alone. Nancy was so excited she could hardly speak when she heard her mam's voice, and she was crying when she joined them in the kitchen later. The next time Nancy wrote to her mam, Ruth pushed a postal order inside for her mother's train fare.

Ruth received another phone call from Hilda, and they arranged to meet at the station the following week. London was heavily bombed a couple of days before she was due, and Hilda was killed. Ruth received the phone call with the news from Hilda's friend Pat.

It wasn't just the fact that Nancy had lost her mam, but what would Ruth do when the war was over? How could she send the child back to London?

Before Ruth told Nancy the bad news, she thought she'd do a bit of digging about her family.

"Do you have any aunties or uncles, Nancy?"

"No."

"No cousins or relatives at all?"

"No, I don't think so. My mam never mentioned anybody."

Ruth decided to have a few words with Alfred before she told Nancy what had happened. They decided that if the child had nowhere to live, they would see about adopting her, if Nancy was willing. First of all, they must report to the authorities. After reporting the situation, they settled on the fact that they would be better waiting until after the war was over, and maybe they could contact any relatives she might have, all being well. Until then, Nancy would remain an evacuee staying with them until after the war.

When Nancy got up the following morning, Ruth had to break the news of her mother's death. Nancy was devastated and took the news badly, which was hardly surprising. She spent most of her time in her bedroom, but came downstairs when she wanted a drink and later for a meal, though her appetite was diminished. Ruth gave her a cuddle.

"Don't worry, Nancy, we'll look after you."

"Yes, but Auntie Ruth, what will happen when the war is over? What will happen to me? There isn't anybody else."

"We'll try to find out if you have any family. Don't worry about it, dear. If there is no family, do you really think that we'd send you back to London?"

Nancy calmed down a little, but she'd break down every so often without warning.

One night when the sirens went, they all moved into the Anderson shelter with an extra chair, which Shirley said she'd use and let Nancy sleep in the cot, as Nora absolutely refused to use the shelter. They could hear the enemy aircraft, and Nancy began to scream. There was no calming her, no matter how hard they tried, and Ruth could see the girl was terrified.

"It's all right, Nancy, don't worry. You'll be safe with us."

Nancy still cried in fear. "No, no, it's a flying bomb."

"I don't think so, Nancy. We don't have them over here."

They couldn't calm Nancy until, exhausted, she fell asleep on Ruth's lap. When the others went back into the house after the all-clear, Ruth stayed where she was; she didn't want to disturb the girl, but followed later when Nancy awoke. This poor child had gone through hell. The following morning, they heard the news that a flying bomb had landed in a farmer's field nearby. Nancy must have recognized the sound.

§ § § § §

Shirley finished junior school, but Nancy had to wait until the following year. As Shirley was saying good-bye and thank you to all the teachers, they were surprised that she wasn't going to the grammar school, but Ruth and

Alfred didn't think it was necessary, so an all-girls secondary school was her next move. Peter was going to grammar school, and Shirley knew there wasn't much chance of seeing him again, as he would make new friends, and he was already a bit of a snob. All the same, she was sad and hurt inside when she said good-bye for the last time. Her world was changing.

Shirley was writing a letter to Jimmy with the help of Nancy, and Jessie was playing with her few toys. Ruth watched her for a while. What a wonderful imagination children had! They could adapt and play with almost anything. Nora said she was going out for a walk, and Ruth felt glad to see the back of her that day.

It took Shirley a long time to write her letter, and Ruth was dying to see what she had written, but she didn't dare ask. She was allowed her privacy unless, of course, she thought she was writing the wrong things, like family and personal things, but Shirley had asked Ruth about what she should write, and Ruth had given her an idea or two, plus restrictions. After Shirley sealed her letter, she ran off to post it with Nancy.

Because of Shirley's trauma of leaving school, Alfred suggested going to the pictures. There was a film in Technicolor on at the Roxy, and he'd overheard Shirley telling a friend about it.

"How would you and Nancy like to go the pictures tonight, Shirley?"

"Can we go to see Maria Montez and Sabu?" she asked. "It's in Technicolor."

"Well, I was hoping to go to the Queens. There's a spy film on there." He laughed when he saw Shirley's face. "I'm only kidding. Go and ask your mam if she would like to go."

"Where is she?"

"She's cleaning the bathroom. It seems I made a mess after cleaning my hands of the printing ink."

Alfred heard Shirley racing up the stairs and thought that at least it would take their minds off Jonathon for a while.

Shirley returned and looked a little disappointed. "Mam says what about Jessie?"

"Tell her I'll get a babysitter if she wants to come with us."

Shirley came back out of breath. "Mam says no! She'll stay with Jessie and wait for Nora to come home."

Alfred was disappointed. "Okay. As soon as we've had our tea then, get yourself ready, and we'll go. We don't want to miss the beginning."

Shirley and Nancy ran upstairs as soon as tea was over and prepared themselves for their trip to the pictures. Ruth could hear them talking and laughing upstairs, and she was glad that Nancy seemed to be settling in, and so quickly.

On the way to the pictures, they called in the corner shop.

"Now then, who wants some sweets?"

"Me, Dad. Can Nancy have some, too?"

"Of course. What would you like, Nancy?"

"What is Shirley having?"

Alfred looked at Shirley questioningly.

"I'll have pear drops, please, Dad."

"Don't you want a change, love?' asked Alfred. "You always choose those, or at least you do when I'm buying."

"But I like pear drops."

"Okay, it's your choice. And what does Nancy want, then?"

"I'll have pear drops, too, please." Alfred pulled a face.

As soon as they sat in their seats in the cinema, the cock began to crow to advertise the Pathe News. It was all about how the war was progressing, and Alfred attempted to forget the problems at home, but the news didn't help matters. He admired Ruth so much, as she never allowed herself to show any emotion in front of the children, and that must have been difficult for her, as he knew her heart was breaking. He breathed a sigh of relief when the big film started and he could lose himself in the story, and he hoped Ruth was coping at home.

Ruth sat darning socks when Nora came home. She looked sullen.

"Is everything all right?" Ruth looked up from her darning.

"I suppose so."

"Been anywhere nice?"

"No."

Nora watched Ruth for a while. "You're good at that, aren't you?"

"Am I, dear?" Ruth looked over her glasses, which were perched on the end of her nose.

"Better than me, anyway. Would you darn my red jumper? It's only a small hole, and I'm afraid of it getting any bigger."

"No, Nora. I'm afraid you will have to do it yourself. I have enough to do." Ruth's thoughts were working overtime. *Cheeky madam!*

Chapter 9

Jonathon was up the following morning as soon as he heard the cows, and there was noise coming from downstairs. There was someone moving about. He could hear feet and voices outside. It was 6:00 a.m., and he dressed, and then made his way downstairs. He felt safe here, if anywhere was safe, but at least it was comfortable and his belly was fed. The water was pumped from the well into a small tub at the front of the house with a tap attached, and this is where they all washed. Jonathon found that French country life was very basic with no bathrooms.

Meals were enjoyed even though the food wasn't always much to write home about, but there was no rush in eating it down. Soup was eaten three times a day with a lump of homemade bread but not much besides; all the same, it was very welcome, as he always had a good appetite. Véronique made the soup with anything edible that she could find. She would often take a walk up the country lanes with a basket and return with it full of he didn't know what. He had seen nettles in her basket, but couldn't name anything else. It always tasted good, though, so she obviously knew what she was doing. She baked only once a month because of the lack of fuel, and it was still a week off to her next baking day, so supplies were coming to an end. Michèle told him that Véronique made pies, cakes, and bread. Jonathon knew about the bread, as this was what they had with the soup. It was round and thick like a car wheel, and she hung it in the pantry, where it slowly dried out. They would hack a piece off to go in their soup each day. Jonathon looked forward to the next week and the promise of such good food.

Yves went into the village to get a cow shod, as there were no horses, so they could plough the land. After, they would visit the local inn for a drink. It was all new territory to Jonathon, and he went along with Yves, watched with interest, and enjoyed the glass or two with him.

On the way home, they hardly saw anyone, and Jonathon enjoyed his new surroundings. It felt good to see so much greenery instead of buildings, streets, and roads. There were no buses, and you hardly ever saw a car unless there was a German sitting in the driving seat.

"Look, Yves, at the rabbits playing over there."

They did have butter and cheese, but rabbits were free food, and Yves would kill one to help with the meals whenever he got the chance. It seemed a shame to kill the rabbits, as they were so lovely and Jonathon always associated them with pets, but with the shortage of meat, it was a necessity. The German army took most of their produce, and they were left with scraps, so any extras from the wildlife were eagerly taken.

The people were very laid-back. His plans were to help them where he could. He'd never worked on a farm in his life, so they would need to teach him a lot of things. He was willing to learn and felt very grateful that they were willing to take him on under the circumstances.

It reminded him of home whenever he heard the chickens in the morning. His first job was to go out and feed them and collect the eggs. They were free to roam, so they fed off the land mostly, but they were supplemented with a little corn. Véronique showed him where everything was, and he found himself enjoying the chore. He loved the way the hens all crowded round him as he put out their food, and again later, as if they were expecting some special treat, but all he had this time was the grit to help make the egg shells hard. It took him back to when he was a child. He was young then, but the memory lingered. There were many more chickens here than when he was young at home and many more eggs to collect. Yves was seeing to the cows at the same time; later, they all met back in the kitchen for a simple breakfast of soup and coffee. To Jonathon, it tasted good. Maybe it was because of the fresh air, or it could be that he had something useful to do at last.

After, he was taken to the land at the back of the house where they grew vegetables and left to do whatever he thought he should. The language was a barrier, but he was willing to learn, and that was the most important thing. Véronique came out later and asked him, using mime, to dig out some potatoes. He enjoyed that chore, too. Rooting through the soil for them, it sometimes amazed him how many he would find attached to one plant. It was very satisfying, and he made himself a pledge that when the war was over, and he had his own garden, he would grow potatoes and vegetables. It was very rewarding.

When Jonathon had enough, he sought out Véronique and gave them to her, and then returned to the garden. Before long, he could smell Véronique's cooking in the kitchen, and by the time he was called for his dinner, he was more than ready for whatever Véronique had prepared. Today it was special, as Yves did kill a rabbit, so they were having a real cooked meal, just like home.

After dinner, Yves put his hands together and placed them on his left cheek and then bent his head to show Jonathon that it was time to go to bed for a nap. Jonathon felt ready for a sleep. After not having had any work to do for a while, he felt weary from working on the land, but he wasn't complaining. He enjoyed everything from working in the garden to eating the produce. Now it was time to lay his head and sink into his feather pillow and sleep. He looked around the bedroom—very basic with bare floorboards and no rugs, but comfortable enough, and definitely an improvement on the woods he first slept in.

Jonathon was constantly on the lookout for enemy soldiers, but mostly for Michèle. After all, she was his only communication, with the language problem. He knew it was important for him to learn French as soon as possible. He only wished he had learned the German language when he was younger, as that would have been very helpful now.

Michèle came to visit and joined them for the evening meal. Jonathon was pleased to see her and found himself watching her at every opportunity, but hoping no one noticed. He was attracted to her, he knew that, and he hoped she felt the same where he was concerned. Yves, Véronique, and Michèle had a heated conversation. They looked angry, and Jonathon wondered what they were saying until Michèle explained they were discussing the German occupation and the horrendous acts they were performing. After seeing how they treated Michèle's parents, he knew he wouldn't be surprised at anything the Germans dished out.

When Michèle left, Jonathon walked with her outside and down the lane a little. He had to be careful, as he didn't want to run any risks for him or the others after they had been so kind. He hesitated, and then placed his arm around her shoulders and stopped.

"I'd better not go any further."

"You're right, it wouldn't do."

"Is there a man in your life, Michèle?" he asked as he held her closer.

"It would be impossible for me at this time."

"You mean with the war?"

"Yes, of course, but there are times that you can't help how you feel."

"Don't you think that you should grab what you can, when you can, because there is no guarantee of a future?"

Michèle went quiet, and Jonathon let her break away, but decided to walk a little further with her. They walked in silence until he stopped again.

"I must go back now, Michèle. I've gone too far as it is."

"You're right, Jonathon…in more ways than one."

Jonathon kissed Michèle, and she kissed him back with a passion. As they parted, Jonathon felt as if he was making progress with her. He liked her a lot.

The following morning, Jonathon was asked to accompany Yves to the cowshed where he showed him how to milk a cow. That was fun, and they laughed about it, but Jonathon wasn't very good at it. Only when the cow complained did Yves stop him. They went for breakfast, and then Yves sent him to hoe around the vines while he pruned the plants. The grapes were almost ready for harvesting and were hanging with the weight. They didn't have too many, but it was hard work, and Jonathon began to miss flying his ship. If only he could climb into the damn thing, he could show the enemy a thing or two. He thought back to his pilot friends, wondering what they were up to and if there were any more missing. He missed their companionship, and he wondered if there were any of them missing him. He would love to know what happened to Roger. He hoped that he'd escaped.

By lunchtime, he was more than ready to demolish anything Véronique placed in front of him, even nettle soup, which he never fancied, but now he enjoyed. He helped Véronique collect the nettles. He was amazed at what they could collect in the hedgerows to make their soup. All this fresh air and hard work were giving him quite an appetite. He could see himself going home unrecognizable with all the weight he may pile on, if it was possible to get fat on mostly bread and soup.

Jonathon was really getting into the French style of living because he was ready for bed in the afternoon. It did break up the day, and when Yves shouted to him later to return to the vines, again he was ready.

They hadn't been outside for very long when Véronique came running towards them, shouting in a panic. Jonathon couldn't understand until he heard the sound of a vehicle. Yves pointed to the ditch at the side of the field, and he ran towards it. Véronique picked up the hoe and took over from Jonathon. He lay in the mud at the bottom of the ditch, his heart beating so hard he felt it would come through his chest when he heard the German voices. Had they come for him? Maybe he'd been seen by someone and reported. It could have been when he was with Michèle, as he could forget himself when he was with her. He flattened himself as much as he could into the ditch. It was soft and slimy, and again he wished he knew what the voices were saying. He didn't dare peep over the ditch for fear of being seen, but for all he knew, Yves and Véronique could be telling the Germans where he was hiding. Jonathon hoped there was enough ditch to hide in, and he began to pray as he crawled along the slime on his belly.

It went very quiet for a while, but Jonathon stayed where he was and waited for the all clear from Yves or Véronique. He heard voices again and some laughing, too, but from further away. Eventually, he realized the soldiers had left, and Yves came over and waved his arms to show he was safe. Yves laughed when he saw the state of Jonathon. He was covered in mud, and he shouted to Véronique, who also laughed, but beckoned to Jonathon to follow her to the house. On the way, Véronique showed him the chickens and some eggs and explained in mime that they were the reason for the soldiers' visit. Véronique told him to strip off his clothes, and after she had poured a few buckets of water over him and washed his hair that was congealed with mud, she brought him a towel, and Jonathon dried his naked body and made his way upstairs to get dressed, while Véronique took over the job of getting his clothes clean. There was no bathroom; the water had to be heated first and the toilet was in a shed at the back of the house, but nothing was wasted here, as the proceeds were used on the garden as fertilizer. As Jonathon dressed himself, he thanked his guardian angel again. That had been a close shave, and it made him realize that he mustn't get too complacent.

Chapter 10

The following morning, Shirley gave a full commentary to Ruth over breakfast on the film she saw with her dad the night before. Later when Shirley and Nancy left to go to the park, Ruth thanked Alfred for taking them.

"Sorry, Alfred, I just couldn't concentrate on a film, but the children enjoyed it."

Alfred touched her arm. "I know."

After Alfred went to work, Ruth took the post that had been delivered that morning. There was a small parcel from Jimmy, so she placed it on one side for Shirley to open later. She opened the mail addressed to her and Alfred, as he didn't mind her doing that. There were just bills and one order. They were scraping through okay, and that was good, as there were others depending on them for a wage. After that, she thought she would clean one of the bedrooms upstairs and make all the beds.

Ruth picked up Jessie and took her upstairs with her. "Play quietly, Jessie, because Nora is still sleeping." Giving her a few toys to play with in her cot, she did her chores.

It was almost noon when Nora came downstairs. The girls came back for their dinner, and Alfred joined them. After Alfred had returned to work, Nora put on her coat.

"I'm going out."

"Are you going anywhere nice?" asked Ruth

"I'm meeting a friend." Then Nora left.

After Ruth washed the dishes, she took Jessie upstairs with her and walked into Jonathon's bedroom. Ruth looked around. If only she'd known that Jonathon would go missing, she wouldn't have washed those clothes he left for her, they would have still smelled of him, but it's too late now. Making the

69

bed, which now belonged to Nora, tears sprang to her eyes and trickled down her face. He wasn't dead, she told herself, only missing, and he could be fine and well. She must remember that and keep faith. Ruth dried her eyes and then went back into her own bedroom and lay on the bed. Was it possible to absorb his present feelings? Where was he? Was he hurt? If only she was there to help him if he needed her. "Oh, God, please look after my son," she prayed quietly. She slowly got up from the bed. At least she could make sure the bedroom was clean when and if he did come home, but she would leave everything exactly as he had left it, as near as possible anyway, if or when Nora left.

In the afternoon, after Jessie had gone to bed for her afternoon sleep, Ruth went into the printers' side of the property and helped Alfred to finish an order.

"I'm sorry to hear about Jonathon." Marion, the full-time assistant, looked a little uncomfortable.

"Thank you, Marion, but we're hoping he'll turn up safe and well."

"That's good. After all, he could be. You never know."

Ruth could tell from her voice that she didn't really believe it. After all, when a pilot goes missing, it usually means that his aircraft has been shot down. Ruth couldn't believe that, wouldn't believe that; she was going to be strong. Alfred came and put his arm around her shoulders. He bent close to her ear.

"Are you okay?" he asked.

"I'll survive." Ruth went back inside the house.

It had been an ordeal keeping a brave face, but she must. Ruth also had decided that the sooner she went out and faced everyone, the better. Life had to go on, and she had her girls and husband to look after. She would try to think positively. Jonathon would come home, maybe not for a while, but he would come home.

Jessie was awake, so Ruth prepared her to go out. After putting on her coat and picking up her basket, Ruth walked to Mary and Peter's shop. They needed to know about Jonathon, and she may as well get it over and done with. Opening the door, she could see they were busy, so she hung back a while. As soon as she got the chance, she told Mary she had something to tell her—something private. Mary led her into the back of the shop and made a cup of tea for them both.

"Now, what's on your mind, Ruth? It must be something serious, as you don't often want to come and talk to me in private." Ruth burst into tears and Mary rushed to her side. "Whatever is it, sis?"

"It's Jonathon. He's missing." Ruth attempted to compose herself.

"Where?"

"I don't know where. In my own mind, it's France, but I don't really know." Ruth broke down crying again, and Mary put her arms around her.

"My God!"

"I know. It didn't say dead, just missing."

"That could mean anything, as you know...after what happened to Billy."

"Oh, Mary, it's terrible not knowing. I mean, is he dead, or is he a prisoner? I just don't know, and it's killing me."

"Poor, poor Ruth, you've just got to hope."

Jessie, seeing Ruth crying, started crying, too.

"It's easy to say, but not to do. I must go. Oh, and there's something else."

"What?"

"I have a young woman staying with me who says that she is seven months pregnant with Jonathon's child."

"Oh, Ruth! Are you pleased?"

"I don't know. If it really is Jonathon's child, then yes."

"Don't you believe her?"

"I don't know what to believe anymore. Take no notice of me, Mary. I'd better go."

"Don't go yet, Ruth. Sit a while until you're feeling better and tell me about it."

"I won't get any better, Mary, not until the news improves...if it ever does."

"I'm sure the news will improve. Keep your chin up, dear...for me...please."

Ruth stood and picked up her basket. "I'm going. Pray for me, Mary, but most of all, pray for Jonathon."

"I will."

Mary gave Ruth a hug and watched her go. "Look after yourself," Mary called after her.

Ruth didn't look back—she couldn't, she was crying and didn't want Mary to see her tears. As she walked home, she thought she saw Nora coming out of The White Bear public house with a coloured man. They turned a corner before she got close, but she was sure...then she dismissed it as her state of mind. No, she wouldn't go in that public house; it was a pick-up place. No, she wouldn't do that, not in her condition. When she arrived back home, she switched on the radio. After five minutes, she turned it off again. Ruth found she couldn't concentrate on anything, so she took Jessie into the workshop to see what Alfred was up to.

Alfred needed help, as they were still rushing to get the order finished, so Ruth found Jessie some paper and a pencil and sat her down to draw. She stayed with Alfred and worked hard finishing the order, and then tidying things up, and she felt better for it. This not knowing about Jonathon was driving her mad. If only she knew what was happening with him, she would feel better. How was he coping? Or more importantly, is he alive?

When the order was finally finished, and their cup of tea was gone, Ruth used the guillotine to cut up the trimmings from the paper they'd been using, placed weights on the top, and finished off gluing the ends.

"The children will like them to mess about with. They're handy for the girls who like to make paper dolls. You can sell them for a penny each, Marion, when the glue dries."

Marion nodded. Ruth loved to see the children come in for them, and sometimes if she especially liked them, she would give them a thicker pad.

Ruth took Jessie into the garden while Alfred went back to the workshop to finish off. The garden needed a lot of care, as they were neglecting it. It seemed so pointless when they knew it would only take one bomb and it would all be in vain. Ruth realized she was getting morbid and would have to get out of it. With those thoughts in mind, she began to pull out the weeds again. Maybe she could grow something to eat. A thousand thoughts went through her mind of the First World War when she lived with her auntie, uncle, Mary, and her grandma. Grandma was a good cook and never threw anything away. Her fruit pies were to die for, with pastry that melted away. Now Ruth felt as if she could eat one this very minute, and she licked her lips with the thought. Her sugar allowance wouldn't allow it, though, so she would just have to dream.

Looking around the garden, she wondered if Alfred would agree to have hens. They were tying, but the meat and eggs would help the rations. She would have a word with him when he finished work.

Ruth decided she would make some small cakes with a little of her rations. Carrots would be used to help the sugar, so she stood and grated a few. The smell from the oven tempted her to prepare a pot of tea for when Alfred came back in from the workshop, and she would surprise him with the carrot cakes. Keeping busy was the best thing to do to stop her worrying about Jonathon.

§§§§§§

Shirley came home from school with Nancy and squealed with delight when she found a parcel waiting for her. She could tell it was from Jimmy, and she ran upstairs and threw herself on the bed before she opened it. Nancy went into the garden.

Shirley ripped open the parcel to find a small box, and inside was a ring. It fitted her middle finger. There was a letter, too; it wasn't very long, but it was hers and hers alone. Shirley held it to her chest and made herself comfortable before she began to read it.

Dear Shirley,

I have done most of my training, and they're allowing me home on leave for a few days. I don't know what's happening when I return, but I'm not going to think about that.

I bought you this ring as a thank-you for saving my life. It's only a small gesture, but I thought it was pretty. If it doesn't fit you now, then it will when you grow a little.

I'll pop round to see you and maybe take you to the pictures, if there is one you would especially like to see.

See you soon.

Your friend, Jimmy

Shirley read the letter over and over again and pushed it into her dressing table drawer. Holding up her hand, she viewed the ring. It was like getting engaged, and she felt so proud. Her friends at school would be jealous. Shirley decided to wear it once to school so that everyone could see it, and then she would put it away and wear it when she was out with Jimmy. She imagined his face smiling down at her and looked forward to him coming home, and then she could see him again and thank him for her gift. Running downstairs, she checked on all the pictures that were advertised in the weekly *Reporter* to see which she fancied. Maybe he would be home soon, but he didn't say when. All the same, she was excited and couldn't wait to see him again. Ruth came inside from the garden with Jessie and Nancy.

"Look, Mam, look at my ring. Jimmy bought it for me, isn't it lovely? Look, Nancy, it's from Jimmy."

Ruth admired it, and so did Nancy. "You're very lucky, Shirley. You'll have to make sure you don't lose it. I think that would upset Jimmy, so look after it well."

Ruth pondered the gift. It was more than likely just a gift, and she hoped there were no undercurrents. It worried her for a while. When she told Alfred her thoughts, he dismissed them.

"I was thinking, you know, I don't think there is anything wrong with that lad, and I don't think it's a sinister gift. He seems a really nice boy...very likeable."

Ruth had to agree with him.

Shirley saw Jimmy the following evening when she was looking at the advertised photographs at the front of the picture house with Nancy. It was Jimmy's voice she heard first. He couldn't see her, as Nancy was almost blocking his view, and because he wouldn't expect her to be there, he wasn't looking. Shirley was glad he couldn't see her. Jimmy was with a girl, and he was looking down at her and smiling. He looked happy, and for the first time in her life, Shirley felt jealous. Tears sprang to her eyes as she watched him pay the cashier for them both to go upstairs in the expensive seats. It cost much more upstairs, and he never took her there. He always took her downstairs where it was cheaper.

"Come on, Nancy, let's go home."

"I thought you wanted to see what was on."

"It doesn't matter now. Come on." Shirley turned to go, and Nancy followed her.

Shirley didn't want any supper that evening and couldn't wait to go to bed. She felt ill, and Ruth worried about her and followed her upstairs to tuck her in.

"Aren't you feeling well, dear?" Ruth asked.

"I'm okay, Mam."

"Have you written a letter to Jimmy yet? I see you received one from him."

"No, he's home on leave."

"Oh! When did he get home?"

"I don't know, but I saw him tonight."

"Will he be coming here for you?"

"He said he would, but I don't know. He was with a girl tonight."

"I see." Ruth bent over and kissed Shirley on her forehead.

Ruth went back downstairs. "I think our Shirley's growing up, Alfred."

"I know she is, but what makes you say that?"

"I think she has a crush on Jimmy."

"Jimmy from the air raid?"

"Yes."

Nothing more was said, but Ruth felt the hurt for her daughter.

Nora came home for her tea, a little late, but hungry. She asked if she could have Shirley's meal, too, as it was spare. Ruth agreed. Better not wasting it, and Nora was eating for two. Ruth wouldn't ask Nancy if she wanted it, in case she ate too much again.

§ § § § §

Jimmy called to see Shirley early the following evening. Ruth answered the door and invited him in.

"Is it okay if I take Shirley to the pictures again, that's if she wants to go?"

"It's okay with me, but you'd better ask Shirley."

"Where is she?"

"Her dad asked her to do some proofreading for him."

"Can I go through?"

"I'll come with you. Nancy, can you watch Jessie for me? I won't be a minute."

Ruth led the way because she wanted to see Shirley's face when Jimmy appeared. Ruth wasn't disappointed as her daughter's face lit up.

"Jimmy! I won't be long. Can you wait?" Shirley asked breathlessly.

"Course I can. I'm not going anywhere else."

As soon as she was able, Shirley left the printing shop and hurried back to the house where she rushed upstairs to have a wash and prepare for her outing with Jimmy.

Returning downstairs, Shirley asked, "Where are we going?"

"Don't you want to go to the pictures?"

"There's a Lassie film on. Can we go there?"

"If that's what you fancy, and it's okay with your mam and dad." Jimmy looked at Ruth.

"It's fine, Jimmy. Just take care of her if the sirens go, dear," Ruth said.

"I will." Jimmy offered Shirley his arm, but she was too shy to take it.

Ruth watched them both walk up the street and breathed a sigh of relief. "Happy about that?" asked Alfred.

"It does seem odd, a young man taking our Shirley out."

Jimmy presented Shirley with some pear drops. "I thought I may as well buy some for you. It will save us calling at the shop on the way there."

"Thank you. You know I like them, don't you?"

"Now will you link my arm?"

Shirley linked his arm now that he'd asked her to, but she was still a little upset at seeing him with that girl.

Jimmy took her to the Queens. Shirley saw Peter go into the cinema ahead of them, and he went to pay to go upstairs with his friend.

"Can we go upstairs, please, Jimmy?" Shirley asked sheepishly. She thought if he could take a young woman in the posh seats, then why not her?

Jimmy looked surprised. "If you want to."

"I want to." Shirley looked up at him and smiled triumphantly. What would Peter think when he noticed her with a young man? Would he be jealous? "I've never been upstairs at the pictures before, and I've always wanted to see what it's like," Shirley said as they walked up the steps.

"And now you're going to find out. I hope your dream won't be shattered."

Shirley smiled to herself. "It won't be," she looked up at Jimmy. "Believe me."

Ruth was still worrying about Shirley being with Jimmy, and she went back into the garden with Nancy to take her mind off things. Alfred joined her after putting Jessie to bed.

"I wish I didn't listen to Nora. I can't stop worrying about Shirley again."

"She's right, though, about young men. We will have to watch her, I suppose."

"I don't think he'd do anything out of hand, do you really, Alfred?"

"You just never know."

Ruth worried about that all evening and was relieved when she heard Shirley and Jimmy's voices outside.

Chapter 11

When Michèle called in the evening, Jonathon was relieved. He was expecting her earlier and felt disappointed when she didn't turn up, but now that she was here, he was elated. Yves and Véronique told her about Jonathon and the German soldiers, and she laughed when she was told about Jonathon in the ditch. She explained to him that the Germans were allowed to take meat, eggs, chickens, and fresh vegetables from Yves to feed their men, and they weren't allowed to refuse them.

"I needed to see you today, Jonathon, because I'm going away."

Jonathon's heart sank. "Where are you going?"

"I have orders to join the resistance again. Their orders are to blow up a bridge to hold up the enemy." Michèle noticed the look of disappointment on his face. "I think you'd better come with me, Jonathon. You can help us. After all, you can't stay here forever. My orders are to take you towards the coast to Ruffec soon, so why not now?"

"Why Ruffec?"

"You will be looked after, and they will arrange for you to escape."

"How?"

"At this stage, you'd better not know. You'll find out soon enough."

"Where is Ruffec?"

"We must make our way towards La Souterraine first. There are many German military at Limoges, so we'll try and keep away from there. We must keep a low profile."

"What happens then?"

"The less you know, the better."

Jonathon prepared for the journey. He washed the clothes he stood in and bathed himself all over. He knew it could be a while before he would get the chance again. Véronique touched his hair and pretended to cut it, so he nodded his head. He hoped that he'd got it right and she was asking if he wanted her to cut his hair. She went into the sideboard and came back with scissors and motioned him outside. When she wrapped a towel around his neck and started cutting his hair, he knew he'd got it right. He felt better, and Yves gave him a wolf whistle. He thanked Véronique and Yves for having him, and then he set off with Michèle as soon as the night began to fall. Jonathon felt a little disappointed that he would miss the food treats, but he soon got over that, as he had Michèle for company instead. She told him they had a long walk before they could rest. They cut over fields and sometimes sat or lay on the grass to rest. It was great being free to wander. Michèle was a good conversationalist, and Jonathon felt sad that he had to discover France in the middle of a war. When they both settled for the night, it was under a hedge, and they lay close to each other for comfort. He put his arm around her shoulders, and she responded by turning towards him and placing her arm across his middle. They listened to the noises of the night and looked up at the stars.

"I wonder how long this war will go on, Jonathon."

"I wonder if I will get back to my ship. I would love to be in it now and sort these Gerries out."

"At least I know you're safe when you're with me." Michèle snuggled into him.

"And is that important to you?"

"To know you're safe? Yes, it is."

"Yes, I'm safe for now, but for how long?" Jonathon muttered under his breath, "There are different types of danger."

"What do you mean? Do you think I am dangerous?"

"You know what I mean, you little minx."

They lay quietly in each other's arms for a while.

"What are you thinking?" Jonathon asked.

"I was thinking of the Jews and mostly the children. It is so sad."

"It is?"

"The Germans are murdering them or sending them to their camps to finish them off. They're so cruel."

"Can we do anything about it?"

"Not at this moment, but I would love to see an end to all this heartache."

They were both silent for a while, deep in their own thoughts.

The following morning, it rained, so Jonathon and Michèle stopped at a farm. It was dangerous, but a necessity. The farmer and his wife dried their clothes and asked them to join them and their family for lunch, but they declined, so instead they gave them a warm drink and allowed them to rest until the rain eased. They had a dog that loved to be petted, but for no reason, it stopped, and standing very still, looked at the door.

"I think he's heard something," Jonathon said. "Dogs have good hearing. Maybe we'd better be off, Michèle." Jonathon stood up and held Michèle's arm. "Come on."

When they set off again, it wasn't long before they heard the sound of a truck speeding towards them.

"Quickly," Michèle pushed Jonathon towards some trees, "Hide. I think someone's informed on us."

They ran into the trees and hid quickly. They couldn't run the risk of making a noise; they had to keep quiet.

"Jonathon, I think they must have seen us," Michèle whispered.

Jonathon watched as two of the soldiers left the Jeep, while the one remaining sat behind the steering wheel. He could feel Michèle stiffen as the soldiers came closer, and he took out the knife from his side pocket and let his finger run down the blade. He was ready.

As one of the soldiers came level, Jonathon stepped forward; the look of surprise on the soldier's face gave Jonathon time to grab him, and they both fought for supremacy, and then Jonathon took over and stabbed him. While Jonathon was fighting the soldier, Michèle jumped on the other one and tried to disarm him. He was amazed at Michèle; she had guts, and he admired that. Jonathon grabbed the soldier from off Michèle, and then finished him off, too. He picked up one of their guns and shot the soldier in the Jeep, and then threw the gun in the bushes. They didn't wait to see if they were all dead, but set off running. They had to put a great distance between them before the soldiers were found.

Michèle and Jonathon were exhausted by the time they found a well and stopped running to take a drink.

"Are you all right?" asked Michèle.

"That's the first time I've killed anyone hands on."

"Don't feel sorry. They would have killed us with no hesitation."

"I know, but it worried me *because* it didn't bother me. I never thought that I could kill someone so easily and with no regrets."

"It's called war, Jonathon. Anyway, it's time we took a rest."

They lay down under a tree at the side of a wall and tried to sleep. Jonathon was listening, even in slumber, and was aware of any noise. The feel of Michèle close to him was disturbing. As he lay there, a picture formed in his mind. For the first time in his life, he had seen the eyes of someone who wanted to kill him, and it preyed on his memory.

When they awoke early the following morning, they walked on towards the next village, but kept low, watching and listening for any German involvement. They were hungry, but had no money except for a few francs Michèle had in her pocket that would just buy them bread. After a while, they reached a village, and Michèle walked into the *boulangerie* while Jonathon waited around the corner. There were a few waiting to be served, and she listened to the conversation. One man angrily talked about the German soldiers, but no one joined in. Michèle noticed the fear in their faces and realized they were too afraid to pass an opinion. Michèle asked for a *pain* and left, brandishing the bread so that Jonathon could see she had food. Outside the shop, she observed the man and took notice where he lived.

Jonathon helped Michèle eat the bread. They were both ravenous, and it hardly filled them. When it was dark, Michèle went to seek the man from the *boulangerie* and knocked on his door. Jonathon didn't know what was said, but Michèle came to collect him from where he was waiting for her.

"Come, Jonathon."

Jonathon followed her inside the house and found the man busy making them a meal. It smelled delicious, and he stopped and shook hands with Jonathon and gestured for him to sit at the table. He spoke in French, but Michèle translated for him.

"He said there are those who hate the Germans and are willing to help anyone escape, and there are those who hate the Germans, but are too afraid to do anything. They know they can be shot or sent to the camps if they are found collaborating."

"Tell him, Michèle, how grateful I am that he is willing to help, but I don't like to think that he is putting his own life in jeopardy."

"I don't need to tell him that. It goes without saying."

Jonathon looked at the man. "*Merci*," he said, and the man grinned back at him.

"*Soyez le bienvenu*," he replied.

"He said, "Welcome, Jonathon," Michèle said before Jonathon asked.

After their meal, they made a move to go, and the man put his hand into his pocket and gave them a few coins. Michèle refused at first, but the man insisted. She kissed him on both cheeks; Jonathon shook his hand; and they both left.

Before Michèle and Jonathon left the village, they slipped into the church. The door was always open for everyone, Michèle said. They were alone, and they sat and rested there. It was peaceful, and Jonathon admired the inside and the paintings on the walls.

"Aren't they beautiful?"

"They are," Michèle said. "They're very old and were discovered not all that long ago."

"It makes you feel safe here. It's so calming."

"It's not, Jonathon. The Germans wouldn't hesitate to come for you here. They don't recognize the church as a sanctuary."

Jonathon and Michèle talked in whispers in case anyone overheard them. They stayed there until they thought most people would be in bed. Jonathon felt sad at leaving the church, as he felt at peace within those walls, but they had to go. They walked about two miles until they found a good bush they could sleep under. Jonathon tried to make it as comfortable as he could by removing any hard sticks, and they both laid down together. He put his arm around Michèle, and she cuddled into him. They discussed their day and chances of survival. Up to that time, they both agreed they had been lucky, but it was a guess as to what the future held.

The following morning, they bypassed La Souterraine and kept to the woods as much as possible. Sometimes, they came across a well where they could refresh themselves, but they knew that food was a problem. They had to go without something to eat until they couldn't stand it any longer, so they risked their lives and found some very brave farmers who were only too willing to give them a meal.

"Where are we going now?" asked Jonathon.

"We're making tracks for Bellac. We have a long way to go yet."

They met with other French resistance on the way and helped them with their missions. One was to attack the German soldiers and bomb the bridge they were protecting, but Michèle had now become more intent on Jonathon's escape. Jonathon asked a favour of André, who was in charge.

"The next time you get in touch with London, can you tell them that Jonathon Turner is well and trying to get back home, please? My family will be worried to death and should be told." André agreed.

They found a barn to sleep in for one night, and after they had made a bed in the hay, they both undressed and made themselves comfortable.

Michèle lay next to Jonathon and snuggled into him. "*Je t'aime,*" she whispered in his ear.

"What does that mean? You're not the first woman who has said that to me."

Michèle went quiet for a while. Jonathon nudged Michèle. "What does *je t'aime* mean? Are you going to tell me?"

"It doesn't matter," Michèle replied.

"Yes it does. Tell me, you *peu sorcière.*"

Michèle nudged Jonathon. "A little witch, eh! I am, am I? And where did you learn that?"

Trying to speak with a French accent, Jonathon repeated what Michèle had said earlier. "You'd better not know. You'll find out soon enough."

"Tell me, Jonathon, who were the other women who said *je t'aime?*"

"Women! There was only one. It was an English lady I once knew."

"Did you know her well?"

"I did."

"Is she waiting for you when you return home?"

Jonathon's mind wandered to Ann for a short while before he replied. "No, she was killed in a bombing raid."

"Oh, Jonathon, I'm so sorry. Have I upset you?"

"It doesn't matter."

"I'm so sorry."

"It happens."

"When you reach home, will you forget me?"

"I don't think so."

"You will. There will be plenty of ladies after you. Ladies like pilots."

Jonathon laughed. "You still haven't told me what *je t'aime* means."

"And you still haven't told me how you knew what *peu sorcière* means."

Jonathon confessed. "I asked one of the men from the resistance how to say 'you little witch' in French. Now it's your turn. What does *je t'aime* mean?"

"I love you."

Chapter 12

Nora got bigger…and lazier, much to Ruth's disgust. She never moved anything; she just left everything where she finished using it, for Ruth or the family to move. Ruth would work hard, tidying up, sweeping, and polishing, and Nora would make the house look untidy again in no time. Ruth looked forward to the birth, and then maybe Nora would be less untidy. Then again, she thought about all the dirty nappies and realized that Nora would more than likely expect her to wash them. It would still be nice having a baby about, so maybe it would be worth it in the long run. Shirley couldn't wait to become an auntie, and Ruth could only imagine being a grandmother. When she went shopping, she avoided looking at anything regarding babies. Maybe it was because she wasn't overly keen on Nora, but she didn't know. Ruth told herself it was because it was unlucky, but there was something missing. How she wished Jonathon were there; at least he should have warned them if he could, instead of the silence. She didn't even know whether he was alive or…no, she wouldn't go there. If only she knew. Alfred didn't say much about the oncoming birth, so Ruth didn't pursue the conversation.

Jimmy called on Shirley once more before returning to camp. Ruth knew that he was spending time with a girl, as she had seen them out together when she called on a friend, but she didn't tell Shirley. After all, she felt glad he was interested in girls of his own age; she would be worried if he wasn't. Eventually, Shirley waved him off, and then very excitedly went to tell Ruth about the ring that Jimmy had sent her.

"It's a friendship ring, Jimmy said, so that I won't forget him. Isn't it lovely, Mam?" Ruth looked at the ring and nodded her approval.

"Are you only going to wear it when you see Jimmy?"

"I think so. I'm frightened of losing it."

Shirley began to write to Jimmy a few days after he left. Ruth could see that she had a real crush on him and hoped she wouldn't be too upset when Jimmy met the girl he would marry. Girls can be so serious with things like that. She would need to keep a keen eye on her.

Alfred made a poultry house with nest boxes on the outside to make collection of the eggs easier, and it would save them getting their shoes dirty. He also added a run for the birds. Six point-of-lay pullets were the next addition. Alfred and Ruth watched them pecking at their food, and it stirred a memory that took her back a few years. She wondered if this unborn grandchild would love the chickens like Jonathon did. It would be nice to have a little Jonathon running around the place. It would be lovely to have a baby around, any baby, male or female, again, but she secretly wished it didn't belong to Nora.

Spending time in the garden was relaxing. At least it gave her something else to think about and take her mind off Jonathon. Jessie helped Ruth to prepare a plot to grow vegetables, or at least she tried. She hoped it wasn't too late to grow the seeds. It took Ruth so much longer to do it, but the fresh air was good for the child—and her. Jessie was given radish seeds, and Ruth told her where to sprinkle them. Ruth allowed Shirley and Nancy a small plot, too, and they planted tomato and lettuce seed. It was a trial, as she had never grown anything before except pink and red roses, so it would be interesting to see how they progressed.

When the hens began to lay eggs, they were collected with much glee by Jessie. Ruth made sure that Jessie did the morning check for eggs and Shirley and Nancy the evening. Ruth would make sure the eggs were all clean before placing them into a bowl, and soon they had enough to sell, and the family was grateful for them.

As Nora became increasingly bigger and nearer to her due date, Ruth became tempted to look at baby clothes. They had a few used ones given to them by friends and customers from the business, but Ruth thought she should buy the baby something for immediate use after birth. Her wardrobe left a lot to be desired, but she would manage for now. After much thought, she bought two nightdresses, two vests, and nappies, later adding a shawl that had been used for Jessie. She couldn't understand Nora, as she hadn't prepared for the baby at all. Maybe she knew someone who could give her a pram; if not, then she and Alfred would have to provide her with one.

Ruth took Jessie into the garden to feed the chickens and Jessie shouted to her, "Mam, Mam, my wadishes are gwowing."

Ruth looked and found that they were. Jessie was so proud. It had taken Ruth all her time to stop Jessie from digging them up to see if they were growing, but now she had the proof. Jessie watered them with a jug that Ruth provided for her.

Alfred took the girls to the wakes that was always on the marketplace and visited Ashton every August. Ruth didn't like the wakes, as it was too noisy with the loud music. The girls loved it; they walked around the fair taking it all in. They met their friends and swapped tales of what they'd seen and which rides they intended to go on while Alfred kept busy with Jessie. Alfred bought them black peas from a stall, which they all enjoyed, and then they came to the caterpillar. Jessie loved that ride best and laughed as it blew their skirts up, but their favourite bit was when the hood came over and no one could see them; that was exciting.

"You know, Nancy, the big boys bring their girlfriends on here and kiss them when the hood comes over," Shirley said.

"Do you think that'll ever happen to us, Shirl?"

"I hope so."

Alfred took Jessie on the dodgems, or bumper cars. He liked the dodgems, and Jessie laughed every time they were bumped by someone, but laughed even harder when her dad bumped someone else.

Alfred gave them some pennies to roll down the little wooden chutes on a side stall. They tried to get them on the biggest money signs, but didn't manage it. Jessie got one on a tuppence square, but that was the best they could do, and they watched as the man took his long scoop and dragged their money away.

Next, they tried to win a goldfish by throwing a dart, but they didn't have any luck there, either.

"What on earth do you want a goldfish for?" asked Alfred.

"Why not, Dad?" Shirley answered with disgust.

Alfred had a go, but he didn't win one, either, and Shirley wondered if he missed on purpose because he didn't really want one. Then they all stopped to watch a sideshow of a man willing to wrestle anyone who took up the challenge.

"Go on, Dad, go and wrestle him. You'll win. You're strong."

Alfred looked the man up and down and declined. "Not today, love. Maybe some other time."

Alfred did allow them on one more ride, though. After a walk around, they decided they would go on the caterpillar again, and then it was home.

"Nancy really enjoyed the wakes, Ruthie. It did my heart good to see her face when we arrived. She seemed amazed at the noise and was delighted when I tried to win her a prize on a sideshow."

"Yes, she doesn't appear to have had much of a life, bless her."

There was still no word from Jonathon, and both Ruth and Alfred listened to all the news. There was too much bad and not enough good news. Lord Haw Haw and his propaganda, Churchill speaking, and all the latest regarding the war didn't help. They felt better when they listened to "Hippodrome" and the "Penny on the Drum," Tommy Handley, and "ITMA." They needed something to make them laugh and put a smile on their faces.

Shirley was helping Nancy to read. Alfred bought them both comics, and they would swap them. Also, Shirley introduced her to Rudyard Kipling and the story of *Rikki Tikki Tavi,* and she loved it.

As Ruth prepared to go into the garden, Nora appeared.

"I'm off. See you at tea time."

"Oh! Where are you going?" Ruth didn't mean to pry; she was surprised. "Only you're overdue, so don't go too far."

"I don't have to tell you where I'm going or what I'm doing," Nora answered sharply.

"Sorry! I just wondered, that's all."

"I'm going shopping...okay?"

"Fine." Ruth felt hurt and left her to go into the back garden. Maybe she was preparing for the birth and buying things she would need after all, she told herself.

When Nora finally returned, she carried two bags, but took them into her bedroom without saying anything.

Later, when Ruth needed something from upstairs, she noticed Nora's bedroom door was open, and on the bed there was a new dress and shoes with heels.

Ruth wondered why she was wasting her coupons for the purchases that she wouldn't need yet, but didn't dare ask.

§ § § § §

Nora started with labour pains early the next morning. Ruth woke Alfred and made a cup of tea for them all before Alfred took her to the hospital in the car. Nora said she felt sick, so she and Alfred abandoned their tea and rushed to the hospital instead. Alfred came home a little later, telling Ruth that after Nora was examined, they were told that it could be a while before she gave birth.

"So I thought I may as well come home, and then we can go back to bed. What do you think, Ruth?"

"I think you're right. It's going to be a long day, and we're going to need our sleep."

Ruth and Alfred didn't get much sleep and kept asking each other if they were still awake, and then talked about the baby and Jonathon until it was almost time to get up.

"Poor Jonathon may never know that he's becoming a father." Ruth was almost in tears.

Alfred put his arm around her shoulders and cuddled her. "You never know, love, he might."

"What shall we do about a pram, Alfred? Should we buy one for her?"

"Not yet. Wait until the baby's born and everything's okay."

Ruth settled after and managed to get a little sleep.

The following morning, Ruth rang the hospital as soon as she went downstairs and asked about Nora, but they told her she was still in labour. They rang a few times through the day, but the baby still hadn't arrived.

"That poor girl, she must be exhausted," Ruth said sympathetically.

"I bet it's the first time in her life that she is."

"Alfred!"

"Well, it's true, and you know it."

The following morning, Ruth rang the hospital again and asked the nurse if Nora had given birth.

"Are you family?" the nurse asked.

"I'm the baby's grandma," answered Ruth.

"It's a boy, but it's been a difficult birth, and the doctor had to use forceps in the end. The baby is in the premature baby unit, as he isn't well. Don't worry, though, I'm sure he will be fine soon."

"How's Nora?"

"She's resting, but you can visit in the afternoon."

"What weight is the baby?"

"He's a big boy. He weighed nine pounds and four ounces."

"That big? Wow!"

"He's just a little unwell, but nothing to worry about."

"Is it okay if we come and see the baby first?" asked Ruth.

"That's fine. You can only see him through the glass, though, but I'll go into the room and show him to you. Just ask someone when you enter the unit."

"Thank you, nurse, we will." Ruth turned to Alfred excitedly. "It's a boy! He's big. He's more than nine pounds. Hasn't she done well? I hope he looks like Jonathon."

Ruth and Alfred went to the hospital that afternoon after making arrangements for Maureen to look after the children. Ruth was so excited and couldn't wait to see her first grandchild. They entered the unit and were escorted to the room where the baby lay. The nurse donned a white coat and placed a mask on her face.

"We daren't spread any germs until he's fit enough to deal with them."

Ruth and Alfred couldn't see the baby as the head of the cot was under the window and facing the other way. The nurse entered the room and turned the cot for them to see their new grandchild.

"He's black!" Alfred almost shouted. "That's not Jonathon's baby."

Ruth burst into tears. "How could she do this to us?"

Chapter 13

The weather wasn't as hot as it had been, and sleeping outdoors had lost its glamour. Jonathon and Michèle decided to join the resistance for another trip, as they were on the way to Bellac. The resistance heard that the Germans were planning something, and they intended to interfere.

They arranged to meet two of the resistance and found them in the designated place. The resistance carried all the dynamite and wires, and all was going well, and then the German reinforcements turned up. They fought well, but didn't stand a chance against so many, so eventually, Jonathon was captured. Michèle attempted to rescue him, but also found herself a prisoner. It had all been a trick and was well planned. If only they had known. It was one plan too many.

Jonathon was held by the arms, while a burly soldier thumped him; as he doubled up, he was thumped on the back of his neck, which sent him down on the floor. While he lay there, he was kicked all over his body and head until he fell unconscious. He felt himself being carried, but fell unconscious again. When he awoke, he was in bed. Whose bed he didn't know, but it was clean and smelled fresh, and he was alone in the room. He touched his face and felt pain and swelling from the beating. Where was he? If he was with the enemy, they were treating him well. A little later a lady entered the room.

"Hello, young man. How do you feel?"

"As if I've been kicked all over."

"And you have."

"Who are you?"

"My name is Marie. I'm glad to see you're awake."

Jonathon attempted to smile, but found it too painful. "Only just."

"What's your name?"

"Jonathon."

"Are you in a lot of pain?"

"I'm sore."

"I'm sure you are. You took quite a beating. Do you need painkillers?"

"I'm sore all over, but I don't want painkillers. I gather they kicked me around, because my ribs are sore."

"Yes. Like I said, you took quite a beating and are badly bruised."

"Where am I now?"

"You don't want to know, but you're safe."

"Is there anywhere safe?"

"Well, as safe as we can be for the moment."

"What happened to Michèle? Do you know?"

"Who's Michèle?"

"I saw her captured before I was beaten."

"No, I'm sorry, but I don't know."

Jonathon wondered about that. Maybe she had been told not to say, but he worried and prayed that his *peu sorcière* would survive the German soldiers. Then again, he heard the enemy was good at pretending to be English and giving prisoners a false sense of security so they can find out what the English are up to. He would need to be as crafty and make sure that these people were indeed genuine.

"You were brought here by the French resistance, and they told me they had rescued you after you were beaten and left for dead. Does that help?"

"Yes, thanks, but it's a pity they didn't rescue me before I was beaten. Isn't that the story of my life, Mrs....?" Marie smiled. "What do I call you?" asked Jonathon.

"Just Marie." Whether or not that was her name, Jonathon didn't hazard a guess, as the less you knew, the better if you came to be questioned by the Gestapo.

"Is this a hospital?"

"No, but my husband is a doctor."

"I'm glad about that."

"The Germans have taken over a number of *châteaux,* so we moved into this place. Of course, they can take over anything at any time, but until then, we're pretty safe."

Jonathon hardly ever saw her husband. He seemed nice, but he was French and knew no English.

"What do I call the doctor?" Jonathon asked Marie.

"Just call him Doc. He will answer to that."

They were both very kind and gave him the best care they could. Jonathon felt safe in their hands, and he stopped being suspicious. As he slowly recuperated, it became time to leave.

All arrangements were made for him to escape. It wasn't what he and Michèle had planned, but now he was numb without her and just did what he was told.

One of the resistance members came for him and introduced himself as Pierre. Their orders were for them to make their way to southern France, but they were also causing havoc for the Germans by blowing up bridges and railway lines, plus killing a few as they went.

"You must try to hide any bodies as the Germans favour repercussions."

"In what way?" asked Jonathon.

"If you kill ten Germans, they will kill a hundred French people. They have no feelings, as they kill children, too."

They passed through Oradour-sur-Glane, keeping to the woods for cover whenever possible, and then crossed into the Creuse to La Souterraine where they stayed for two days. When they left La Souterraine, they acquired bicycles and made La Celle-Dunoise their next stop, where they picked up equipment from a known sympathizer who gave them guns and ammunition.

As they made their way to Gueret, Jonathon noticed a familiar name, *Le Bourg d'Hem.*

"I've been here before. I'm back to square one."

"Don't you worry, my English friend, and don't get despondent. Your last escape route is no more. There are many traitors, but there is another that we are using."

They swapped their bikes for a car when they reached Gueret. There they were introduced to Antoine, who gave them fake passports and identity cards. Antoine was a printer who had a secret workshop where he would print out leaflets of propaganda to be scattered wherever the Germans were in their numbers. There was a reward for his arrest. Jonathon was never told where his workshop was situated.

"Have you read your papers and realized you now have a new name?" Pierre asked.

"I have. Now you must call me Paul-Henri."

As they were leaving Gueret, they met a Jeep coming from the opposite direction.

"I think someone must have betrayed us. They don't usually come this way without a reason," Pierre said.

They were stopped, and a German soldier checked their credentials. Pierre noticed the man in the truck was a German officer with a bad reputation.

"We must kill him," he whispered. "Kill them all."

§§§§§§

Pierre had been wounded. There had been a fight; it had been very vicious after they attacked the Germans. Jonathon was almost shot, but Pierre saved him in time, and now Pierre had a deep cut in his arm where he'd been stabbed. Jonathon bandaged it as best he could with a piece of his shirt and promised him he'd find a doctor to stitch it.

"No! No doctor."

The Germans were dead, but it had been a long struggle. Pierre was a man to be reckoned with, and he took no prisoners, but the German soldier had been much bigger and stronger than he and managed to take his knife off him. He did his worst before Jonathon managed to stick his own knife into the soldier's back. Pierre was a strong man, too, and Jonathon felt glad of it. They decided to place the bodies of the men in the Jeep that had carried the soldiers and set it on fire. Then they returned to the car and set off at speed through back lanes before someone came to see what had happened. Jonathon had found that killing the Germans was easy. It worried him. He always thought of himself as being soft, but he had found a new character within himself that once seemed alien. He put it down to the war and how it changed people

They found the safe house in Tulle after a hazardous journey, dodging the French Vichy and the German soldiers. Jonathon rested while Pierre found a doctor to stitch his arm. When they received their next orders, it was to make their way to Toulouse.

Jonathon missed Michèle, as he had grown fond of her and her dedication to beating the enemy. He worried about her and didn't like the idea of leaving her behind, because he had developed feelings for her. Michèle was a lovely lady, and he was a sucker for the French accent. He had watched her move with a dignity and poise you didn't find in most girls. Yes, he was definitely going to miss her. He and Pierre were living in the attic of a safe house and eating only to survive, as the owner didn't dare buy more food to avoid suspicion. How he yearned for a nice, big, roast beef dinner cooked by his mam. Roast potatoes and vegetables with tasty, very tasty gravy over a nice big piece of Yorkshire pudding. He could almost smell it.

When it started to go dark, they settled for the night. Jonathon lay for a while thinking. A host of things went through his mind. He wondered what was happening in Ashton-under-Lyne and how his family was coping with the war. Listening to Pierre gently snoring didn't help him go to sleep. Sleep was a long way away for Jonathon. He was always listening for noise of any kind, always on the alert.

As Jonathon and Pierre were preparing to leave, there was a loud banging on the front door, and they guessed right away that it was the Germans. They hurriedly gathered their things together, and the owner of the house moved the box away after they had used it to climb through the skylight on to the roof. Pierre struggled to climb up with the pain from his arm, but Jonathon helped. They stealthily moved across the slates. The owner of the house took his time to answer the door amidst much shouting from the soldiers outside. He told them later that when he did unlock the door, they pushed it so far back he was squashed against the wall and had bruises to prove it. Running through the house, they flung things about and smashed through doors. Eventually, two of them dragged a chair into position, and one of them climbed into the attic. He searched around while the other man watched from the open clap. Climbing onto the wooden box that Jonathon and the others had used, he opened the skylight and pushed his head through to view the roof. Satisfied there was no one around, he returned and joined the others. They left the house, and eventually Jonathon and friends climbed back into the attic.

The owner made them all a cup of tea, while they discussed what had just happened.

"Thank God for chimney stacks is all I can say," Jonathon said. "They come in handy to hide behind."

After Jonathon drank his tea (which, he thought, wasn't as good as his mam's), and it was safe to go, he and Pierre made tracks to leave.

"Thank you for everything." They shook the man's hand. Jonathon never found out the man's name for security reasons.

Jonathon and Pierre left Toulouse, and they now wore black berets as a way of being recognized, if there was any trouble, by the Maquis fighters. They both acquired bicycles and rode to Marseille without coming across any German soldiers. Pierre knew someone in the town, so after hiding their bikes, they risked their lives to get a good night's sleep and some decent food, and then they were off again. They were to meet a man called Alain from the resistance in an outside café. Hiding their bicycles, they found the café and sat at a table, and Pierre ordered a coffee for them. As they sipped it, a Jeep pulled up at the kerb, and three Germans got out. Their eyes searched the tables, but as they took a step towards Jonathon and Pierre, a woman shouted as she walked up to them. She turned her back to Jonathon, and it sounded as if she was complaining about something. The soldiers spoke German, and the lady spoke in French. Jonathon could see the soldiers were losing their temper, and Pierre kicked him under the table to follow him as he sneaked away. They hid in a nearby yard of a house whose gate had been left unlatched, but Pierre locked it behind them. Jonathon peeped through the gap between the door and the wall and watched as the German soldier shouted at the woman and hit her. She was grabbed and pushed into the Jeep. Their eyes surveyed the tables again, and then they all climbed into the Jeep and drove away.

"Poor sod!" Jonathon exclaimed.

"Do you know who that woman was?"

Jonathon shook his head, "No, should I?"

"It was Michèle."

"I didn't recognize her."

"Maybe it's because you never saw her in a dress and headscarf before."

"No! What the hell was she thinking of? Why did she go to them?"

"She was going to surprise you by meeting you here. After escaping, she had arranged to meet us. When she saw the German soldiers, she must have suspected that we were in trouble and gave us a chance to get away."

"I wish I'd known."

"What could you have done? You have a job to do. You must get back to England, and then come and bomb the bastards."

Jonathon felt devastated. "What's going to happen to her now?"

"She could be shot or taken to the camps."

"What can we do to help?"

"Meaning?"

"To help her. We can't just leave her."

"She knew the risks. There is nothing we can do, but carry on trying to win the war. Come."

"No, we can't leave her. I can't leave her to be murdered by these bastards."

Pierre pushed him. "Yes, you can, or she has given her life for nothing."

Jonathon could see that Pierre was serious and angry at his reaction, so Jonathon did what he was told and followed Pierre out of the yard. As Pierre walked swiftly on, Jonathon followed with a heavy heart.

In Marseille, Jonathon was introduced to a young woman who told him that she would get him over the Pyrenées to Spain. It was going to be hard, but if he persevered, he would make it. He would join a group that was ready for the final night ascent to the Spanish border.

When he met the others, he was told that there was a high mountain route into Spain. This particular one had been carefully chosen to avoid any likely contact with German patrols and all official checkpoints. It was with trepidation that they all set off that night.

Chapter 14

Ruth and Alfred returned home with a heavy heart that day after seeing the baby. They hadn't seen Nora, as their feelings were too raw. They both sank into a chair with a weary sigh. It had been a hard day, and the end was not what they expected. There would be no baby, no little Jonathon, and how could they explain that to the girls? Shirley had been so excited at the thought of being an auntie. Ruth couldn't understand Nora. What a devious little soul she was to pretend that the baby she was expecting was Jonathon's. She knew what she was doing, and he going missing played right into her hands.

"I'll put the kettle on," Alfred announced, as if that would make the world all right.

Ruth felt sick. Then she slowly began to laugh. When she started laughing, she found she couldn't stop, until she began to choke and cough.

Alfred looked at her with concern. "Are you all right?"

As soon as Ruth regained her breath, she answered, "Can you imagine what our faces must have looked like when we saw the baby? I was shocked. It's hilarious, really."

"I don't think it's funny, love. Not funny at all."

"Did you like Nora?"

"Well, no, but I knew you were looking forward to being a grandma."

"I'll tell you a secret, Alfred. I didn't like the girl, she was so lazy, and I couldn't understand how Jonathon could have given her a baby."

"Men are very easy to understand, Ruth."

"Well, I must say that I'm glad Jonathon isn't attached to Nora, not in any way now, thank goodness. Admit it, Alfred, aren't you glad it's turned out like this? Let's face it, it's a blessing."

"I suppose so. It's a good job that Jonathon doesn't know anything about it."

"That's what I was thinking, too." Ruth's thoughts turned to Jonathon and what his reaction would be if he knew what Nora had done.

"What happens now? Surely she can't expect us to take her back."

"She's cheeky enough, Alfred, but she's not coming back. I'll collect her things together for when she calls."

"But what will she do?"

"Don't worry about Nora. She'll be all right, believe me, Alfred. I'm not a hard woman, but she has brought the worst out in me, and I hope I never see her again."

"You're right, of course. Now all we have to worry about is telling Shirley."

"I'll tell her when I see her." Ruth thought about how she would tell her. She knew Shirley would be upset, so she would need to choose her words carefully and not go into too much detail.

When Shirley came home with Nancy, after they'd been to the park, Ruth told her the bad news.

"Nora has had her baby, but I'm afraid the child doesn't belong to us."

"Why, Mam?" Shirley looked horrified.

"Jonathon isn't the baby's father like we thought, so Nora and the baby will go and live with someone else, but not us."

"Why? I don't understand. I was really looking forward to being an auntie."

"I know, love, but it's not to be. Not this time, anyway, but I'm sure you'll be an auntie one day."

Shirley looked so disappointed it made Ruth feel very annoyed with Nora.

"I'll write to Jimmy and tell him. I think he's going abroad soon, so I may as well. He should get the letter before he goes." With that, she ran upstairs.

Ruth had been secretly hoping that if it was a boy, he would look just like Jonathon, a kind of Jonathon reborn—some hope! Now she had to face facts, and that was that Jonathon hadn't been in touch, so it looked as if...no, she couldn't face that thought. If only she knew what had happened. It was the not knowing that was eating at her.

Alfred didn't go back to work that day and stayed by her side. He knew she was upset, even though she had said it was funny. He laughed with her at the time, but couldn't see the joke. That Nora had a lot to answer for.

Both Alfred and Ruth went outside to the garden with Jessie, leaving Shirley to write her letter to Jimmy in peace with Nancy. They fed the hens, collected the eggs, and viewed the seedlings.

"Pity we didn't sow them earlier. The radishes may grow enough for us to eat, but I don't think the tomatoes will have a chance. Never mind, we'll know for next time."

They went back inside the house, as it was a little on the chilly side. They talked while Jessie played with Nancy. It was hard to understand why someone like Nora could be so cruel, but some people are devious, and unfortunately, Nora was one of them. Now they had to get on with their lives for the sake of the girls.

Alfred went into the workshop. Shirley soon finished her letter, and it lay on the mantelpiece, waiting for Ruth to put a stamp on it.

"How is Jimmy?" asked Ruth.

"He's okay, but missing Ashton, he said."

Alfred thanked Maureen for looking after the children. There was a congratulation card sitting on his bench, and it brought a lump to his throat. Ruth mustn't see this, because he was sure she'd break down. He told them that they found that Jonathon wasn't the father and left it at that. He watched their faces change from happy to sad, and he knew they must be wondering what had gone on, but he couldn't tell them.

Ruth went upstairs. Going into Jonathon's bedroom seemed strange now. She must return it back to how it was, just in case her son came home. She just hoped that it wasn't another dream that turned into a nightmare. As if she hadn't had enough…

Alfred returned and shouted her name. "Ruth, where are you?"

Ruth came downstairs. "What's the matter?"

"I've been thinking…how about a holiday?"

"Alfred, we can't. We'll need to be here for when Nora comes out of hospital."

"I'm sure one of the others can give Nora her things. In fact, I don't want to see that girl, do you?"

"Well…"

"No, you don't. Don't you give her any sympathy, either. Why should we be here for her? We need to get away for a bit of pleasure for once. It will do the girls a lot of good, too. What do you say, should we take Christmas away, too?"

Ruth's face changed as she thought about what Alfred was saying. "You're right. Why shouldn't we go away for a few days to get over the disappointment we've suffered? There is nothing to celebrate here anyway, not now."

"I'll make a cup of tea while you think about where you'd like to go."

Alfred put the kettle on. Ruth watched him fill the kettle and set the cups and saucers. He was a wonderful man, and she was very lucky. Thinking about the holiday and where to go, she decided to ask the girls for their opinion.

"Your dad said he'd take us away for a holiday, girls."

"Where are we going to go, Mam?" Shirley asked.

"Where would you like to go?"

"I like Blackpool," said Shirley enthusiastically.

"I suppose it's as good as anywhere."

Alfred filled the teapot. "Well, have you decided?"

Ruth and Shirley answered him together. "Blackpool."

Alfred laughed, "Blackpool it is, then."

"What is Blackpool like?" asked Nancy.

"It has a beach with lots of sand, and we can paddle in the sea."

Ruth could see that Nancy was puzzled and didn't understand what Shirley meant. "Have you ever been to the seaside Nancy?"

"No. I have heard about it."

Shirley squealed, and Ruth said, "Then you're in for a treat."

Jessie started singing, "We're going to Blackpool" as she made a tune up to sing to, and chased round the kitchen in high spirits, and her mother wished she had her energy.

Ruth went to find the address where they had stayed before. Her thoughts returned to when she first went there with Alfred. How things had changed since then. After a phone call, she began to prepare for their trip. Alfred's brother said he would see to things while they were away, and he promised to look after the hens and collect the eggs. A few days later, they were on their way.

They hadn't gone far when Ruth realized she had forgotten their ration books. Returning home, they could hear Nora in their workshop demanding her belongings and the key to get into the house.

"They're on holiday, so you'll have to come back when they return," they could hear Alfred's brother say.

Ruth took off her coat, unlocked the door, and walked into the business to confront Nora.

"Alfred has left your stuff, Nora, have you got it? I thought you would be in hospital for a while longer."

"I signed myself out, and now I need to go home."

"Where is your home?" Ruth asked.

"There." Nora pointed to the adjoining door.

"I don't think so," Ruth answered and Alfred joined her.

"I thought you were looking after us, with me having Jonathon's baby."

"How can a black baby be Jonathon's?" said Alfred angrily.

"I don't know. It must be a throwback. I've heard of those before."

"Not in this family, you haven't," Alfred answered.

"I think you'd better go, Nora. I'm sure that one of your boyfriends will look after you, dear." Ruth was insistent.

"What boyfriends?"

"The ones you were seeing while you were pregnant." Ruth spoke softly, trying hard to keep her temper. "I'm soft-hearted, Nora, as you know, but I'm not daft. Please credit me with some sense."

"You can't really expect us to look after you and your child. For goodness sake, have a little decency. We've lost our son and hoped that your baby would fill that gap, but he can't." As Alfred spoke, Ruth was aware that he found it hard to stop the tears so she held his hand.

"I do feel sorry for the child." Ruth showed concern.

"Don't you dare, Ruth." Alfred was shocked. "Now go, Nora, before I call the police. You can leave your things here temporarily, as you have the baby to carry. You can always come back for them. They won't be going anywhere. And after you've picked them up, don't return. We don't want to see you again...ever again."

Nora beat a hasty retreat.

"And don't you dare feel sorry for her, Ruth. She is a callous, sly individual, and we don't want any part of her."

Ruth bent down to look through Nora's things. "She can't have this, I'm afraid," and held up Jessie's shawl. "That is for our first grandchild, if we ever have one."

They went back through the adjoining door, and Ruth put the shawl in the basket for washing and then sat down.

"When are we going to Blackpool?" asked Shirley.

The girls had been good while all the commotion was going on, but now they wanted to be on their way.

"As soon as we've come round, dear. That was an ordeal."

Ruth and Alfred sat and discussed Nora while the children amused themselves, and soon they were on their way again.

"I feel as if we need this holiday, don't you?" Ruth asked.

Alfred nodded. "I'll say...especially now."

As soon as Ruth stepped out of the car in Blackpool, she took a deep breath. The air tasted different. It smelled fresh and clean. It felt good to be back in the friendly boarding house, too, and Ruth unpacked the food that she had brought with her into the cupboard she was allocated. Her ration books were taken away and given back to her later.

They all took a walk along the seafront, and Nancy was thrilled.

"I've never seen the sea before. Isn't it big?"

"I suppose it is, dear…and deep. It's too late now, but tomorrow we'll go paddling. Would you like that?"

"Really? Can I?"

"Yes, of course, and maybe we'll all wet our toes. It will do us all good."

Alfred nudged Ruth and pulled a face at her. He obviously didn't fancy the idea.

Waking to the sound of seagulls always gave Ruth pleasure. Alfred took them all to the beach after breakfast, calling into a shop for a bucket and spade for Jessie, and they sat on the sands. He made Jessie a big sand castle, and she kept going to fill the bucket with water and emptying it into the moat of the castle. She couldn't understand why it kept disappearing, so it kept her busy for a while. After, they all went for a paddle, much to Nancy's delight. It felt really cold, but they had to let Nancy do it, as it was her first visit to the seaside.

"Don't go any deeper, any of you. It's far too cold, so just wet your feet."

Later, they watched the breakers in the sea as they took an evening stroll along the front. It was a little windy now, so the sea was rougher than usual.

"How do you feel about coming for Christmas?" Alfred asked.

Ruth had to think about that. She was dreading the festive season without Jonathon, so it would be easier for her.

"Why not?"

"Do you think the children will enjoy it?"

When they were asked, the children screamed with delight.

"We can have Christmas away, and then have another when we get home where we can unwrap our presents. What do you think about that, girls?" Ruth laughed at their response; their excitement was delightful.

Nancy couldn't get over how much sea there was and talked eagerly about their next visit.

"You do realize, don't you, Nancy, that you won't be able to paddle when we come at Christmas. It'll be too cold."

"Is it as cold here in winter as it is at home?"

"I'm afraid so, dear. We're not that far away."

"I was looking forward to paddling, too. Never mind, I'll still like it," Nancy replied.

The girls walked ahead of Ruth and Alfred, and Alfred remarked how good it was to watch the girls enjoying themselves and how it made their visit worthwhile.

Alfred drove them to Lytham St Annes and Bispham. Another day, they visited Cleveleys. They never went too far, but on their last full day, Alfred suggested visiting Lake Windermere. They had never been before, so they took sandwiches and a flask, buying three bottles of sarsaparilla for the girls on the way to Bowness. It was a lovely day, and they had a picnic in the car as near to the lake as possible. The girls really enjoyed it, and so did Ruth and Alfred. Before they left, they all took a short walk, and then Ruth and Alfred rested while the girls played.

§ § § § §

Life settled down after the holiday with no Nora. It was a shame about the baby. It would have been nice having a young child again, but it wasn't to be. Ruth looked forward to Christmas in Rhyl, as that was where Alfred said he fancied going. It would make a change from Blackpool, but they kept the destination quiet until they were on their way.

It would soon be Christmas, and Ruth and the girls began dressing the tree and putting up the decorations. When they finished, Shirley and Nancy went off to the park to meet their friends.

Ruth had used her rations and made a Christmas cake that the girls had helped to decorate. She had to smile at Jessie's effort, but the child did enjoy doing it, and that's what mattered. The mince pies would wait until the day before they went on holiday.

Shirley came home from the park with Nancy, found a letter from Jimmy on the mantelpiece, and ran upstairs to read it in privacy. After a while, she came down and told Ruth the latest on what Jimmy was doing in the Army. Ruth doubted that Jimmy had told her everything, as he would keep the worst things to himself, she was sure.

The children were getting excited and looking forward to going to Blackpool again, and Ruth hoped they hadn't made a big mistake in booking the holiday in Rhyl.

When they were on their way, Alfred told them where they were going, and at first it was met with silence, but not for long. They were soon excited again, and their conversation changed to places they knew to places they would discover.

The guesthouse looked welcoming, and there was a Christmas tree with presents beneath it for them all. Ruth's mince pies were thoroughly enjoyed and so was the half of Christmas cake. It was an enjoyable holiday, and they were all sorry when it ended. It was different than their usual Christmas, and Ruth thanked Alfred for choosing Rhyl, as it had no memories of Jonathon, so it didn't upset her. He was a thoughtful man.

The following morning, holiday over, they made tracks for home. When they arrived, Shirley found she had another letter from Jimmy.

"I either don't hear from Jimmy for ages or then I get more than one in a short time." Shirley ran upstairs to read it.

Alfred and Ruth dropped their case in the hall and then made their way to the kitchen for a welcome cup of tea. Opening the door, they were met by Jonathon.

Chapter 15

Ruth screamed with surprise and, rushing to Jonathon, gave him a big hug. Shirley came running downstairs to see what all the noise was about and flung herself at Jonathon. Jessie joined her and hugged Jonathon, too. Nancy stood back with Alfred.

"When did you arrive," Ruth asked, "and where have you been? You never wrote to me. You could have been dead or anything."

Jonathon gave his sisters a quick kiss on their cheek, and then wrapped his arms around his mother.

"Too many questions, Mam. How are you?"

"We're all fine. There's so much we have to tell you, you wouldn't believe, but first of all, I want to know all about you, and what you've been up to."

"Later, Mam. Hiya, Dad. How have you been?"

"Let's put it this way, I feel a lot better now." Alfred moved forward and hugged Jonathon.

"And who is this young lady?" Jonathon looked at Nancy.

"This is our new daughter, Nancy. She was an evacuee." Nancy beamed all over her face.

"Was?"

"We'll explain later. When did you arrive?"

"I arrived yesterday, and when I found there was no one home, I went next door to see Uncle Bob and Aunty Beryl. They told me you were away for Christmas. That surprised me, as you never go away for Christmas, so why this time? What's been going on?"

"I told you, Mam, that our Jonathon would come home," Shirley chimed in.

"And you were right, dear, thank goodness."

"Nancy, this is Jonathon, my brother," said Shirley, looking proud.

Ruth couldn't take her eyes off Jonathon. There were so many young men getting killed, and she couldn't believe her luck. He was home…and safe.

"You must tell us where you've been and what happened to you, Jonathon. I'm dying to know."

Jonathon's eyes moved towards Shirley to give Ruth a message. "Later, Mam. It can wait."

Shirley pulled a face. "We had your girlfriend living with us until she had the baby, but the baby wasn't yours after all."

"What girlfriend…and what bloody baby?"

"You don't have to swear, dear, and it doesn't matter now. I'm sure we would all want to hear your news first."

"Wait a minute—what girlfriend, and what baby?"

"She said it was your baby, but it wasn't, Jonathon. We know that now, dear."

"I don't understand, Mam. I didn't have a girlfriend."

"Nora," Shirley broke in.

"Nora! She was never my girlfriend…and never would be. I think her husband was trying to pin that pregnancy on me, but it must have been Nora telling lies. So she's still at it, is she?"

"Not a very nice person," Alfred added.

"You're right, Dad."

"She lived with us," Shirley piped up.

"She what? Here? She lived here?"

"Yes, she had your bed," Shirley added.

"Mother! Whatever possessed you to allow her to stay here—and in my bed! Crikey, Mam!"

"I didn't know, did I? I thought she was genuine…and you were missing."

"Oh, Mam!" Jonathon pulled her into his arms and gave Ruth another hug. "I wouldn't touch that girl. She's just not my type, thank you very much."

"I'm glad to hear it, dear."

"How long was she here?"

"The last two months of her pregnancy."

"I don't believe it, but I'm glad that you realized it wasn't my baby. How did you know for sure?"

Ruth and Alfred looked at each other and grinned.

"It was black." Alfred smiled.

"Black!"

"Yes, dear, but let's not talk about it now. Your room is ready. I have cleaned it since and prepared it again for when you returned. I hoped that you would."

"Like a bad penny, Mam."

"I told you he would come home, Mam," piped in Shirley.

"I know, dear."

"I didn't know the baby was black. You never said. How could it be black?" Shirley asked.

Ruth laughed. "Tea anyone?"

"Yes, and then you can tell me all about this young lady," and Nancy gave Jonathon a big smile.

They spent the rest of the day recapping on the time Jonathon was away, and Jonathon told them about his escape in France, leaving the worst until the girls were in bed.

"It's a lovely country. I think when the war is over, I would like to go and see it again."

"I've never been, have you, Alfred?"

"No. It was a land too far for me in my youth. You didn't get many travelling overseas for holidays."

"That's true," Ruth replied.

"There are many brave people in France, willing to put their lives at risk to help men like me escape. Some have already lost their lives while helping, and there are many more who also will lose their lives. There is a lot going on over there, and they are at the mercy of the German army and the SAS. Even their own have turned against them and are in league with the Germans. I don't know how they manage to live through it, but I applaud them."

"We're lucky here," Alfred remarked.

"You'll never know how, Dad. They have contacts who help people like me, and these are the ones who got me over the Pyrenées. Some are ordinary farming people, some are policemen, and there are others with titles. It's a mixture of people you, or maybe the Germans, would never guess them to be, and that was very helpful to the escapee."

"That's wonderful! So what happened to Michèle?" asked Ruth.

"We'll talk about that later. At present, I don't want to think about her, not while I'm with my family. She was taken prisoner through saving my life. There were too many people who went to the camps and never returned. I just hope to God that she's surviving, and I'll try to find her when this war is all over."

"Poor girl. I obviously owe her a lot if she saved your life." Ruth said a little prayer that night for Michèle and asked God to keep her safe, whether she was in this life or the next.

The following day, Jonathon told Shirley he would take her to the pictures.

"There's a Walt Disney film on. It's called *Dumbo*. Would you take me to see that one, please?"

"I suppose so. Go and get ready, and as soon as we've had our tea, we'll go."

"You don't have to take her to the pictures tonight, Jonathon, if you would prefer to rest for a few days." Ruth looked concerned.

Jonathon placed his arm around Shirley. "These are the pleasures I've missed, Mam, believe me. I want to take her to the pictures. I would sometimes lie and think of you all in this room. I'd think about my bed, of course I didn't know that Nora was occupying it at the time, and I'd think about your endless, enjoyable cups of tea, Mam, and the roast you cook on Sunday. I missed you all so much. I missed my friends and..." he looked at Shirley "...and taking Shirley to the pictures." Jonathon gave his sister a squeeze.

As soon as Shirley finished her tea, she ran upstairs and came down again in her favourite dress, wearing the ring that Jimmy had bought her. It was the first time she'd worn it without being with Jimmy. She decided that she'd wear it on special occasions, and this was one.

"You're wearing Jimmy's ring, I notice. We didn't tell you about him, did we, Jonathon?" Ruth winked at him.

"No, you didn't. Who's Jimmy?"

Shirley went closer to Jonathon. "He's my friend, and he bought me this." Shirley held up her hand for Jonathon to see.

Jonathon stared at the ring and looked closely. "Where did he get this?"

"I don't know. He sent it to me in the post."

"Why? What's the matter?" asked Ruth.

"It looks like a ring that I bought for a girl I intended to marry. Let me look, Shirl? Can you take it off your finger?"

"I'm sorry I showed it to you now." Shirley struggled to take it off her finger, and then passed it to Jonathon.

"It is the same one. I scratched our initials on the flank of the ring. Look, they're there." Jonathon showed it to the others. "It's Ann's ring. They told me that this was an individual ring and there wasn't another like it, so just to make sure, I scratched our initials." Jonathon was excited and couldn't stop babbling.

"What happened then?" asked Ruth.

Jonathon now looked serious. "It's okay, Mam. She was killed in an air raid...at least I thought she was. We had been to the pictures that evening and there was an air raid, but after I left her and went to bed, there was another, and that's when she was killed. It was when I was in Bournemouth."

"I wonder how Jimmy came to buy it then." Ruth frowned.

Jonathon looked far away. "She was buried under a lot of rubble. They must have found her body and taken the ring off her finger."

"Ugh! I don't think I want it now." Shirley shuddered.

"Your friend Jimmy wouldn't know the history. It's ironic, though."

"I shall be asking him about it when I see him again," said Shirley in disgust.

"So will I, sis. How old is this boyfriend of yours, anyway?"

"Eighteen, unless he's had a birthday since."

"I don't understand. How come she's going out with an eighteen year old, Mam?"

"She's not his girlfriend like that. He's just a friend, and I'll explain again. Just leave it for now."

"He's gone abroad to India, so it will be a while before you meet him." Shirley frowned. "I'm sorry, Jonathon, but I'm not expecting to hear from Jimmy for a while. Do you think he'll be okay?"

"I don't know, Shirl. More than likely."

"I hope he is."

"Oh, well. Come on, kidder, let's get moving. Here." Jonathon pushed a paper bag into Shirley's hand, and when she opened it, she squealed in delight.

"Pear drops."

"I know you like them, but we'll still have to call at the shop for Nancy."

"Not yet. I'm taking the ring back upstairs. I really don't want to wear it now."

Shirley disappeared for a few minutes and returned wearing her jacket. Jonathon offered her his arm and then his other arm to Nancy, who was all ready to go. They both giggled as they walked out of the house, and Ruth watched them with Alfred.

"I wonder what the story was there," Ruth looked at Alfred.

"Sounds sad," he answered.

§ § § § §

Jonathon sat looking at the screen in the picture house and thought back to Bournemouth and Ann. What happened that made her ring for sale? Maybe some petty thief took it off her finger when they brought out her body. Or…did she escape? No, that couldn't be. The man said there were no survivors—and the place was just rubble. He couldn't concentrate on the film at all. The film ended, and he ushered Shirley and Nancy outside to make their way home.

"It was good, wasn't it?" Shirley asked.

"Great!" Jonathon answered. He realized that he didn't have any idea as to what the film was about, but thought he'd better seem enthusiastic for his sister's sake. "Did you enjoy it, Nancy?"

"Yes, thank you for taking me. Dumbo was a lovely elephant, but I like dogs. I wonder if I will ever have one."

"Perhaps, when you marry and live happily ever after," said Jonathon.

When Shirley and Nancy went to bed that night, they talked about the picture they'd seen, how they would both like a dog, how beautiful Maria Montez was, and last of all, Jonathon.

"He's nice, your brother, isn't he?" Nancy said wistfully.

"Do you think he's good-looking, Nancy?"

"Yes, I think he is."

"Ooh, you want to marry my brother. I'll tell him."

"No, don't, Shirley."

Shirley laughed. "Don't worry, I'm only kidding."

The following day, Jonathon began to make enquiries regarding Ann. He must find out what happened to her. Maybe he could start by finding her friends and asking them. Then Jonathon was called back to take over another aircraft. He had been back from France for a few days before he went home on leave, and now it was time for him to return. There was a war on, and he knew his duty. His dedication was stronger now that he'd been in France and seen how the Nazis treated the people there. If only he knew where Michèle was, if she was still alive, he could go out of his way to bomb the damn Germans away and help to free her if that were possible.

Jonathon's mind kept drifting to Ann. Was she alive? If only he knew what had happened to both women in his life. Then he wondered whom he would choose if he had a choice—but there was now no doubt in his mind.

§ § § § §

6 June 1944

"'D-Day' Normandy Landings"

The Allied forces landed. Where the last battles had been fought, the towns had suffered with the bombing day and night. Roads and railways were destroyed and so many people had lost their lives as the fighting in the villages and streets continued. A shortage of food and fuel made everyone hungry. There were many refugees searching for somewhere to stay that was safe. Jonathon would often see long strings of people on the move to who knows where.

The air defence used many squadrons to support the invasion with serviceable aircraft, plus additions. First, there was the day and night air defence, the anti-aircraft command, troop concentrations and marshal areas, including beaches, shipping routes, and embarkation ports. There was air-sea rescue in the channel, protection of the coastal command aircraft during anti-submarine warfare, and anti-shipping operations near the French coast, also operation night-intruder aircraft over the continent. Finally, they were to provide fighter cover for daylight bombing and airborne forces operations and to suppress enemy air and sea activity in Brittany to Pas-de-Calais. Air defence of Great Britain had a huge combination of tasks that directly affected every part of the air war over the channel and Normandy beachhead and much, much more.

Chapter 16

15 December 1944, *Glenn Miller's Plane Lost* was the headline in the evening paper. As he was a great bandleader, it was a major disaster. His "Moonlight Serenade" took on a different meaning.

16 December–23 December 1944

"Battle of the Bulge-Ardennes Offensive"

There were many bombs dropped on Manchester from the Luftwaffe. On Christmas Eve 1944, Germany launched flying bombs at Manchester. The attack went wrong, and twenty-seven people in Oldham were killed by a stray bomb. Manchester was safe from the V-2 rockets as the city was out of range.

Jonathon was back in the air in a mosquito, only him and the navigator-bomb aimer. It felt good to be back in a ship, even though it was night-time. He made himself as comfortable as he could and tried to relax. He felt good, especially knowing he was on the way to France with a group of other planes. He hoped the flight would be fruitful, very fruitful. He had a lot to make up for, and he was ready. They had been briefed on the target, time, the number of the group, the bomb load and their type to be used, plus the route to the target. The information had been given to them just that afternoon, plus what weather to expect and the expected enemy reaction to their visit. His pockets had been emptied of anything that the enemy would find useful, and his parachute was in position. He had been there before, so he knew how important it all was, but still he had butterflies in the pit of his stomach.

He waited for the flares that were sent from the heavy aircraft and dropped his bombs towards them. How he wished he could see what was happening down there, but he could only guess at the devastation, panic, and hopefully the obliteration of the German army. He hated the Germans!

He felt good when he arrived back and stepped onto solid ground, even if it was covered in snow. He would never have thought that he could get pleasure from killing people, but when they happened to be the hated German army, it was different. Killing them could be saving friends, family, and many others. At least he survived and brought the ship home, not like the last time. When he sat down to his operation meal of egg and chips, he really enjoyed them. He felt as if he'd achieved something. Maybe he had made a difference that night, maybe not, but he sincerely hoped he had. His only fear was that he bombed people he knew, like Michèle. It was highly improbable, but who knows!

The war had lasted much longer than was expected, and there had been many casualties, both theirs and enemies.' Everyone was getting frustrated with it all. Things were happening that made you think it couldn't go on much longer, but it did.

Time marched on with many more casualties, and they heard that Alan, who served his apprenticeship with them, had been killed. There were many who lost their lives and sometimes along the grapevine they would hear of their bravery under fire. Some were rewarded with a medal, but it was little compensation after losing someone close in the family. War was such a waste of time and lives. It's a shame there are always greedy people who want to start one, and mostly, they're still alive at the end of it—it's the working man who suffers the most.

Jonathon kept in touch with his family, but didn't tell all that was happening. There were military plans in operation, but as yet they didn't know what. He found that a number of his friends had been killed, and he made new acquaintances. Everyone was expendable, it seemed. Roger didn't make it, and that was bad. He had been a good man, and more importantly, a good friend. The enemy had a lot to answer for. There was never enough time to grieve as his services were always needed, so he had to get on with it and keep on hoping he would still be alive when it was all over. There were more night-time raids and more pilots killed on both sides. It was endless. He welcomed letters from home telling him all the news there, and he hoped and prayed that his home would still be intact when the war was over.

Shirley was working now and thoroughly enjoying it. Ruth wrote telling him that her ambition was always to be a shop assistant in Arcadia, the co-op, in Ashton. Even though there were much better offers after her dad had used his contacts, she still wanted to be a shop assistant, so she was happy to get the job she was offered there. Jonathon knew that his dad always secretly hoped that Shirley would go in an office and learn typing and accounts, then she could be a help in the business. Typical girl, she had her own mind and wouldn't budge. Nancy left school and eventually received employment in the office of Arcadia, like Shirley. Maybe Nancy could learn the necessaries there, and that would please his dad. Jonathon was aware that the girl tried very hard to please his dad. She was obviously very fond of him and grateful for what his parents had done for her.

Soon Jonathon was on leave again, and this time, he was determined to find out what happened to Ann. How did Jimmy come to have her ring, and how strange he should give it to Shirley? What happened there? What if she was still alive? He would start in Dukinfield. Maybe the town hall would know.

When he arrived home, there seemed a different atmosphere, one of hope maybe, as everyone talked about the end of the war that couldn't last much longer, as they were winning. He went into the garden to help with the chickens. There were so many memories attached to these birds. The most recent being of Michèle, and his mind became full of her memory. He wondered if she was still alive, and if so, what was she doing at this very minute.

He caught a bus and made his way to Dukinfield town hall. It was a good start to begin his enquiries. It felt warm, and the sun shone, giving him a feeling of excitement.

Jonathon turned off King Street near the town hall and onto the little road of small terraced houses. He knocked at the door of number fifteen and waited. Would Ann be here now? Was she still alive? His heart was beating fast with expectancy. He thought he saw someone look through the window, and shortly after, the door opened. The butterflies in his stomach were going mad, and he held his breath for a moment.

"Does Ann Meredith live here?" he asked.

"Yes." The woman looked like Ann, so Jonathon guessed it to be her mother.

"Is it possible to speak to her, please?" Jonathon felt excitement move up to his throat. She can't be dead, after all.

"She's not in."

"Could you tell me where she is stationed? I'm an old friend."

"Hello." A woman's voice from behind him made him turn round, and there was Ann limping towards him. "I thought it was you. I was walking behind you up King Street and saw you turn right."

Jonathon took her in his arms, and they laughed and kissed until it brought tears to her eyes.

"I can't believe it." Jonathon grinned at her. "I thought you were dead."

"Thank you, Jonathon."

"Sorry!"

Ann laughed. "I did see you at a railway station when I was going back to hospital after recovering from my injuries. I realized that you must have thought that I was dead, as I never heard from you, and I couldn't contact you because I didn't have any idea where you were."

"I was shot down in France, and it took me a while to escape, but what about you? I saw the building you were in, and it was flattened in the bomb raid. How did you survive that?"

"I was on secret work in the cellar of the building that night, luckily. That was how I managed to live through it. There were only two of us who made it."

"Were you badly injured?"

"I lost my front teeth, broke my nose, right arm, left leg, and two broken ribs, hence the limp."

"You poor thing."

"I have a confession to make, Jonathon, and I feel awful about it."

"And what could you have done wrong, I ask you?" Jonathon laughed.

"When I was being rescued, I was aware that someone was pulling the ring off my finger, but I couldn't do a thing about it, as I was only semi-conscious. So, Jonathon, I'm afraid I lost the ring…your ring. I'm sorry!"

"I've heard of those leeches, but that's the least of my worries, and it does explain some things."

"Really, what?"

"How my sister came to be wearing it."

"My ring?"

"Yes, but that's another story."

"Jonathon, we must talk. I have so much to tell you."

"I think it's time you came into the house," Mrs. Meredith chimed in. "Come in, young man, and I'll put the kettle on."

"We'll come back, Mam, but first I think we'll go to the park."

"Okay, see you both later."

Ann's mam went back inside, and Ann and Jonathon walked to the park. While they chatted, Ann took him up the steps and into the circle. They sat down on a bench and watched the birds in the fountain.

Ann turned and, looking into Jonathon's eyes, held his hand with both of hers. "I needed to speak to you alone. I thought it would be better this way. You know war changes people, Jonathon, I'm sure you will agree. I've changed, and I'm sure you have, too. Things happen. Things change you." Ann cleared her throat. "I was taken to hospital, and I was in there for quite a while."

"I'm sure you were, with all those injuries."

"There was a doctor…Barrington, and he was special. He looked after me. I mean, really looked after me, much more than was necessary."

"And so he should have. You are special."

"He sat up through the night with me, held my hand when I felt bad, and really helped me through the worst. He was so kind." Jonathon lifted her hand and kissed it.

"I owe Barrington so much, and I fell in love with him. I'm sorry, Jonathon."

"I see. No worries, Ann, and thank you for your honesty." Flippantly he added, "But you have broken my heart," and he placed his hand on his chest. Ann laughed, but he could see the tears in her eyes. Jonathon took out her handkerchief from his pocket. "Do you remember this?"

Ann took it, unfolded it, and then noticed her initial in the corner.

"The blood stain was mine, the night of the raid when we left the shelter. Do you remember, Ann?"

"I do. And you kept it all this time?"

"It was for luck…plus your memory. I thought you were dead and looking after me up high as long as I had that in my pocket."

Ann smiled. "Did it make you feel safe?"

"It did, actually."

"Then it served its purpose."

"I suppose you're right." Jonathon put his arm around her shoulders. "Are you happy with this Barrington?"

"Yes, I am, Jonathon, very happy. He's really lovely. Have you met anyone else?"

Jonathon noticed she still had unshed tears in her eyes.

"I did. She was French…Michèle, but the Germans took her prisoner."

Ann leaned over and kissed him on the cheek. "Poor Jonathon. What happened to her, do you know?"

"No, I don't, unfortunately. I don't hold much hope, though, they were cruel bastards…and she was saving my life at the time."

Ann stood up. "Try to find her if you can, Jonathon. Or else you will always wonder what happened to her."

Jonathon and Ann walked slowly back to her home, and then hugged each other.

"I intend to make enquiries regarding Michèle. She was a brave woman, and I owe her a lot."

They hugged each other for the last time, and the tears ran down Ann's cheeks.

"At least we'll always have the lovely memories, Jonathon."

"You're right. All the best for the future with Barrington."

"Thanks and the same for you. Hope you find your Michèle."

As Jonathon walked to the bus stop, he could feel the tears trickling down his cheeks. He and Ann were never meant to be. Now there was Barrington, and he so hoped Ann would be happy with her doctor. Meantime, he would try to find Michèle because he didn't realize until now how much he loved her. There had been no Ann for a long time…since…not long after he met Michèle. Now he knew what he must do as soon as this damn war was over.

The war was changing. Germany was declining, and 8 May 1945 marked the date when the WWII Allies formally accepted the unconditional surrender of the armed forces of Nazi Germany and the end of Adolf Hitler's Third Reich. It was the end of the war in Europe. The atomic bomb dropped on Japan on 6 August 1945 was the beginning of the end.

Chapter 17

2 September 1945

"Japan Surrenders

(VJ Day, Victory over Japan Day)"

General Okamura Yasiyi submitted surrender to Douglas MacArthur and Admiral Chester Nimitz on the USS Missouri in Tokyo Bay.

Ruth made herself a cup of tea the morning after, and when they had all left to go to work and school, she sat sipping her tea, while looking at the fire and thinking. She read the headlines from the day before and hoped Jonathon was okay. How long would it be before this war would all be sorted and her family would be free of danger? It was a blessing that the Anderson shelter would be defunct. She knew she would need to go to the shelter to clean and take the furniture out at some point, but not now. That would be a long-awaited pleasure. Taking her cup and saucer to the sink, she began to wash the pots. When she had tidied everything away, she put on her coat, picked up the brush and shovel, and left the house. The Anderson shelter was a chore she'd be glad to see the back of. If only they had known when the German planes were going to come, they could have lit the paraffin stove in readiness and made it cosy, instead of having to use it when it was so cold. The thought of all those horrible nights being all over gave her a spring in her step. What was she cleaning it for? They wouldn't be using it again. Carrying the brush and shovel back to the house, she replaced them into their places, and it felt good. The garden did look better than it had, but there was still room for improvement. Maybe now that the war was over, she would try and tidy the place more and grow something interesting, instead of allowing the weeds to take over. New plan, new ideas, and the old disappointments—she never seemed to have the time, but she must make an effort.

It was many weeks before Shirley received a letter from Jimmy, and it had another foreign stamp on it. She couldn't wait to open it, but she ran upstairs for the privacy of her bedroom first. Jimmy had a lot to tell her, as his letter was longer than usual.

Dear Shirley,

It's hot in India, very hot, and living in tents doesn't help. Getting acclimatized was bad enough without all the work, but I'm still here. We only work in the early morning or late evening, as it's too hot in the afternoon. We moved once again, a trip of more than thirteen hundred miles across India, which was a very hot and dusty trip. We went right across India via Indore, Mhow, Jhansi, Cawnpore, Allahabad, and Benares to Ranchi, where the division was concentrating. It was a long stop, so that we were ready in case the Japanese made a landing on the east coast in the Bay of Bengal. India's heat and smells will never be forgotten by any of us, I'll tell you.

The monsoon came next, which lasted a few months when everyone lived with the damp, and except for the few cases of malaria, we didn't take much harm.

After this we went for jungle training, and believe me, Shirley, bamboo leaves do not keep out the rain.

Next it was Calcutta, where we lived in luxury in Tollygomge, one of Calcutta's suburbs. Now it's Burma and the word "Japanese" is a dirty word.

Hope to see you soon when this bloody war is over.

Look after yourself.

Love from your special friend, Jimmy

Shirley cried and decided not to show the family the letter. He had told her a lot and after Jonathon had told her about censorship, Shirley wondered if Jimmy had overstepped the line, so she kept it to herself, except for Nancy.

Jonathon was on his way home. Ruth planned a party for him and invited the family and his friends. He looked forward to seeing the family again and all his mates. *It would,* he thought, *be good to have a pint with them all and swap tales.* He had a lot to catch up on.

The train was busy, but he managed to find a seat near the window. Everyone seemed to be talking and laughing together; spirits were much higher than they had been, and the train was stuffed with baggage, but he was quiet as he thought about his future. What had happened to Michèle? Was she still alive? He owed her so much. If it hadn't been for her...he felt cold at the thought. If she was murdered, did she suffer? No, he mustn't think like that. He must find out for sure, and then he could make plans.

As he walked home, he could see the big V sign on Hartshead Pike on the top of the hill, all lit up and looking proud in the twilight surrounded by fields. He had spent many happy hours around there when he was a child. The war was now ended, and it felt great, and who knows, maybe he could spend many more happy hours up there with his own children if fate was kind.

All those soldiers, sailors, and the lads from the Air Force would soon be home, too, to join their families. There were flags everywhere and bunting across the streets. Parties were celebrating the end of the worry and loss of life, and Jonathon couldn't wait to get home. Life was changing and for the better.

He was met at the door with many hugs and kisses, and most of all, there was laughter.

"What a relief now you're home, Jonathon," Ruth said as she hugged him. "We can begin to live again."

Jonathon still felt as if his life was on hold, or it would be until he found out what happened to Michèle. As soon as all the excitement died down at home, he would find out what he could.

The party in the next street that was planned included all the people living there with no exceptions. They all had a part to play, and all the neighbours put their heads together to plan it and make it a party to remember. As Jonathon's family lived on a main road and there would be too much traffic, they had been invited to join in the street party, too, because they were allowed to block off the street and make it safe.

When the day came, the excitement from the children couldn't be hidden. They enjoyed every minute. With no danger of the sirens going off and having to run for the shelters, everyone had slept well the previous night. They were learning again how to enjoy life. Everyone brought out their tables and lined them up in the middle of the street with their chairs. Sandwiches were provided, plus cakes and biscuits for both children and adults, made from their rations. There was pop for the children, and someone brought a gramophone and records. Someone else brought out their wireless, and they all danced to the music. The children ran around playing their games. There was a lot of laughing that hadn't been heard much over the last few years, and everyone was having a good time. The neighbours had all pulled together in the war, and now they were letting their hair down together. At last the war was over, and it was time to celebrate. There was beer and high spirits, and they laughed and danced with each other far into the night. It was a memory to keep. Some of the children had been taken home and put to bed, but they watched from their bedroom windows, as they didn't want to miss anything.

Shirley laughed at Jonathon when he danced with Mrs. Scott, who was very fat, and he couldn't get his arms around her, but he got his own back when Bert Shawcross asked to dance with Shirley. He had fancied Shirley for a while, but she wouldn't have anything to do with him until now, as she didn't like to refuse him on an occasion like this. Jonathon pulled faces at her behind Bert's back, and Shirley looked daggers at Jonathon.

Everyone had done their best with the decorations; they went over the top and didn't care, with their Union Jacks hung from windows and bunting dancing with each little breeze displayed across the streets, and they added balloons, too. There were parties going on everywhere, not just on their street. It had been a long war, but now the fear was over. Jimmy was still in Japan and unable to get home, and Shirley longed for the day when he would return, and she could wear his ring again now that Jonathon told her that Ann was still alive. She never met Ann, but she hoped one day to meet Michèle, as Jonathon spoke about her a lot.

Rationing was still going on and would be for a long time yet, and people were still queuing for their needs. Life was beginning to change for the better. If you could afford a holiday, then it was a good time to have one with no fears of sirens. There were more weddings planned, and everyone began to relax and make plans for the future.

Jonathon could soon be home to stay, but for now, he had itchy feet and couldn't settle. He told Ruth that he wouldn't go back to work in the workshop until he had returned to France, as he must try to find Michèle. He had bad dreams, as sometimes he could be heard shouting in his sleep. Ruth told the girls it was through the war, and what had happened.

Jimmy didn't write to Shirley anymore, but she still held hope for the day he would return.

The Anderson shelter in the back garden became Jessie's den; she was now seven years old and growing fast. Ruth still had to keep it clean and free of spiders, much to her regret. Shirley and Nancy were working and were blossoming, looking very adult as their figures filled out. Ruth allowed them to wear a little lipstick and silk stockings. When Ruth took them for a pair of shoes, Shirley pressured her to allow them to have a pair of Cuban heels. Nancy did work in an office and was learning about accounts and typing, just as Alfred hoped. In her spare time, she helped Alfred to run the business, both on the accounts and the printing. She was a boon, and Alfred blessed the day she entered their lives. Nancy's family hadn't come forward, so she was a permanent member of the family until someone turned up, unless she didn't want to go with them, and that was possible. Ruth didn't think she would ever want to leave them now anyway. She called on Mary for advice.

"They're growing up so fast, Mary. It's frightening."

"They do, Ruth. Look at Barbara. We've had our arguments, but you have to allow them to have their own mind, with a little help, of course."

"Now you know, Mam, that I'm perfect in every way." Barbara smiled and tried to look angelic.

"You'd better keep reminding me, because I keep forgetting, funnily enough." Mary smiled and winked at Ruth. "Kids."

"I don't want them to grow up, Mary."

"You can't stop them."

"I know. Alfred and I have made enquiries about Nancy. Up to now, there are no living relatives that they can find."

"And do you want them to be?"

"Of course, if they will love her."

"Like you, do you mean?"

"Yes, like me and Alfred do...and the girls. I think Shirley would miss her most."

Ruth worried about Nancy, more than she let on to the others, and wore a permanent frown on her face every time the girl's name was mentioned. What if someone did turn up and claim her? What would they do? They would take her away to London never to be seen again.

Jonathon left the RAF for good and eventually left for France, taking the ferry. He made his way to Paris. Maybe he could find out what happened to Michèle there. He found there were many displaced people. The prisoners who were repatriated had nowhere to go. He couldn't find anything about Michèle and hoped that didn't mean he'd lost her forever. There were terrible stories circulating, but he held on to the hope that Michèle would be okay. She had to be. He had to find her.

Returning home, Jonathon still had itchy feet. He couldn't settle. He had to know about Michèle. One morning, he told Ruth he was going to Datchet near London in his pursuit of her. He felt sure that if he could find her aunt and uncle, they would know where she was.

It seemed a long train journey for Jonathon. There were many servicemen with their kit bags on the train. Going off their cheery conversation, they were on their way home. The smoke from their cigarettes was almost choking him. He didn't grumble. Goodness knows they deserved the pleasure after the grueling war. He managed to find a seat and stared through the window, his thoughts on what he hoped to find when he reached Datchet. The not knowing about Michèle was driving him crazy. It didn't take him long to find her aunt and uncle, as he remembered some of the details that Michèle had mentioned about the area where they lived. It was a nice village, but Jonathon didn't notice, as he was too busy concentrating on finding Michèle. What happened to her, and where was she?

When Jonathon did eventually knock on the door and ask Michèle's aunt and uncle about her, they insisted that he come in for a while and join them for tea while they talked about it. They made him very welcome, and Jonathon had the impression that they had brought out their Sunday best for the table. A white cloth with beautiful china took pride of place. Their rations must have really been used up, as Jonathon enjoyed the sandwiches and homemade scones and cake. When tea was over, they took out much-loved photographs and showed them to Jonathon. They were of Michèle when she was a little girl and showing them to him only made Jonathon want to find her even more. She had obviously been a beautiful child and had given her aunt and uncle a lot of pleasure.

"How did you know Michèle?" they asked.

It was obvious to Jonathon that they loved her like a daughter. He told them all about him being shot down in France and how they met.

"I love Michèle and won't settle until I find her or at least find out what happened to her, if that's the case, and I hope it isn't."

"We haven't heard a thing from her or my sister and her husband. We don't know what's happened to them, either."

"I know." Jonathon swallowed. Why was he the one who had to tell them that he thought they were both dead? He explained what had happened and left them to wonder about their fate. There were tears shed, and Jonathon had a lump in his throat that didn't leave him until he was on the train home.

Shirley greeted him home with the news that Jimmy was back from Burma, but he was ill in hospital.

"He's promised me he'll write often now and come and see me when he's home."

When Jonathon went upstairs to unpack, Ruth joined him in his bedroom.

"Did you get to know anything, son?" she asked.

"No, they hadn't heard anything at all. They didn't even know that her parents had been taken away. They were nice people, and I had to break the news about her parents. That wasn't nice."

"What will you do now?"

"I'll need to go back to France. I have to know what happened to her, Mam. I'll never rest until I do."

"Have you enough money to go?"

"Yes, I'm okay."

Ruth hugged Jonathon. "I feel for you, dear."

"I know."

Shirley was writing a letter to Jimmy at the kitchen table when Ruth returned downstairs. Her cheeks were flushed, and her face now had a permanent smile across it. Nancy was reading in one of the fireside chairs, and Jessie was playing Ludo with a friend of hers at the other side of the table. Ruth could hear them arguing about the rules as she stood at the sink washing the pots. She smiled.

"Some things never change," she said quietly to herself.

Alfred came in from the business, "Get the kettle on, love, and let's have a cup of tea." He joined her at the sink and whispered in her ear. "Shirley is looking happier now that she's heard from that Jimmy. I think he'll have the surprise of his life when he sees her."

"Why's that?" Ruth asked puzzled.

"She's a young woman now. Not the little girl anymore. I think he'll be pleasantly surprised…and we'll have to keep an eye on her, too."

Ruth nodded. "You're right; I've been worrying about that."

Chapter 18

Jonathon made his way to the Limousin. He'd left the war and forces behind him, and he was now a free man. He found the house where Michèle once lived. There was another family living there, so he made his way to the house where she had taken him after her parents were taken away. Things didn't look much different—they must have been lucky—and he knocked on the door. He asked them about Michèle, and they told him that they hadn't seen her, and then the lady brought out a letter and showed it to Jonathon. Although he couldn't read it, as it was all in French, he recognized the signature at the bottom...Michèle. He looked at the date, which was recent, and then the address at the top of the letter. After asking them for pen and paper, he copied the address, and then they insisted that he stay the night. They talked well into the night and shared a bottle of wine before Jonathon went to bed. He left the following morning after thanking them and promising to let them know when he found out anything, and then made his way to Paris and the address at the top of the letter. He was relieved that at least he was getting somewhere.

Jonathon got off the train and headed for the area where she lived. He hoped she was still there. He would be devastated if she'd moved on. Walking down the street, he looked around at the crumbling buildings. The RAF had done a good job, but now he felt sorry for the Parisians. He stood outside of the building and checked the address. This was it. He looked up. It had obviously been bombed, as there was only part of it standing. He checked the address again. Looking at it, no one would suspect that anyone lived there. It was pouring with rain, but he didn't notice as he looked for anything that would confirm anyone lived there. The flats looked unkempt. What would he find? Where had she been, and what had happened in her life that had brought her to this? There was a lift, but it didn't work, so Jonathon made his way up the stairs. It smelled musty and damp and was littered with waste paper, urine, and anything else they couldn't be bothered putting in the dustbin. His steps echoed, and the cold seemed to penetrate through his clothes. Someone was playing a record, and it sounded like Marlene Dietrich singing "Lili Marlene." The concrete walls bore messages in paint, but he didn't understand what they said. The only word that he recognized was *Nazi* and just to make sure they were understood, they painted swastikas beside it. It was two floors up, and when he reached the flat, he stood and looked at the door for a few seconds. Would she remember him? Would she want to see him? The door of the flat was losing its paint. The number had been scrawled on by some budding artist, and not a very good one. There were swastikas painted on that, too, and it looked as if a good push would open it. He knocked and waited.

The woman who opened the door looked haggard. Her face was thin and drawn, and her eyes were dark and sunk in. She had obviously had her head shaved, but her hair was now growing, but only just. She looked scrawny and ill, and her clothes were rags. He could hear a child in the background calling to her.

The woman turned towards the child, "Taire, le chéri." Then she looked at Jonathon with empty eyes.

"Pardon, madame, parlez-vous l'anglais?"

"Oui."

"I'm looking for Michèle. Do you know where I can find her, please?"

Her face looked as if there was no life left in her as she answered, "I am Michèle."

He was horror struck and stared into her face. It was impossible. This poor wretch couldn't be his Michèle. His Michèle was voluptuous and beautiful. Could it be…?

"You are Michèle?"

"I am Michèle, Jonathon. Don't you remember me?"

"Yes." Jonathon sighed with the relief of finding her, but felt empty inside. What on earth had happened to her? He could feel anger mounting at the thought of what the Germans had done. "May I come in?" This wasn't what Jonathon was expecting. In his mind, and he had been over this so many times, when or if they met again, they would fall into each other's arms, but this…this isn't what he imagined at all.

Michèle opened the door to allow him inside, and Jonathon sat on the nearest chair. Had he made a mistake? She didn't appear to be interested in him.

Her flat was very basic and shabby, and the few pieces of furniture looked as if they had seen better days and many of them. The curtains were torn and hanging on the side of the window. A broken piece of mirror hung on the wall very precariously. There wasn't a comfortable chair to sit on, as they were all hard-back chairs only suitable for a kitchen, which she didn't have. He noticed a gas ring on a bench at the side of the sink, and the sink had the one tap.

The child, a boy, who looked about two years old, came and stood in front of him. Jonathon looked into his face.

"Is this your child?" Jonathon asked.

"Yes."

"Are you married?"

"No."

"Who's the father?"

"You are."

Jonathon must have shown the shock in his face. This isn't what he was expecting at all. How could he be the father? Thinking about it, it was possible. It happened only once, but yes, come to think of it, it was...possible.

"Are you sure?"

"Oh, yes, I'm sure. What is it that you're trying to say? Are you accusing me of being a whore?"

Jonathon jumped up and put his arms around Michèle. "That never went through my mind."

"Well, that's what I'm accused of with my people. They say I'm a whore."

"I don't understand."

"They shaved my head. They stripped me and painted me with swastikas in tar, and then paraded me through the streets and the square like an animal." Her eyes began to fill with tears. "They accused me of living with a German officer and having his child."

"And did you...have his child, I mean?"

"It is your child, yours, Jonathon. I pretended it was Jan's, the German officer's baby, to save our lives. I didn't have a choice. It's your child, only yours." Michèle was sobbing uncontrollably by now.

"Oh, Michèle. What have they done to you?" Jonathon could feel the tears pricking his eyes.

"I told Jan that our son had been born prematurely, and he believed me, as he was so tiny. I'm sorry, Jonathon, but I had to do it," Michèle sobbed.

"It's all right, it's all right," he soothed. "I'm here now, and no one will hurt you again as long as I have breath in my body."

Jonathon hugged her for a while until she calmed down, and then he turned around and picked up the boy, who was clinging to his mother's skirt and watching them closely. "Now, then, let me take a look at you." The boy had Michèle's eyes, but his features were definitely similar to his. He looked at the child's hands. He didn't have the deformed lump that he had, but that was a bonus, and then he looked down at the child's bare feet and laughed when he noticed his little toes that bent inwards, a perfect replica of his. Oh, yes, he was definitely his son.

Jonathon's voice was a whisper, "Tell me about it." Michèle sat on a chair, and Jonathon moved his chair closer. Jonathon held her hand. "Don't be afraid. You saved my life. I know that, so I owe you."

"Is this why you're here, because you owe me?'"

"I love you, Michèle." Jonathon kissed her. "You know I do."

"Do you, Jonathon, do you really?"

Jonathon nodded his head. "My poor, poor Michèle." He kissed her again. "Did you ever find out what happened to your parents after they were taken away?"

"No. I did try to find out, but it was very difficult. I suppose I shall never really know."

"Oh Michèle, I'm so sorry."

Michèle shrugged her shoulders and began to open up her soul. "When I arrived at the camp, they placed me into work detail. That was good. Otherwise, I could have been shot. I was taken to a room where there were other women, and that's where we had to allow them to do the shearing and haircutting. We were told that this was so we wouldn't get lice. We were shorn everywhere by both male and female Kapos—you know, the trustee inmates?—and the SS. They were disgusting! The Germans depended on the Kapos carrying out orders issued by the Nazis. They were rough and often as brutal as the SS. Some were Jewish and even gave out harsh treatment to their fellow prisoners. Many didn't have a choice. They knew that if they failed to do their duties, it would have meant punishment and even death, but to me, they seemed to enjoy what they were doing. I must admit I was terrified, and it was so humiliating. They also used a rusty razor blade that made us bleed. The Kapos or the SS did their work quickly, shaving pubic hair as well. Our clothes were ripped piece by piece off our body, and then we had to climb onto a table where the women held us down, while others inspected all our natural body openings." Michèle burst into tears again. "It was awful! They took away our identities and our dignities. They took away everything that made you an individual. Those pretty women with beautiful hair soon looked like melons with ears. Their eyes burned a hole in my memory forever. They were eyes full of fear. It was a living nightmare. After that, the soldiers taunted us. They were disgusting!"

"Oh, Michèle, I love you so much." Jonathon kissed her cheek and her neck. "You put up with that, and all through saving my life. Where did Jan, the German officer, come into it?"

"He entered the room after. They had us all lined up, and he came and inspected us. Then he told them to send me to his house. I was terrified as to what he intended to do with me."

"And?"

"One of the Kapos took me to his house, and we waited for Jan. When he came, the other man left, and Jan showed me the cellar where I was to sleep."

"The cellar! Was it bad?"

"Filthy! But I cleaned it up as much as I could. I managed, but it was very cold. By the time Jan was born, it was cleaner, but still freezing down there, so he would sleep cuddled up next to me. It wasn't ideal, and I was so afraid of smothering him, but it was too cold for him to sleep without me by his side."

"So how did you become Jan's sleeping partner?"

"Jonathon, I was his prisoner to do with whatever he wanted to do. There was nowhere to run. No escape. No help. I couldn't refuse."

"What was he like?"

"I will not go into that. It is far too painful a memory."

"How did you convince him that this was his child, when he looks so much like me?"

"I told him that he looked like my father...and I called him Jan, which finally convinced him."

"Was he better with you then?"

"I did better than most, but I was still a prisoner. I was expected to keep his house and entertain his friends. I was not allowed to refuse to do anything he asked or I would be threatened with death and beaten. He could be kind sometimes, but I was always under stress."

Jonathon held her again. "Oh, Michèle, I'm so sorry."

"It wasn't your fault."

"Would you come home with me to England? I'll look after you and our son." He suddenly realized what he'd said, our son, and that felt good.

Michèle trembled beneath his hands. "Oh, Jonathon, if only you knew how much I dreamed of this. It kept me alive through that terrible time. And now you're here."

"We can get married and live with my parents until we get our own place. I know the family will love you. That's if you want to."

"Really, Jonathon, would you marry me even now?"

"What a silly question. Of course I'll marry you—the mother of my son. Why shouldn't I?"

"Even after my living with Jan?"

"Yes, of course. After all, it wasn't your choice. What happened to Jan. anyway?"

"There was a raid, and he was killed. Luckily we weren't together at the time. He had sent us down to the cellar because he was going to entertain women, and he was in the garden preparing."

"Bastard!" Jonathon muttered, and then a thought went through his mind. Hopefully, it was a bomb from his aircraft that had killed Jan. He'd like to think so, and he would keep that thought.

"Can I stay here with you and Jan?"

Michèle looked surprised. "If you want to."

"Oh, I want to, Michèle. I want that more than I have ever wanted anything in my life."

"I didn't think it would be your ideal place to stay."

"You'll never know how ideal it is."

"But I am open to being attacked at any time, that is why I am living like this," and she waved her arms outwards. "You don't think I live like this by choice, do you?"

Jonathon swallowed to stop him swearing. "I'll protect you now."

The money he'd taken with him didn't stretch to a hotel, but he did manage to buy a secondhand blanket that they wrapped themselves up in when they were cold and put it on their bed at night. He stayed with Michèle for a while until things were sorted for them all to go to England. Someone did try to break into the flat, but hastily withdrew when Jonathon challenged him. They both suffered verbal abuse at times, but slowly Michèle began to relax again, and Jonathon heard her laugh for the first time after he had been with her a few weeks. It was a good sound. Jan also seemed a much happier child, too.

§ § § § § §

When they eventually caught the ferry for England, Jonathon felt relief, and when the sight of the white cliffs of Dover came into view, Jonathon knew the bad times were over, and he wrapped his arms around them both and gave them a squeeze.

"We're almost there, Michèle. Welcome to England...and home...and safety." Jonathon hired a car, and they visited her aunt and uncle in Datchet on the way home. There were a few tears shed by all of them, and her aunt and uncle insisted they stayed with them for a couple of days. Meanwhile, Jonathon telephoned his parents.

"Dad, it's Jonathon."

"Hang on, son. I'll get your mam."

"Jonathon, where are you?" His mother's voice sounded relieved, and Jonathon guessed she'd been worrying.

"I'm in Datchet with Michèle and her aunt and uncle, and Mam..."

"Oh, Jonathon, that's wonderful."

"Mam…I also have my son with me."

"Your son? What do you mean?"

"Michèle had my son while she was a prisoner."

"You didn't tell me she was expecting."

"I didn't know, Mam, but she was, and they're both with me."

Ruth burst into tears. "When are you coming home, dear?"

"Tomorrow. Can you get everything prepared? Jan is two years old, so he'll sleep in my bedroom with me and Michèle."

"We'll be ready, dear."

"See you tomorrow."

The house was in turmoil as Ruth and Alfred prepared for Michèle and Jan. The girls were thrilled to bits to find they were aunties after all and couldn't wait to see the little stranger and the French lady.

When Jonathon and his family arrived at the house, they found bunting and a welcome home sign on the door. It was a joyful reunion, and Ruth, Alfred, and the girls welcomed them with open arms. Shirley picked Jan up.

"Hello, my little nephew. So I am an auntie, after all."

"I'll say, and you should see his toes, Mam. They're just like mine."

Ruth went quiet. Jonathon didn't have feet like hers, so they must be like his dad's, but he would never know.

"We had to fight to get Michèle out of France. I don't mean physically, but it was a mental strain. I never want to fight any more bloody battles again, as long as I live. I've had enough."

Again, Ruth thanked her blessings as she had been so afraid of Jonathon having a violent nature like his dad. The dad he would never know anything about. Thankfully, though, her son had her characteristics.

Ruth showed them to their bedroom, which had the usual double bed, but now there was a cot close to it. She knew a joiner, a customer of theirs, and he had made Jan a small wooden train. Jan loved it.

"Puff, puff," he called as he pushed it around the floor on his hands and knees.

No one needed to know the trauma that Michèle had known. They didn't tell anyone the full details, but just mentioned that after saving Jonathon's life, she was made a prisoner. Both Jonathon and Michèle had nightmares when the war was relived, but they gradually settled.

The family loved Jan, and Ruth was elated at the thought of becoming a grandmother at last. He was a lovely child, a little imp who crawled into all their hearts and embedded himself there. Jan soon forgot his life with the German officer, because he began calling Jonathon Daddy.

Jonathon started working in the business again, and Nancy started working there, too. After getting a job in the office at Arcadia, because Shirley worked there, she found she didn't like it because she wasn't working with Shirley, so she asked if she could change her job and work with Alfred. At least she could help him with his accounts and also help in the workshop. Nancy said she would go to night school if necessary to learn how to do the accounts if Alfred wanted her to. Ruth thought that maybe she still needed the family around her to give her confidence, and as orders were coming in more now that the war was over, they did need more employees. Everything seemed to be fitting in nicely, and then one evening they all sat down for their meal, and Jonathon made an announcement.

"Michèle and I want to get married. We can't have a big wedding as Michèle has Jan, but it will be the best we can do under the circumstances. We still want you and Jessie to be bridesmaids, Shirley, and you, Nancy, if you will. I was also going to ask Barbara."

Shirley screamed with pleasure and went over to both Jonathon and Michèle, planting a kiss on their cheeks.

"I've never been a bridesmaid before," Nancy said.

"When do you plan to have the big day?" asked Alfred.

"As soon as possible. We have nothing to wait for…except maybe a house of our own.'

"Are you going to buy one?" Ruth asked and dreaded the answer, as she knew she would be losing them.

"No, we're planning on renting for a while, and we've been told there's one not very far away. We're going to view it. Aren't we, my sweet?" Jonathon put a protective arm around Michèle's shoulders.

"Would you like to come with us, both of you?" Michèle asked. "You can give us your opinion."

"We'd love to, wouldn't we, Alfred? Shirley and Nancy can keep an eye on Jessie for us, can't you?"

"I suppose so." Shirley pulled a face. "I'd rather come with you, though."

"I'm sorry, but we can't all of us go, love. I think there'll be enough with four of us," Ruth said.

They walked round to the house and down a wide alley that had an arch above the entrance. It was situated back behind the yards belonging to the houses on the main road. There were three very old houses all together, two semi-detached and one detached. The one they were after was a semi-detached. It was dark inside and lit with the old gas lighting. There was one main room and a tiny kitchen with a brown slop stone sink with one cold tap and stairs to the top floor. Upstairs were two bedrooms, but one was so bad with woodworm that it wasn't safe to walk on. The house was damp and dirty, and you could see mouse droppings on the floor. There was no back door, and at the front, they had to walk past the detached house to find the one toilet the three houses all shared. It was almost condemned.

"I know they have plans to condemn it, but it will do until then," Jonathon said.

"Are you sure you want to live here?" Ruth looked perplexed.

"I have lived in similar places," Michèle said.

"You mean in the prison camp?"

"No, in France."

Jonathon looked it over. "It'll be fine, Mam. It just wants a bit of plastering and paint. It'll get sorted. We'll take it, if you agree, Michèle," and she nodded.

"Are you sure, Jonathon?" Ruth looked a little dubious. "You know you can live with us until you sort yourself out."

"Thanks, Mam, but no. We have to be independent at some time, and this is it. We can't live with you forever."

"But what about Jan?"

"What about Jan?" asked Jonathon.

"Surely you can't expect to bring a child up in here?"

"It'll be fine by the time we've finished with it. And a child belongs with its mother and father. Don't you agree?"

"Of course, dear. As long as you're sure, but you know you're always welcome at home."

"I know, Mam. Don't worry, we'll be fine." Michèle was laughing and looked really happy, and Jonathon nodded. "We'll take it. Then when it's all ready, we'll get married and move in."

Ruth was happy for them, but a little dubious, as she had become quite fond of Michèle, and although she didn't want to lose them, she knew it was inevitable one day, but the house…what were they thinking of?

"What are you wearing for the wedding? You can't wear white, not with having Jan, it just wouldn't do. You'd have people talking, and they can be nasty at times."

"I'm going to wear a suit, but as it's my first," Michèle turned to Jonathon and smiled, "and the only wedding I'll have, then I'll want my bridesmaids."

"And why not?" added Alfred.

"I have been saving my clothing coupons," Ruth chimed in, "and I've begged and bought them from one or two sources, so we should be okay as long as we don't go too mad. We'd better start on the arrangements as soon as possible," Ruth added with a big smile. "I believe the new registrar Mr. Voidt is foreign, sexy, and lovely, too."

"Now then." Alfred pulled a face, and Ruth laughed.

Chapter 19

Shirley received a letter from Jimmy on her half-day off. Jonathon was out on a delivery, and there was only Ruth downstairs, as her dad and Nancy were working and Jessie was at school, but she ran upstairs to read her letter in privacy.

Dear Shirley,

I know letters aren't coming through very often, but it's not because I don't want to write to you. I'm in Burma. Sometimes, we ride the elephants, but it's not all fun. The Japanese know how to hide themselves and keep giving us shocks. The little blighters seem to be everywhere. I think they're trying to frighten us, but they don't know we English, we're strong as bulldogs, they won't frighten us.

It's very dense and hilly in the Burmese jungle. There are airstrips for the airplanes and gliders to land, and that's how we managed to get here behind the Japanese lines. We were in columns of men, and we have mules, many of them, to carry the heavy equipment. They carry the wireless sets, as we have RAF operators. The rest of the equipment we carry on our backs. Believe me when I say that we don't carry anything we don't need. Our food is dehydrated so it doesn't give us away to the Japs with the smell and smoke, and it's lighter to carry.

Our job is to blow up bridges and railways and anything else to make it difficult for the enemy. We ambush the little blighters in villages and wherever we can find them. We don't *take prisoners with being on the move, and anyway we couldn't trust the Japs, crafty little devils!*

Our food and supplies are sent to us by dropping them from a plane where there is a clearing in the jungle, and that is repeated every three days.

Can't wait to come home and take you to the pictures again. I do enjoy your company, my little lifesaver.

Love, Jimmy

Shirley looked at the letter for a while, and as it had no date, she wondered when he wrote it and how long ago. He was home now, so he must have written it a while ago. She heard someone enter the house and voices downstairs, and then Michèle called to her, so she left the sanctuary of her bedroom and went downstairs.

"Are you and Nancy coming with us for the bridesmaids' dresses?"

"Oh, yes, please." Shirley was excited. She'd never been a bridesmaid before. "What colour are we having?"

"We'll just wait and see," Michèle replied with a smile. "It all depends on the materials Aunty Mary has for us to choose from, but I'm sure your Aunty Mary will help."

"Is Barbara meeting us there?" Shirley asked.

"Oh, yes, she can help us, too. I suppose she'll have a good idea about these things now," Michèle said.

"And I'm hoping Mary will have coupons to spare for Barbara's dress."

"I'm sure she will, knowing Mary," added Alfred.

They went into the workshop and told Nancy to go and get ready while Ruth sorted herself out, preparing the tea for when they returned. By this time, Jessie had returned from school so Ruth, Michèle, Shirley, Nancy, and Jessie all waved to Alfred and went to catch a bus. Alfred offered to drive them, but they preferred to leave him at home in case he had a long wait. They needed time to choose their outfits and not be hurried by a man.

Shirley noticed a stranger outside the house and whispered to her mam, "That man on the corner keeps watching me."

Ruth looked at him. He looked smart and well dressed, and as he stood at the side of a car, she gathered that belonged to him, too. "It's your imagination, dear. Why should he be watching you? He's more than likely waiting for someone." Ruth didn't think he was a danger.

"He's always there when I come home from work lately. I don't think it's my imagination, Mam. He just stands there watching me, and I can feel his eyes burning into me as I pass him."

They all chose their outfits for the wedding after a lot of mind changes and giggles, and Mary promised they would be ready in time.

"Don't worry. I'll help my mam to get them ready," Barbara added, as she was excited at the thought of being chief bridesmaid.

The following morning, Shirley received two more letters. She ran upstairs to read them in privacy. They were from Jimmy again and she couldn't see the dates. Shirley opened the first one.

Dear Shirley,

Had a bad time with the mules. They are a great help, but the old saying is so true when they call them stubborn. They had an awkward mood on them, broke loose, and smashed the radios, making them unusable, and we couldn't report our position back to base for our supplies. It was six days before we could contact another column to let them know where we were. You can imagine how hungry we were by then!

Now it's the monsoon season, so it's raining all the time. We are always wet and take off our socks, ring them out, and then put them back on our feet. We have just been given lightweight hammocks with a groundsheet and mosquito net combined. They're looking good. Maybe we can get some sleep now. I sincerely hope so. Mind you, I'll still need to sleep with clothes on and be ready for action. I've been carrying the Tommy gun, which is great for this jungle. I've had some close shaves, I'll tell you. One of them was when we set up an ambush leading from a village where we knew the Japs were. We were told not to fire until we were given the order. We waited, it was thick jungle, and we saw Japs walking towards us. Out of the blue, there was a loud noise. One of the men hadn't kept his gun clean, so it didn't perform as it should. The Japs immediately hid in the jungle, and everyone started firing. I felt something hard hit my back. It was a hand gre-nade. I picked it up and threw it back where it had come from. It must have been faulty because it didn't go off, thank goodness, or I wouldn't be able to write to you now. The gun-ner was charged because he had allowed the gun to rust through lack of cleaning. Poor bugger got a beating for that.

If you don't get letters for a while, please don't give up on me.

Yours, Jimmy

Shirley thought about how he ended his letter and wished he meant what he said. She did worry about him, and it was obvious he was going through a bad time. Reading his letters made her realize how he came to be ill. Then she opened his next letter.

Dear Shirley,

Things aren't good. Clearing the Japs from a village, we found English prisoners. They were starving, so we gave them food.

Now we are in India. We arrived by rail and road, and of course, our feet. We met up with some Americans. What a lot of food and supplies they had! Bread, which we hadn't seen for ages, was much enjoyed, and we thanked our lucky stars that we were back in India again. We shaved our beards off, showered (that felt good), and received a new lot of uniforms. We were sent to a vacant camp and had a well-earned rest.

Our toilets are a trench dug out in the ground. These worked out fine until after having a smoke, I dropped the cigarette end into the trench and it exploded. It seems the RSM had put some mortar bombs down the trench he wanted to get rid of. Can you imagine it? "Killed in action on the toilet."

Hope you're all well and looking after yourselves.

Hope to see you soon.

Love, Jimmy

Shirley read the last letter again. He was hoping to see her soon, so why couldn't she see him? How ill was ill? She tucked the letter back in its envelope and put it away. As she walked downstairs she began to sing, "We'll Meet Again."

"Can you slip to the shop and get me five pounds of potatoes, Shirley?" Ruth asked.

Shirley ran outside, and there was the man on the corner again. She went back inside the house.

"Mam, that man is there again."

Ruth hurried to the door and looked outside. Shirley was right, the man stood on the corner again, and this time, she saw him look towards her, and then turn quickly away. Before he got back into the car and roared off, Ruth went back inside and took off her pinafore, checked herself in the mirror, and left the house. She walked towards the man.

"Excuse me. Is there something I can help you with?" she asked the stranger.

Shirley joined her mam on the corner and placed her arm around her waist to give her support.

"Sorry if I've upset you but…" he looked at Shirley, "Is your name Nancy?"

Shirley went to answer, but Ruth stopped her. "No, she isn't. Why do you ask?"

"I'm looking for a Nancy Howarth. Do you know her at all?'

"Why are you looking for her?" asked Ruth.

The man was immediately excited. "Do you know of her?"

"Maybe," Ruth answered, "but why do you want her?"

"It's a long story, but…I'm her father, Andrew Howarth."

"Well, I know that's not true because her dad was killed, she told me."

"Oh, my goodness! Is that what Hilda told her?"

"I think you'd better come inside."

Ruth led him into the house, and Shirley kept close by her side.

Ruth made a pot of tea, and they all sat round the table. "Now, then, I think you'd better start at the beginning, don't you?"

"Hilda and I married and lived in London. We'd only been married a year, and there was a chance of promotion if we moved to Manchester, so I agreed with my superiors to go, and then told Hilda when I arrived home. I thought she'd be excited."

"So you didn't discuss it with her first?"

"No, and don't tell me that was a bad decision, because I know it was now. I was young, headstrong, and foolish. Unfortunately, Hilda was headstrong, too, and we both didn't know how to say the one little word that would have made such a difference—sorry. So I left and made the move to Manchester alone. I was sure that she'd follow me."

"But she didn't."

"No."

"How could you leave Nancy?"

"I didn't. I didn't know she was expecting. In fact, even Hilda didn't know it at the time. Pat, her friend, told me."

"Yes, it does seem to happen sometimes."

"I went to a show in London two weeks ago on a night out with colleagues and bumped into Hilda's friend, Pat, and she told me I had a daughter. I was thrilled to bits. I've been standing on that corner for a day or two watching and trying to find the courage to ask you if you were Nancy," he said, looking at Shirley.

"So Hilda didn't let you know you were going to be a father?"

"I didn't leave a forwarding address, and she didn't get in touch with the insurance company. She knew she could get in touch with me through them, but she didn't. I suppose it was pride."

"So you live in Manchester still?"

"Closer than that, I live in Denton. If only I'd known."

"So many *if onlies*," Ruth commented.

"I agree."

Ruth sat back and looked at Shirley.

"I really thought that you were Nancy, you know," he said to Shirley.

"What do you think, Shirley?" Ruth asked.

"I think Nancy would be thrilled to bits to find she has a dad."

"Then we'd better tell her."

"Can I tell her?" asked Shirley.

"Don't tell her yet, just go and ask her to come in. Bring your dad, too."

Shirley rushed into the workshop and returned to the kitchen, followed by Alfred and Nancy, who were both looking a little sceptical. They looked surprised to see a strange man sitting at the kitchen table with Ruth. Ruth motioned them to sit down as she poured them a cup of tea. Shirley just sat there grinning from ear to ear.

"Do you know who this is, Nancy?" Ruth asked.

"No, should I?"

"This is your father."

"I'm not a Catholic."

Ruth and Shirley laughed. "Not that kind of a father. I mean he's your dad."

"I don't understand," Alfred said. "I thought he was dead."

"Believe me. I'm very much alive and so delighted to be meeting my daughter at last." He looked at her with pride. "You're very much like your mother, you know."

Nancy's eyes had been looking at Ruth and then her dad and couldn't quite understand what was going on. She knew that her mam told her that her dad was dead, so how could this be him? "Why are you doing this? Why are you saying you're my dad when he's been dead a long time? I never even knew him, and you are taking advantage of that."

"Here me out. Let me explain, Nancy." Andrew then went through the whole story. "Can I add that I was thrilled to bits when Pat told me I had a daughter?"

Nancy sat quietly for a few minutes taking it all in. "So what happens now? I live here...and my work is here, too."

"I've not come to make you unhappy, girl, I just want you to know that you have a father, and I love you. What happens now is entirely up to you, but I hope you will allow me into your life. That's all I ask."

Andrew sat back and took a deep breath. Ruth noticed there were tears in his eyes.

"I live in Denton with my partner, Mabel. I never divorced your mam. I think the intentions were always there to find Hilda again. Anyway, I've been with Mabel for..." he paused. "It must be ten years now. She's a lovely woman, and she's dying to meet you. And...we have two boys and a girl together, so they're your half-sister and -brothers."

"I have a sister and two brothers?" Nancy brightened up.

"You do."

Nancy squealed with delight. Her eyes were all over the place, looking first at Ruth, then Alfred, and then her dad and Shirley. "I don't know...I don't know what to do."

"May I say my two-penneth?" Ruth asked.

Andrew looked pleased. "Please do."

"As far as I can see, I think it would be a good idea for Nancy to think about this. It's been a shock for her. If you could give her a few days to think about it, then I think it would be for the best."

Andrew got up from his chair. "I think that's a good idea, do you think so, Nancy?"

Nancy breathed a sigh of relief and nodded her head. "Please."

"Then I shall leave for now. I'll call again next week, if you think that will be long enough?" He looked at Ruth. "I don't want to lose her again."

Ruth left her chair and escorted him to the door. "I'm sure once she gets used to the idea, she'll love having you in her life."

§ § § § § §

The house was ready for Jonathon and Michèle to move into. It had been a rush, but it was looking as nice as possible. It was plastered and painted. There was a coconut matting on the floor with some furniture they had bought and some that had been given to them. All the other bits they had gathered together for their new home.

Nancy still lived with Ruth and Alfred, but her dad came to visit her every weekend. She looked forward to his visits and spending time with him. The next time he visited, he took her shopping.

"When you feel ready to meet Mabel and your sister and brothers, just say, Nancy. They all can't wait to meet you."

"I think I'm ready now, Dad. Now that I've got to know you, it'll be okay."

"Next time I visit, then. I'll pick you up on Friday after tea and bring you back Sunday after tea, if that's okay. Do you mind sleeping at our house?"

"No, Dad. I'm ready now to stay with you and my new family."

"If you want to come back early, I'll understand. It's all up to you. I won't push you."

"That's all right, Dad."

"If you change your mind meanwhile, then that's okay, too."

"I don't think I will. Not now." Nancy squeezed his arm. "I'm beginning to look forward to meeting them myself."

"That's my girl."

Later that day after her dad had left, she told Shirley all about the time she had spent with him, and what the plans were for the following weekend.

"If only my mam was here, too, Shirley, my life would be perfect."

The following weekend, Andrew picked his daughter up in his car and took her to his home. Nancy was excited, but her tummy was making her feel sick with nerves. What if they didn't like her? What if she didn't fit in? She might not like them, so what would she do then? When her dad pulled up at the kerb, her new family all came out of the house and stood at the garden gate to greet her. They looked nice. The girl, Kate, was very much like Mabel, and one of her brothers, Arthur, looked like her dad. The older brother, Timothy, or Tim for short, didn't look like either of them, but he had a lovely smile and looked friendly.

Nancy was ushered into the neat semi-detached house, where she was greeted by a dog that looked like a spaniel, and Nancy was over the moon.

"I didn't know you had a dog."

"But *we* do," said Andrew, pulling his face.

"Go on with you. You know you love him," Mabel said, laughing.

"What kind is it?" asked Nancy.

"It's a mongrel," Kate said, ruffling the dog's head. "Aren't you, Monty?" The dog wagged its tail and gave a little bark. "He's called Montgomery, really, after the general, but it was too much of a mouthful so we shortened it."

"I'd love a dog," Nancy said wistfully.

"And now you have one. We don't mind sharing, do we kids?" Andrew said.

"They don't mind at all." Mabel smiled.

They all made an effort to make her welcome. Mabel showed her Kate's bedroom, which had two single beds.

"Would you mind sharing the bedroom with Kate, Nancy?"

"No, that's okay, as long as Kate doesn't mind sharing with me."

Kate was enthusiastic. "Mum and Dad bought a new bed for you, so it should be nice and comfortable."

"Oh, thank you very much. That's lovely," Nancy said, looking at Mabel.

It did look inviting, and the bedroom looked cosy. Andrew had asked Ruth what Nancy's favourite meal was, so when she sat down for her tea, she was pleased when Mabel brought it into the dining room.

"Ooh! Potato pie, I love that."

Mabel and Andrew looked at each other and smiled.

Chapter 20

The wedding day arrived, and Shirley was the most excited of them all. Michèle had chosen a navy suit, and the bridesmaids were all in blue. Their bouquets weren't overlarge, but looked lovely with their choice of flowers. Barbara looked efficient and ready for her role of chief, and Nancy was nervous.

Jan looked cute in his white outfit and was thoroughly enjoying all the attraction he was receiving.

"You all look beautiful," Ruth exclaimed.

"And so do you, my love," added Alfred.

"Oh, go on with you. We can't spend all day talking," Ruth said as she made her way to the front door. "Are we getting in the car? You can come back for Michèle and the bridesmaids after you've taken Jonathon, me, and little Jan to the registry office, and we'll take Jessie with us, too; that will save the crush."

"If that's what you want." Alfred was always agreeable.

"Your dad and Mabel and family will meet us there, Nancy. Your mam and dad said they may be a little late, but not to wait for them, Barbara."

"Typical of my parents." Barbara turned to Nancy. "It's the business, you know, you can't always get away when you want to." Nancy nodded.

Ruth turned to her future daughter-in-law. "Come here, Michèle, before I go." Ruth kissed her on the cheek. "Hope you have a wonderful marriage with Jonathon. You deserve it."

Michèle hugged Ruth back. "I hope I do because Jonathon deserves it, too. I just hope I'm good enough for him."

"Don't even think that." Ruth touched Michèle affectionately on her cheek, and then turned to Alfred. "Come on, dear, let's go."

Ruth felt a little guilty about not telling Michèle and Jonathon about his dad. Would she want to marry Jonathon if she knew his dad murdered someone and committed rape? Was she right in keeping that secret? Why did she have this continual worry, when it wasn't her fault? Pushing it to the back of her mind, she smiled and commented to Alfred, "Don't they all look lovely, Alfred?"

"They do. It's a proud day for us."

When Michèle appeared in the registry office, she looked radiant. There had been a considerable change in the girl from when Ruth was first introduced to her. Then she had no confidence at all; although she still had a way to go, she was much improved. Ruth felt sure that it was all a matter of time.

Shirley beamed, and Jessie looked very grown up. Nancy looked worried and admitted after that she was afraid of doing the wrong thing and spoiling their day. Their dresses were such a lovely blue, and the girls looked beautiful, so much so that Ruth wanted to cry. Alfred must have known how she felt, because he found her hand and held it tight throughout the ceremony.

Jan kept pointing at Michelle saying, "That's my Mummy."

Jonathon kissed his bride and the registrar, Mr. Voidt, asked if he could give her a kiss, too, and everyone laughed as he hugged her. When they made their way outside after the ceremony, Michèle broke down and sobbed uncontrollably.

"Michèle, what's the matter?" Jonathon put his arm around his wife's shoulders. "Why are you crying like that? Is it such a bad thing marrying me?"

Michèle couldn't speak and just shook her head.

Ruth held her and whispered in her ear, "Is something the matter?"

Michèle sobbed even louder. "You don't understand." Breaking away, she ran off, with Jonathon closely on her heels, but Ruth stopped him.

"Michèle," Jonathon called out to her, "talk to me."

Ruth put her hand on his shoulder. "Something's spooked her, dear. Leave her for now. She may want to be alone. Leave her to calm down."

Jonathon later found Michèle on their favourite bench in the park. "Why did you run away from me?" he asked.

Michèle could see that he was hurt. "It wasn't you who upset me, Jonathon."

"What, then? My Mam had everything all set out at home for us all to enjoy a buffet. It isn't easy with the rationing. You could at least have come home with us...and...I don't know what Nancy's family thinks."

"Jonathon, you just don't understand."

"Make me."

"I can't."

"Why not?"

"Don't try to make me, Jonathon, ple-e-ease."

"Women! I'll never understand them."

Jonathon left her in the park. Michèle said that she needed to be on her own for a while, so he respected her wishes. He found everyone at home worrying about her, and they all asked if she was okay. Everyone was very quiet, and it wasn't as it should have been. It was miserable, and they all waited patiently for Michèle to return home, as Jan was beginning to ask for her.

When Michèle did come home, Jonathon could see that she had been crying again. She put up her hand as a gesture for him not to ask. They all looked relieved when Jonathon told them it was just nerves, but he knew there was something seriously wrong. He would need to tackle her about it later.

Nancy and her family were in the front room of Ruth and Alfred's house. The room was only used on special occasions because of the fuel. Today it looked its best. The furniture was well polished, and the fire burned a welcome to them when they opened the door.

"I'm glad that's over," Nancy breathed a sigh of relief.

"Don't say that, Nancy," said Andrew. "I hoped you'd be a bridesmaid again soon."

"Whom to?" Nancy asked.

"Well...now I know about your mam, I thought I'd make a decent woman of Mabel and marry her."

Nancy felt a lump in her throat, but swallowed as she realized how difficult it must have been for Mabel in this day and age not being married. "That would be lovely, Dad."

Mabel showed her excitement. "I think it's about time we did get married, with the children and all. Don't mention it to the neighbours, though, they think we're married already," she laughed.

"I'm going to be a bridesmaid, too," added Kate.

"I'm not," said Timothy, pulling his face.

"No, but we're going to get new suits, aren't we, Mam?" Arthur was excited at the thought.

"When are you being married? Have you set the date yet?" Nancy asked.

"No," Andrew said.

"But it will be soon," added Mabel.

"I wonder what's happened to Michèle." Nancy was concerned.

"Wedding nerves, perhaps," Mabel answered.

Jonathon couldn't wait to go home. Something had ruined their wedding day, but he didn't know what. He and Michèle left his parents' house earlier than they intended.

"Are you going to tell me what upset you, Michèle?"

"Please don't ask, Jonathon."

"Surely you can tell me. I'm your husband now. There should be no secrets from each other."

Michèle burst out crying. "I can't tell you. You wouldn't understand."

"I will."

"You couldn't. You don't know."

"That's why I want you to tell me. For goodness' sake, Michèle." Jonathon was getting a little impatient.

"I can't."

Jonathon left her to cry. He was angry. Their wedding day was in ruins. What reason could she have to be so upset? Everything had gone well. All the family and the few friends were all in good spirits…except for Michèle. He couldn't understand it. He apologized to everyone, making excuses, and Nancy left with her new family, promising to return in a few days.

Over the next few days, Michèle settled down, and Jonathon didn't pursue it. She soon returned to almost her normal self. There was a little underlying tension, but Jonathon dismissed it as something he would need to adapt to. If she didn't want him to know, then she didn't want him to know, and that was that.

The following day, Shirley received another letter from Jimmy, and she couldn't wait to go upstairs to read it. Tearing open the envelope, she straightened it out on the bed.

My dear Shirley,

We've heard that the war with Germany is over. That's one down but another to go. I don't know how long the war with Japan can go on, but I'm hoping it won't be too long. It's great to know that families and friends will be safe now. We will continue to fight until the Japanese army surrenders. Preparations are being made to go back to Burma now, and we'll be on the move soon.

More news. Someone has just told me that the Americans have dropped the atomic bomb on Hiroshima and Nagasaki and the Japanese have surrendered. This is great news. Home, here we come and raspberries to Burma. I've had enough. I've been away too long, and me and everyone else are ready for a break, a real break.

See you soon, I hope.

Love, Jimmy

§§§§§§

One day Jonathon delivered a parcel of private printing for a customer who needed it urgently and decided to go home for a cup of tea before going back to work. He was surprised to find Michèle and the registrar talking on the doorstep.

"Hello there," Jonathon called out from a few feet away.

The registrar turned quickly and looked at Jonathon with annoyance, but changed his face quickly and smiled at him as Jonathon reached them both.

"Oh, hello, young man. I thought I'd just call and see how you were both getting on with married life."

Jonathon looked from Michèle to the registrar and couldn't decide what was going on, so he put his arm around Michèle's waist.

"We're fine." Jonathon looked straight into the man's eyes, but found them cold with no response. "Is there anything else we can do for you?"

Again, the registrar gave Jonathon a sickly grin. "No, I'll just get on my way."

Jonathon watched the man walk back under the arch to the main street. There was something going on, and he intended to find out what. Registrars don't usually go around checking on people they've married, or at least it was news to him. When he shut the door, Michèle burst into tears.

"I think it's time we had a little talk, don't you?"

"I feel so ashamed, Jonathon."

"Why, what have you done?"

Michèle cried so much, Jonathon couldn't get any sense out of her. Her babblings were uncontrollable. Not only did her shoulders shake, but her whole body trembled. Jonathon dreaded, even though he had to know, what she would tell him.

Sitting her down on the settee, he sat beside her and put her head on his shoulder as he held her tightly.

"You must tell me what is upsetting you, Michèle."

"I'm trying, Jonathon." Finally, she took a deep breath.

"I don't care what it is, I just need to know. I love you, Michèle, and nothing will ever change that."

Michèle looked into his face, and then held his head between her hands. "Nothing?"

"Just tell me."

"It's nothing. I'm still suffering from the camp, and I have…what do you call it…regression?"

Jonathon hugged her for a few minutes, but doubted if what she was telling him was the truth.

§ § § § § §

Shirley received another letter from Jimmy, but this time, it had an English stamp on it.

Dear Shirley,

I'm home! Not in my own home. I'm in England, but in Liverpool. Due to the conditions we lived in, I was taken ill, so I'm recovering in hospital. I should be here a while, but I'll come and see you when I come home. Home is such a lovely word, and I've missed it so much. War is not a nice word, and I hope I'll never see another.

It's so long since we went to the pictures together, but it won't be much longer now. I suppose you've changed since I last saw you, but in my mind you're still the same sweet Shirley I knew then.

See you soon.

Love, Jimmy

Shirley looked at the address at the top of the letter and immediately showed it to Ruth.

"Do you think I can go and see him in hospital?" she asked.

"I don't know. Let me think about that."

§ § § § § §

"What on earth is she doing?" Alfred asked. He and Ruth sat in the car waiting for Shirley to join them. It was Shirley's half-day off, so she was taking advantage of it to see Jimmy, while Nancy worked and Jessie was at school.

"Oh, Alfred, you know what young girls are like. She's had a crush on Jimmy for years."

"That's true. She's taking a long time to get ready, though." Alfred fidgeted. "This car is getting past its best."

Ruth ignored him. "She hasn't seen Jimmy for ages, so she wants to look her best."

Alfred sighed and made himself more comfortable. "Women!"

Shirley appeared, and Alfred breathed a sigh of relief. Picking up the handle of the crankshaft, he got out of the car and began to start the engine. When he got back inside, he rested for a few minutes. "These modern cars are a blessing, have you seen them?"

"Yes, Alfred."

"At least you don't have to knock yourself out, using a crank to get them started."

"Don't worry, Alfred. We'll renew ours as soon as we can."

"You just turn a key, and that's it."

"Stop dreaming, and let's get going."

It was a long trip for Shirley, as it seemed to go on forever. Normally, she would have enjoyed the drive, but she hadn't seen Jimmy for so long. She just couldn't wait to see him, and the butterflies were flying around and around in her tummy until she felt sick with anticipation. What would he be like? Would he have already met someone else? Had he missed her, really missed her like she had missed him? Would he still think of her as a kid? For goodness' sake, he could be married, for all she knew. The hospital loomed, and when she finally left the car, her legs wobbled beneath her.

Shirley walked through the hospital and onto Jimmy's ward and looked around. She couldn't see him, and she asked a nurse where he was. The nurse pointed to a bed at the end of the ward.

As Shirley walked towards Jimmy, she hardly recognised him. He wore the beginnings of a beard and still his face looked thin. He'd lost a lot of weight; she could see that his arms looked like skin and bone as they relaxed on the counterpane. He was so changed, it was no wonder she didn't recognize him. Jimmy looked at her, big eyes in a small face, and she could see his surprise when she stopped at his bed.

"Hello, stranger," Shirley whispered.

Jimmy was still surprised. "Hello."

"Don't you recognize me, Jimmy?" Shirley asked.

"No, should I?"

"It's Shirley. Look…" She showed him the ring she wore on her finger. "Recognise it?"

"Shirley!" His mouth gaped open, and his eyes opened wide. "But…you're a woman."

"I'm sixteen. Are you pleasantly surprised?"

"Very." He whistled. "You've grown into a smasher. Turn around and let me take a good look at you."

Shirley spun round, and then sat on the chair at the side of the bed. "And you need some special care. You look terrible. What have they done to you?"

"Thanks very much," he answered sarcastically.

"Oh, Jimmy, I don't care how you look. I'm so pleased to see you." Shirley felt shy and awkward, "I've missed those visits to the pictures."

"It will be resumed as soon as possible."

"Tell me how and when you arrived here."

"The night before we all came home, there was a party, and what a party! I was sent to Dodali, just outside Bombay to pick up a ship for home. We all christened it Doolali, as that was how it was affecting us. It was a basic camp, nothing there, and we waited there for six very long weeks. The time dragged. Once we knew we were going home, it seemed endless. We just couldn't get away quick enough. Finally, we picked up a troop ship to sail for England. What a relief that was. We sailed across the Indian Ocean through the Suez Canal and through the Mediterranean, and that's when the storm hit us. It was bad, and I stood at the front of the ship as it went through the very rough seas and wondered if after all we had been through, the ship would sink and we would all drown. Your mind plays tricks on you in those kinds of situations. But we arrived at Southampton, and although anxious to get off the ship, we were not allowed. We had to wait until the powers that be agreed to let us go. I was finally discharged on February 11, 1946, after five years' service in the Army. Anyway, how did you get here?" Jimmy asked.

"Mam and Dad brought me."

"Where are they?"

"I don't know. Outside...somewhere."

"Well, go and find them. I'd like to see them."

Shirley left the ward for a short time and came back with Ruth and Alfred. They stayed with Jimmy for a while, and he told them what he'd been doing in the Army, or at least some of it.

"I'm sorry, but you must leave now so that he can rest," the nurse urged.

Ruth and Alfred then left Shirley and Jimmy alone for the last few minutes.

"Nice to see you, Jimmy," Shirley said as she got up from her chair beside the bed.

"Thanks for coming." They both stared at each other in an awkward silence, and then Shirley took the bull by the horns and leaned over to kiss him on the lips.

He turned his face so that she kissed his cheek instead, but his arms went round her. They hugged each other, and then Shirley broke away.

"Please don't forget me, Shirley."

"I never will."

Shirley could feel Jimmy's eyes watching her as she walked down the ward. She turned and gave him a little farewell wave.

"Write soon," he called after her.

"I will," Shirley answered and hurried into the corridor outside.

There were tears running down her cheeks that she had to hide from Jimmy. He looked so skinny and poorly, she felt sorry for him, but she was happy...deliriously happy that he wanted to hold her. Why wouldn't he kiss her, though? Did he still think of her as a child? Perhaps she was being juvenile. There could be a future for them; she mustn't give up, and all the way home, Shirley thought about the way he hugged her.

The drive home was more enjoyable for Shirley. Although she didn't do much talking to Ruth and Alfred, her thoughts were busy. Somehow everything had taken on a different look. Life was getting brighter and more promising.

Chapter 21

Jimmy and Shirley wrote letters to each other often, and Shirley started to catch a train to go to see Jimmy once a week.

"When are they going to allow you home?" Shirley asked one day.

"Where's home?" he answered.

"Your gran's house?"

"She died when I was in Japan, so the house is let to someone else now."

"How unfair, when you've been fighting for your country. They could have at least let you keep the house."

"My name wasn't on the rent book."

"What happened to your parents? You never told me."

"That's because I don't know."

"I don't understand."

"I was an abandoned child. I wasn't wanted."

"What about your gran? Where does she fit in?"

"She was my saviour. It was her doorstep where my mam left me...well, on the porch actually, so I was out of the weather. Gran told me I was left wrapped in a towel. I called her my gran, but she was no relation, really."

"Aww! Poor Jimmy! Have you tried to find your parents since?"

"No, what's the point? If they didn't want me then, they won't want me now."

"You never know. Things happen, and they could have had many reasons. Maybe the father didn't want to know, and she knew she couldn't look after a baby on her own. Or it could have been that they were too poor to bring up a child, or...or...she could have been raped."

Jimmy grunted. "Thanks very much for that. You're making it worse. Anyway, I'll never know. I was abandoned, and unwanted, full stop."

"Did your gran adopt you?"

"She said she fought for me tooth and nail, because at first they said she couldn't keep me, but she won in the end."

"Where did the name Jimmy come from? Was it the name your gran gave you or your mam? Did your mam leave a note telling your gran that was your name?"

"It was my gran's late husband's name."

"And now you're all alone with no family?"

"Well, there's always Sue, I suppose."

" Is that your Gran's friend?"

"She was always part of my life."

"Aww! And then you come back here, and you're still fighting a war."

"It's a bit different here. The Japs were unbelievable."

"Why?"

"Oh, Shirley, you have no idea."

"Then tell me."

Jimmy took hold of Shirley's hand. "I saw too much regarding the Japs. Once we came across women tied to the ground, and their arms and legs were stretched out. They'd died a horrible death by the soldiers. We had a Burmese guide who knew the country well, and that was a help. In fact, I don't know how we'd have managed without him. They were daft enough to send us officers from England, who were a waste of time. They knew nothing, no experience of the jungle warfare. And not only that, none of the Africans had much idea either. They were useless. It was a shambles, believe me. Like I said, we had to carry everything on our backs. We had a choice to shave or not to shave, so most of us ditched the razor. After all, washing was a problem in itself. With all the rain and mud in the monsoon, we became a scruffy lot. I bet the Japs could smell us coming. Although the K rations weren't all that good, we managed to make something out of next to nothing with the dehydrated food and cans of stuff. There was a lot of animal life in the jungle, too. Monkeys scared us to death at night with their chattering, because they sounded very much like Japs. They put the fear of God in us sometimes. Leeches were the most horrible things—they wanted blood—and the only way we could get them off was by burning them with a cigarette. If you pulled them off, they left their fangs behind and then they'd fester."

"Oh, Jimmy, you have been through it, but what are you going to do now?" Shirley felt devastated.

"I don't know. I'm not thinking about it yet."

On the way home, Shirley thought about it a lot. As soon as the opportunity arose, she broached the subject with her mam and dad. "I don't know where or when Jimmy's coming out of the hospital because he has no home."

"No home? Where did he live before?" asked Ruth.

"With his gran, but she died when he was in Japan."

"Oh, dear. Poor lad."

Shirley sat quietly for a while and waited to see if her mam would get the hint, but she didn't. Ruth picked up the evening paper and began to read it.

"Do you think that he could come and stay with us, Mam?" Shirley asked from behind the newspaper. "He could have Jonathon's room, couldn't he?"

"Who, dear?"

"Jimmy, Mam. Who else?"

Ruth didn't answer for a while. She didn't like the idea, but she did feel sorry for the lad. "Is he ready to leave hospital?"

"Well, I don't think so, but if he is, could he?"

"It's difficult, Shirley."

"Why? You wouldn't mind, would you, Dad?"

"Whatever your mam decides is fine with me, you know that."

"Just leave it for now, Shirley, and see how things go. It could be all decided for you anyway, dear," Ruth said.

"What do you mean?"

"Things have a strange way of sorting themselves out."

Shirley snorted with annoyance and went upstairs to her bedroom.

§ § § § § §

Michèle wasn't as happy as she could be, and Jonathon worried about her. Was it the camp memories that took over her life, or was there something else she wasn't telling him? He loved to hear her sing. Many times he would waken to her singing. She had a beautiful, sweet voice, and he missed that, as she didn't sing anymore. Her spontaneity had disappeared.

Trying to concentrate at work was getting more and more difficult. His dad was very understanding. Jonathon was sure that he knew he was going through a bad patch in his marriage, but didn't say anything. He was so wrapped up in his thoughts that everything came automatically. The hours melted away without him noticing. His only respite was when there was an urgent delivery and he had a break away. He always ended up at home seeing Michèle.

Both Ruth and Alfred knew there was something wrong, but they didn't ask. They worried about their son's marriage and hoped he and Michèle would sort things out.

"Jonathon has a continual worried look on his face, Alfred. What is he like at work?"

"He hardly ever laughs now. He seems unhappy."

Alfred didn't like to tell tales, but he thought Ruth should know. Sometimes, he would send Jonathon out on an emergency delivery. It wasn't urgent, really, but he thought it might help Jonathon sort himself out and give him a much-needed break.

Jonathon bought Michèle flowers and small gifts, and she seemed happy enough, but then she would drift off again into her secretive self. It was hard to penetrate her mind and understand how she felt. Maybe another baby might help, a girl perhaps; she would have something in common with a girl. He went to see the doctor about her, and he arranged an appointment for her to see him.

Michèle was annoyed at Jonathon for making arrangements for her to go to the doctor.

"I'm not ill, Jonathon, so why should I see the doctor? You should have asked me first."

"But there's something wrong. I thought it would be good to make sure you're okay if you had another child."

"A child? No, Jonathon. I don't want another child. Not yet. I couldn't cope with another baby. No, Jonathon…please."

"I thought you could have a little girl this time. You'd like a little girl, wouldn't you?"

"A girl is not guaranteed, Jonathon."

"I know, but I thought it would be worth trying."

Was it such a hardship for Michèle to have another child? A little sister or brother for Jan? Didn't she love him anymore? Jonathon was upset. He didn't understand her attitude. What was the matter with her?

He began to look at property for sale. It would be nice to buy a semi-detached with a garden for Jan to play in, but he knew they couldn't afford that. He thought that maybe it was the house that was getting Michèle down. He looked at a lot of property, mostly small terraced, but he couldn't buy one without Michèle's approval, and they couldn't really afford any of them, terraced and definitely not semis, anyway.

After Jan was put to bed, Jonathon and Michèle would sit and listen to the wireless or read books and magazines, but quite often he would find himself watching her instead. Sometimes, she would question him.

"Haven't you read that yet?"

"Er, no, my mind keeps wandering."

"Slow coach, where is your mind going?"

"You have no idea," Jonathon would say.

He took her out for the day with Jan to see if he could please her. When she was away from home, she was a different person. She was the old Michèle, a fun, witty *peu sorcière*. Why was she so different at home?

After a heated argument when they arrived home, Michèle finally agreed to go with Jonathon to see the doctor. He examined her, listened to her heart, took blood and urine samples, and talked to her for a while.

"Come to see me next week, Jonathon," he whispered as they left.

Michèle still insisted there was nothing wrong, but Jonathon worried all week about her and what it could be. Was she ill? He hoped not, but then again, if she wasn't, then what was her problem? *It must be him,* he thought, *something had gone wrong.* He hoped it wasn't that she had gone off him, as being separated from her and Jan was unthinkable.

Sometimes, Jonathon would sit in the park. It was peaceful there, and he could think about things. If only he could afford a nice little semi with a garden. He felt sure that could be the answer to their problems. He would watch mothers with their children and wished Michèle would come here, too, but she would hardly leave the house.

Jonathon would sometimes pop upstairs and just look at Jan asleep in his bed. He was a miracle! How his son and Michèle had both survived through the war was a miracle. If only he'd known. No, he didn't…wouldn't…couldn't lose him. He couldn't lose either of them, not now, so he dearly hoped Michèle hadn't found someone else.

Jonathon found himself looking at other men with suspicion, especially Voidt. Was it him she was having an affair with? He always seemed to be around. He knew his mam thought the man was sexy, so maybe Michèle did, too. He was a foreigner, but then again, so was Michèle. It could be Voidt.

Jonathon went to see the doctor again for her results. "There is nothing bodily wrong with Michèle," the doctor told him. "She appears to be quite healthy. I honestly have no idea what's wrong with her."

"Then what can it be?" asked Jonathon. He wasn't happy with these results. He knew Michèle had problems regarding the war. There were times when he would be wakened by her tossing and turning in her sleep and talking; even though he couldn't understand what she was saying, he knew she was having a nightmare, and he would shake her awake. Then she would lie in his arms until she fell asleep again, but there was something else, he was sure. He came to the only conclusion. She didn't love him anymore, but that thought was too painful, so he pushed it to the back of his mind.

A few weeks passed, and Jonathon went to see the doctor again about Michèle.

"If you think there is something wrong, then maybe it's in her mind," the doctor said. "Jonathon, you must realize that the girl has gone through a lot. Is she worried about her health?"

Jonathon shook his head. "She doesn't appear to be."

"Then I suggest she see someone who deals with mental problems. Would you like me to make an appointment? Michèle doesn't need to know he's that kind of a doctor."

"No, leave it for now, and I'll see how things progress. Thank you for seeing me. I don't like being a nuisance, but I know there's something wrong. If this problem persists, then I shall contact you again," and Jonathon left the surgery.

Jonathon couldn't have Michèle seeing a psychiatrist; she deserved more than that. He was sure there was nothing wrong with her mind. Whatever was bothering her he would sort out himself, if at all possible. If only he knew what he was going to sort out.

When he was close to home, he saw Mr. Voidt walking towards the archway that led to his house, so Jonathon hurried to catch up to him and grabbed his arm. "Hello, there. We keep meeting around here, don't we? Are you well?"

Voidt looked surprised. "Hello, Jonathon. Yes, it is surprising, isn't it? I've just been visiting a friend. Nice to see you," he said as he rushed off past the archway.

Jonathon watched Voidt walk away. He didn't trust that man, and he didn't like the thought of him and Michèle being on his visiting list. He must be told somehow. He didn't like to upset anyone, but most of all, he didn't like the idea of the man upsetting Michèle. His wife had been through hell, and she didn't need any more in her life.

Michèle was happier today and was glad to see Jonathon.

"Jan is so funny, Jons. He's doing little things that I know I do, and he's starting on you now."

"What do you mean?" Jonathon showed surprise.

"He's started holding his left ear when he talks sometimes, just like you do."

"Didn't think you'd noticed."

"I know it's when you get nervous, and yes, I had noticed."

"Does Jan do it when he gets nervous?"

"I think he does, but he does it anytime anyway."

Jonathon picked up his son and cuddled him. "Like father, like son."

When he arrived back at the workshop, his mother joined him. "I've just seen Nora when I went to buy some bread, Jonathon. She's looking well...and so is the baby."

"It wouldn't do for me to see that woman. I'm still angry about the way she barged in here claiming that she was expecting my child."

"She asked about you."

"She's cheeky enough."

"Nora also asked me if you would pass Jan's clothes and things on to her child when Jan's finished with them."

Jonathon was flabbergasted. "Cheeky madam! Not a hope."

"Don't be bitter, Jonathon."

"Bitter doesn't come into it."

"Nora also told me that she was moving to Manchester."

"Manchester! Why the heck would she want to move there when she must know the Germans liked to bomb it? It's a real mess now."

"I don't know, unless she has a boyfriend who comes from there."

"Who knows? That woman never fails to surprise me."

Chapter 22

Shirley was visiting Jimmy again. She had found it difficult getting up that morning for the early train, so she was still sleepy. Concentrating on the scene before her, she watched the people going to and fro and wondered where they were going and what they were doing. She took a guess at some, and then smiled to herself, wondering what people would guess about her, until a young couple came and sat opposite her. They were obviously in love with the way they looked into each other's eyes. Trying to avert her eyes and focus on the view from the window, she couldn't help but notice the young man holding the girl's hand throughout the journey. Shirley wondered if Jimmy would ever think enough of her to do that. Her mind went astray, and imagination came into play. What a pity that Jimmy hadn't taken her on the caterpillar in wakes week, she was sure she'd have enjoyed a kiss. If only . . .

This journey was getting to be a regular weekly trip, and that took up most of her pocket money.

Shirley thought about when she married. Would it be to Jimmy? She hoped so. *I'd like at least two children, but maybe four, two boys and two girls,* she thought to herself. Maybe two of those could be twins. She shifted uncomfortably and hoped the couple hadn't noticed her vacant stare. Smiling at them, she got up and moved to another compartment so that they could be alone.

Ruth worried about Shirley. "Do you think I should stop Shirley from seeing Jimmy as often?" she asked Alfred.

"You know I leave things like that to you."

"Well, yes, but I would like your opinion. I mean she's spending most of her money on these train trips. She's letting her life pass by, when she should be enjoying it. She should be going out with her friends...enjoying life, meeting boys her age, not rushing about catching trains and buses," Ruth finished with exasperation.

"If you're worrying about it, then have a talk with her."

Ruth thought a lot about Shirley and Jimmy and wondered if she would be doing the right thing if she mentioned it to her daughter. She knew Shirley had spirit and could rebel against her wishes, making things worse. Perhaps she'd better leave it for now and take her own advice about things sorting themselves out.

When Shirley returned home, Ruth could see she was full of anger with the way she slammed the door when she came in, then slammed her handbag down on the table and threw herself into the nearest chair.

"What's the matter, dear?"

"Nothing," Shirley answered sharply.

"How's Jimmy?"

"He said he's feeling better, but he doesn't look much improved to me. He says he can't wait to get out of hospital, but he still looks ill, Mam."

"Isn't that a good thing, him wanting to leave hospital? Doesn't it mean he's feeling better?" Ruth was puzzled.

"I thought so until today. I thought that at least I'd see more of him, but I won't."

"Do you want to talk about it?"

"No!" Shirley got up and walked away, but not before Ruth noticed the unshed tears in her eyes. Then Ruth heard her running upstairs.

When Ruth went up a little later, she could hear Shirley crying in her bedroom. Should she try to comfort her? Maybe not. It was awful hearing her crying and knowing there wasn't anything she could do about it.

It was the following day, when Shirley sat having an early breakfast with Ruth that she told her mother what had happened.

"I'm sorry about yesterday, Mam, but I was so angry. When I walked onto Jimmy's ward, I saw Audrey, a nurse, talking to him. I thought she seemed too close at the time, but as I reached his bed, I could see there was something going on between them. It was the way they were looking into each other's eyes."

"You could have been mistaken, Shirley. You could have been imagining it."

"I would be talking to him and suddenly notice that his eyes weren't looking at me, but at Audrey. It was very unflattering."

"It might not mean anything."

"Mother, I know you see me as your little girl, but I'm not stupid. There was something between them. When she was around, Jimmy's eyes followed her. I felt daft, sitting, watching, and I did think of turning round and coming home."

"How was he with you then?"

"I suppose he was normal."

"I see."

"What does that mean?"

"What *you* mean is you were jealous."

"No…well, yes, I suppose I was…but it hurt, Mam."

"Shirley, I think everyone goes through the feelings of jealousy at some time in their lives."

"Were you jealous with Dad?"

"Yes, I remember vividly once when I felt jealous, when I saw him holding hands with a friend of mine, but I got over it like you must."

"Did Dad two-time you?"

"No, he didn't. Your dad wasn't the type to do that. No, I was with Jonathon's dad at the time, but it was then that I realized I was fond of your dad, too."

"Mother!"

"I know, but you're not always in charge of your feelings. Some things suddenly hit you."

"Do you think there's something going on with Jimmy and that nurse, then?"

"I don't know, dear. Time will tell."

"Oh, Mam, I do love him."

"I know."

"By the way, I saw Nora in Manchester the last time I went for the bus in Piccadilly."

"How is she?"

"We didn't speak. She was busy."

"Oh, what was she doing?"

"What girls usually do in Piccadilly, she was looking for men."

Ruth was shocked. How did her daughter know about these things? And what about Nora's baby? Now that Shirley had told her about Nora, she felt bad at asking the girl to leave. Perhaps she should have shown her a little more kindness. Her thoughts turned to Shirley. She is growing up. Of course she would know about these things; she's a young woman now.

Alfred and Nancy came in for their morning cup of tea, so Ruth and Shirley's conversation ended. Ruth felt sorry for her daughter and hoped things would sort themselves out soon. Shirley had loved Jimmy for a while now, and it had changed from puppy love. Her daughter was quite mature, maybe not in years, but definitely in her mind. Ruth remembered the pangs of jealousy she felt all those years ago when she saw Alfred holding her friend's hand, and they weren't nice feelings.

Shirley collected her things together and went off to work. "Don't tell Dad what I said, will you?"

"Don't worry, I won't."

"See you, Mam." The door closed behind her.

Shirley still went to see Jimmy in Liverpool. He talked about the nurse, Audrey, a lot, and he finally told Shirley that Audrey had offered him a home.

"You're going to live with her?" Shirley asked with disgust.

"She said I could. That would sort out the problem of where I was going to live for now."

"You can't."

"Why can't I?"

"Y-you hardly know her."

"She knows me very well," he answered grinning.

Shirley understood the implications, but preferred to ignore them. "You can't."

"I think it's a good idea, Shirley. She said she'd look after me until I was ready to find work."

"What about me?"

"You're my special girl. We'll always be friends."

Shirley walked out of the ward in disgust. Friends! She didn't want to be his friend, she wanted more than that, and she wanted very much for him to feel the same about her. How could he do this to her, after she visited him in hospital every week without fail? Idiot! When would she learn? Everyone treated her like a child. She wasn't a child. She was a woman with a woman's feelings. Couldn't they see she was a grown woman? Were they stupid? Shirley went home feeling very deflated and determined she wouldn't go to see Jimmy again. She confided in Nancy, who gave her the sympathy she needed.

"He doesn't deserve you, Shirl. After all you've done, too. All those letters you wrote to him when he was in Japan. No, he doesn't deserve you at all."

When her friend Margaret asked her to go dancing at the Jubilee Hall in Dukinfield on Saturday, she agreed. It would make a change, and they didn't get the fights that sometimes happened at the Palais. She liked the Jubilee Hall. They caught a bus, and all the way there, Shirley wished she hadn't agreed to go, but as soon as she entered with Nancy and Margaret, she saw Peter, her childhood crush. Would he remember her or be indifferent?

When the band began to play, the girls sat on the side of the dance hall and waited to see if they would be asked to dance. It didn't take long before a good-looking lad asked Margaret to dance. Shirley hoped Peter would come along and ask her, but he didn't. Soon Nancy and Shirley were up and dancing with young men, and Shirley forgot all about Jimmy, or at least she kidded herself that she had. It was a good night at the Jubilee Hall, and Shirley was asked to dance many more times. As the night wore on, Peter at last came and asked her to dance the last waltz. It did seem strange as he placed his arm around her, but she liked the feeling, even though she could feel every nerve in her body tremble. They smooched, and she wrapped her arms around him. They danced cheek to cheek, and he did remember her as they talked about their school days. Finally, he asked if he could take her home.

Conversation was difficult, as their lives had changed, and Shirley found that they had nothing in common. His attraction began to wane, as he showed off and asked her questions in a foreign language that he explained was French—Shirley had another word for it, but kept it to herself—and then he would laugh at her when she couldn't answer. He was a stuck-up idiot! They had a different education, and he was speaking of something she knew nothing about, and he knew it.

When he kissed her goodnight, she was disappointed. There was no electricity between them at all. Nothing like when Jimmy kissed her. Peter was…childish. He asked if he could take her to the pictures the following evening, and she heard herself say, "No." No, after all these years of having that crush, now that she had the chance, she was refusing him. Something had happened in the meantime.

She had grown up.

For a while, Shirley stayed at home and didn't go out with her friends, until Margaret came around and asked her to go to a special factory dance that was local. Shirley agreed after a lot of persuasion. There was one young man, Ken, whom she took a liking to, and he asked her to dance. He stayed with her all night and then took her home.

Whenever Shirley finished work, Ken was waiting for her. He brought her flowers every Saturday and bought her small gifts.

When the wakes came, Ken took Shirley, and they walked around for a short time. Ken tried his luck on a couple of sideshows, but didn't win anything. When they passed the caterpillar, he nudged her.

"Do you fancy it?"

Shirley remembered the fun she had with the family in the past and agreed, so Ken found a carriage and paid for the ride. When the hood came over and he tried to kiss her, it took her by surprise. This had never happened to her before, even though she knew the boys did that when they had the chance. She didn't like it and decided she didn't like him anymore, so she ended it that night.

"Have you finished with Ken, dear?" Ruth asked.

"Yes."

"Why? He seemed a nice boy."

"He put me on a pedestal."

"You didn't like being on a pedestal?"

"No, not really."

"Why?"

"I got lonely."

"Silly thing!"

"He was just too much, Mam. He didn't leave me alone. I had no breathing space."

"Or is it because he's not Jimmy?" asked Ruth.

Shirley shrugged her shoulders. Her mam was right, but she hadn't even admitted it to herself.

The following morning, Shirley received a letter from Jimmy.

Chapter 23

Dear Shirley,

I thought I'd better let you know that I've left hospital, and I'm now living with Audrey and her family. They're nice people and look after me very well. Audrey has been a brick helping me like this. I don't know what I'd have done without her.

Hope your family is well and you're enjoying your job. Think of me sometime, as I'll always think of you.

Write to me.

Your special friend, Jimmy

Shirley looked at the address at the top of the letter and felt like screwing the letter into a ball and throwing it into the fire, but she didn't. Any letter from Jimmy was still special, so she tucked the letter back into the envelope and took it upstairs as the tears ran down her face. How could he? How could he go and live with that nurse? She would hate the name Audrey for evermore.

Margaret came to see her, and Shirley took her upstairs with Nancy and showed them the letter.

"Oh, Shirl, you must be dead upset." Margaret was very sympathetic.

"I am. What do you think of that?"

"After you've gone to see him in Liverpool, Shirl...you're angry, aren't you?" She looked at Nancy. "She is, isn't she?" Nancy nodded.

"Too right I am. I suppose I've lost him forever now." Shirley couldn't stop the tears from running down her cheeks.

"Don't cry, Shirl. You never know, it might not work out with that nurse." Nancy put her head on Shirley's shoulder.

"Come to the Palais with me on Saturday. You might meet someone else," Margaret urged.

"I don't want someone else, Margaret. I just want Jimmy."

"You never know, you may meet somebody. I've seen a lad I like. He's dead good-looking and reminds me of Stewart Granger."

"Stewart Granger?" Nancy looked puzzled.

"Knowing my luck, I'd end up with a Boris Karloff look-alike," Shirley said sardonically.

"Shirley!" Margaret said laughing. "You wouldn't at all. This lad I like is tall and fair, and I'm going to ask him to dance if he doesn't ask me soon.'

"Margaret, you can't do that," Shirley sounded horrified. "You wouldn't?"

"I know, but I really like him."

After a while, they went back downstairs, but now Shirley was curious to see this boy who had taken Margaret's fancy.

"If I go to the Palais, are you coming, too, Nancy? Your dad wouldn't mind, would he?"

"No, of course not. It won't matter for once if I just go and see the family on Sunday for lunch. I don't need to sleep, and besides, I want to see this Stewart Granger look-alike, too."

§ § § § §

When Saturday came, Shirley and Nancy took their time to get ready, doing each other's hair and make-up and swapping clothes until they felt they looked their best. It gave Shirley something else to think about, and she enjoyed it. Margaret called for them, and they walked down to the Palais. There were many others walking in front of them who were obviously going to the same place, and they took note of what they were wearing and passing comment on anything they really liked. When they got inside, it was very crowded and they had to push in to use the mirror in the ladies to reapply lipstick and check their hair. They joined the crowd that stood at the side of the dance floor and watched the dancers; Shirley asked Margaret if the Stewart Granger look-alike was in. He wasn't, so Margaret kept a look out for him. When he did arrive, she pointed him out. Shirley couldn't see the resemblance, except he was tall, but she didn't mention it. After a while, he came and asked Nancy for a dance. Margaret was devastated, but Nancy got up and danced with him. When Nancy joined them after, Margaret bombarded her with questions. Nancy laughed at first, but eventually confessed why the young man asked her to dance.

"He only asked me to find out all about you."

"And what did you tell him?" Margaret urged.

"I told him that you were wonderful, but didn't like boys."

Margaret yelled, "You what?"

Nancy laughed. "I'm kidding. I told him that you seemed to like him, too."

"You shouldn't have said that, either, but I suppose it's better than the other," Margaret added, "much better than the other," and laughed.

"Stewart Granger" danced with Margaret for the rest of the evening, and she allowed him to walk her home. Nancy and Shirley walked home together, but Shirley admitted that she had enjoyed herself, and the evening had kept her thoughts of Jimmy at bay.

Nancy was on holiday for a few days and was spending it with her family. Taking a walk with Monty was a new experience, and she loved it. Her brothers had complained about taking the dog for a walk, so she gladly took over the role. Sometimes, Kate came with her, and other times, she was alone. The dog was very well behaved, so he was no trouble. Also, it gave her a chance to discover the territory her family lived in.

They were a lovely family, and Nancy got on well with them. Timothy was the comedian, and his humour was very dry. Arthur couldn't do enough for her, and Kate…was Kate. She was her own girl and never failed to surprise Nancy with the things she said and did. Mabel was a very kind lady, and although Nancy could never call her mam, she was as close as she could be. Her dad was everything she would expect a dad to be, tolerant, understanding, and loving. She was a lucky girl!

Weeks passed, and Shirley had stopped writing to Jimmy. She didn't want to know how comfortable and happy he was with Audrey. She didn't want to know anything more about Audrey. Audrey was welcome to him, she kidded herself, but underneath she was heartbroken.

Nancy started courting with a lovely lad. His name was Harry, and she urged Shirley to come on a double date with them and his friend, but Shirley refused. She went dancing occasionally with Margaret to the Jubilee Hall when her boyfriend worked away, as Nancy stayed with her own family at weekends. Sometimes, Shirley would allow a young man to walk her home and arrange to go to the pictures on the following evening. Through the week, she would visit a friend's home or go for a walk with Nancy. When Nancy and Harry became a permanent feature, Shirley would stay in and read in her bedroom quite often. Jimmy's letters would get an airing, and she still shed a tear when she read them.

Shirley began to collect the *Red Letter* magazine on her way home from work and would read with interest of other women and their views of men, hoping they would enlighten her problem with Jimmy in the stories they printed. Also, she would enter the competitions and occasionally win. If it was household things, she would place them in her bottom drawer for when she married, if she ever did.

Eventually, both Margaret and Nancy were courting seriously, so on Saturday evenings, she went dancing to the Jubilee Hall in Dukinfield alone. Although she was on her own, she soon got to know many of the girls there and joined a group of them. They included her with everything they did, and she found herself going for a drink with them on occasional evenings. Shirley didn't drink much, so a glass of cider was more than enough for her, but at least she was getting out and about.

Shirley began to enjoy herself and decided that she had grieved for Jimmy long enough. He wasn't her Jimmy anymore. He belonged to Audrey. She had to get him out of her system and move on.

A trip to Blackpool was organized by one of the girls on a Saturday. They were going dancing at the Tower Ballroom for the evening. It made a change, and Shirley looked forward to it. They all took the train and intended to make their way to the Tower, until one of them suggested they walk down the Golden Mile first. All the different sideshows fascinated Shirley, as she had never walked the mile at night before. It was an education that she quite enjoyed. That night she had a little more to drink than usual, so she was glad to get into bed when she eventually arrived home.

On Sunday morning, Shirley was in bed suffering with a headache.

"Never again," she muttered to herself, and her thoughts turned to Jimmy. If she were with him, she wouldn't have drunk any alcohol, and if she did, he wouldn't have allowed her to drink too much. She had to give up the idea that they would live happily ever after. He was with Audrey, and she had to accept it. She wondered if she would ever meet him again and hoped they would, but when she was happily married with someone else, otherwise it would break her heart. Would she ever meet anyone else? Somehow she doubted it. A spinster's life would be hers. There was a snag, though, as she wanted children—Jimmy's children, unfortunately. She could always marry a man just for children. No, that wouldn't be very nice.

Shirley realized there were voices coming from downstairs, but it was muffled, and she couldn't hear them very well. A short while later, there were footsteps coming up the stairs, and Mam opened her bedroom door with a small paper bag in her hand.

"Oh, you're awake? These are for you."

Shirley sat up quickly, and her mother thrust the bag into her hand, and then left with a smile on her face. Opening the paper bag, she found it was full of pear drops. She frowned and wondered who had bought them. She still liked them, but her taste had changed, and she much preferred chocolate now. Was it Jonathon? Curiosity made her get up. Slipping into her dressing gown and slippers, she went downstairs.

Opening the kitchen door, she asked "Where have these come fr—?" and looked straight at Jimmy, who was standing by the table.

"Do you want a cup of tea, dear?" Ruth asked.

Shirley stood transfixed as she and Jimmy both stared at each other.

"What are you doing here?" Shirley asked. "And where's Audrey?"

Jimmy hesitated, and then took a step towards her, while Ruth made the tea and poured out three cups, placing two of them in front of Shirley and Jimmy.

"I've come to see you…and Audrey's at home. Where else would she be?"

"Are you going to marry her?"

"No! I don't think her husband would like that."

"Is she married now?"

"She's always been married. Well, as long as I've known her, anyway."

"I don't understand." Shirley waited for an explanation.

Jimmy closed the gap between them and stood close to Shirley. "I thought I'd pop round and see what you're up to."

"Not a lot." Shirley found herself tongue-tied as she looked up into his face. Couldn't he see how much she was aching for him to put his arms around her?

"How about you, Jimmy?"

"I wanted to see how my best girl was."

"I'm fine."

"Don't I get a cuddle?"

Shirley went closer, and Jimmy wrapped his arms around her.

"Silly girl. What am I going to do with you? There was never anything between Audrey and me other than a deep friendship. She is quite a woman." With trepidation, Jimmy started to kiss her face and neck, and Shirley struggled free of him.

"Then why did you go and live with her?"

"I was ill, Shirley, very ill, and Audrey has a big heart. I had consumption and didn't know if I would live or die. You know I had no home and no one to look after me, and believe me I needed someone to care for me. There was Sue, but it would have been an imposition to ask her, even though she's told me in no uncertain terms that I should have felt that I could. Audrey thought it would be easier for me to live with her and her husband, John, and little boy. John is a very good man. Very understanding and a terrific doctor, too. He's helped me to get a job in the hospital. Also, it was easier for the hospital to keep their eye on me, and I could save a lot of travelling."

"Are you cured now?"

"Strong and hearty. Come here." Jimmy pulled her close.

Again he began to kiss her cheek and neck, and Shirley allowed him to do it. She felt as if she was dreaming as she placed her arms around his neck and offered her lips. Ruth silently slipped out of the kitchen to leave them alone.

"I thought you didn't want me anymore. I thought you and Audrey were together and I'd lost you."

"I know. Under the circumstances, I thought it was better if I didn't put you straight. At least if anything happened to me, you were getting on with your life."

"You devil! Why? You really made me suffer, do you know?"

"I wasn't sure that I would survive at the time."

Shirley looked at him, horrified! "I didn't know you were that ill. You never said."

"I know I didn't. It was best that way."

"Oh, Jimmy. I wish you'd told me. I went through hell."

"You were jealous, weren't you?"

"Too true I was...and look at me still in my pyjamas. I must look an absolute mess. My hair...if I'd have known you were coming, I'd have been dressed."

"You're gorgeous just the way you are." His face changed, and he looked serious. "There isn't anyone else, is there? I never thought to ask."

"Oh, Jimmy!"

Chapter 24

Shirley and Jimmy spent a lot of time alone in the front room talking it all through. He told her he was staying with Sue while he was here.

"Sue's been great with me, right from as long as I can remember. I was as much at home with her as I was at Gran's. At first, she lived with her mam and dad, but they were old when she was born, so they've gone now. She's smashing. You'd like her."

"Is she married?"

"No, and is that green-eyed monster working overtime again?"

"I just wondered, that's all."

"Sue's much older than me, and we didn't have that kind of relationship anyway."

"How much older?"

"What are you like?" Jimmy bent over and kissed her. "Behave."

"I'm just curious, that's all.'

They went for a walk to Stamford Park so they could be alone. Shirley was elated and couldn't believe what was happening. They talked about their plans for the future, but Shirley noticed she wasn't mentioned in his plans. He said that he worked in the hospital in Liverpool, but when he met the right girl, he would ask for a transfer to the hospital where they chose to live. Could that mean Ashton-under-Lyne, she wondered?

Shirley lay in bed the following morning, thinking about the day before and how lucky she was, Jimmy had returned to her, and everything was looking great. He was staying here in Ashton, and she was happy. Shirley wondered if he was still in bed and what he was thinking. How did he really feel about her? Was he serious? She couldn't believe what happened yesterday, and she felt glad she hadn't turned her back on him and given up. It almost happened, but not quite, and now they were a couple. Jimmy and Shirley…it sounded good.

"Are you getting up, Shirley?" Ruth called up the stairs for her.

Shirley didn't want to get up; she wanted to stay where she was and think about yesterday and Jimmy.

"Coming," Shirley called back to Ruth and, climbing out of bed, put on her dressing gown, and went into the bathroom. This morning she was extra careful that she made a good job of her hair and gave her teeth a good brush. She tried breathing into her hand and then smelling it to see if her breath was fresh, but it didn't work, so she left it to luck.

When Shirley came to dress herself, she took extra care about her clothes. She must look her best for Jimmy. They had both waited a long time for this, so she had to look good. She tried on a few different things before she came across her lucky dress. Whenever she wore it, she had a good time. It was this dress she wore when she met Peter again at the Jubilee Hall. Come to think about it, that wasn't a memorable experience. She thought again about yesterday. Jimmy looked gorgeous. She'd forgotten how handsome he could look. She put on her lucky dress after all, as it felt comfortable, and maybe fate would be on her side today. Shirley went downstairs.

"Good morning, sleeping beauty," Ruth said as she looked up and down at her daughter. "You've been busy up there, but I'm glad you're wearing that dress. I've always liked you in that."

"Thanks, Mam. I thought I'd better be ready for when he comes to pick me up."

"Where are you going?"

Shirley shrugged her shoulders, "I don't know."

"As long as you're with Jimmy, eh?"

"Something like that, yes." Shirley smiled at her mother. "So, do you and Dad like him?"

"He seems a nice lad. You like him, and that's all that matters, really."

"Yes, I know, but I like to think I have your approval, too."

"You have, dear."

After Shirley had finished her breakfast, there was a knock on the door. When Ruth went to answer it, she found Jimmy standing there with a bunch of flowers. Ruth told him to come in, and he walked to the kitchen and opened the door where Shirley stood alone and gave them to her.

Shirley gave a nervous laugh. "What are these for?"

"For the girl I desire."

Ruth came up behind him. "And we'll have none of that," she laughed as she took the flowers off Shirley. "I'll put these in water for you."

Jimmy went closer and kissed Shirley on the cheek. "Good morning, beautiful."

Shirley couldn't believe this was happening. She must be dreaming.

"Good morning, Jimmy." Shirley felt shy and awkward. Did she look all right? She caught her reflection in the mirror on the wall. She seemed to be okay.

"Sue would like to meet you, Shirley, so she's invited us both to tea. Is that okay?"

Shirley felt a little dubious. What if Sue didn't like her? If she didn't, it could put Jimmy off her.

"Must we?"

"Shirley! Of course we must. I think that's really nice of her...don't you?"

"It's just that we have so much catching up to do ourselves."

"We'll have the rest of our lives to do that."

Shirley was taken aback. Does that mean that Jimmy wanted to marry her? He must have it in his mind for him to say things like that.

"You're right. Yes, we can go for tea. I'm dying to meet her, and it is nice of her to want to meet me."

§§§§§§

Shirley and Jimmy went shopping first. They looked at many things, and Jimmy bought her a pink blouse and a necklace with pink stones of the same colour. She was thrilled with her gifts and wished she had worn a skirt, and then she could wear the blouse right away.

Jimmy then took her to the house where Sue lived. Shirley stood outside and waited until Jimmy opened the garden gate for her. The privets were trimmed and neat, and the garden was tidy. Shirley wondered what Sue would be like, and she imagined her to be quite old and plump with graying hair. Sue wasn't what she expected. She was slim, and although older, nowhere near as old as she expected her to be, and she had fair hair. Shirley was introduced to Sue and found her easy to talk to. The woman had made a special effort and presented them with a lovely meal, which they both enjoyed. After, Sue had a record collection that she allowed them to rummage through. Jimmy came up with a record that stirred memories for him.

"Hey, I remember this one. You used to play it a lot, Sue."

"You remember that?"

"I do."

Shirley noticed that Sue had tears in her eyes.

"Play it, Jimmy."

"It has a special meaning, doesn't it?" Shirley whispered, and through Sue's tears, she nodded.

When they cleared the table, Shirley offered to help Sue with the washing up in the kitchen while Jimmy played the records he'd chosen.

Shirley wiped the crockery while Sue washed the pots. "I hope that tune didn't upset you too much, Sue. It's the last thing we'd want to do."

"It brought back memories—some of them good, and some of them bad. I cried for both of them because I'm an idiot."

"If you're an idiot, you're a lovely one."

"Aww, bless you. You know, I think we're going to get on fine, don't you think so?"

"There's no reason why we shouldn't. I think we both love Jimmy, so we have that in common."

To Shirley's surprise, Sue burst into tears. "You would share him with me, wouldn't you? I couldn't bear to lose him."

"Of course I would. You won't lose him."

Sue dabbed at her eyes. "There's something I should tell you. I think it's time I did, now that my parents are gone and, of course, Gran, bless her.' Sue left the sink and sat on one of the kitchen chairs and motioned for Shirley to sit next to her.

"I'm Jimmy's mother."

Shirley was more shocked than surprised. "You're not old enough." Shirley realized that Sue was serious. "Are you really? Does Jimmy know?"

"No, not yet. No one knows. I haven't told a soul. I was only just fifteen when Jimmy was born. When I found out I was expecting, which was difficult as I was naïve and knew nothing, I couldn't tell my parents. They were very strict and couldn't have lived with the scandal. I wore loose-fitting clothes. You know, no belt and sloppy jumpers and blouses. My parents thought it was puppy fat. They never guessed."

"What do you think would have happened if they had found out?'

"It doesn't bear thinking about, but I'm sure they would have insisted that my baby went into a home, and I couldn't have that."

"What about Jimmy's father? Didn't he have something to say about it?"

"He was as naïve as I. I don't think either of us knew what we'd done until it was too late. Then along came Jimmy."

"How awful! Mind you, I'm glad."

Sue smiled. "Yes, he's a lovely lad, and I'm proud of him, but it was awful. When I started with labour pains, I didn't know what to do at first, and then I knew my friend's parents were away for the day, and she was on her own in the house. I'd already told her I was pregnant, so I ran over. I told her I thought I was having the baby, and she helped me to deliver him in the bathroom. It was easier to clean up in there as there was oilcloth on the floor. No one would guess what had happened after we finished. My friend scrubbed it clean. It wasn't easy, as we were both kids with no knowledge of giving birth, but we managed."

"Who was your friend?"

"It doesn't matter now, as she has died, but she was a good friend, and I knew I could count on her to keep quiet about it…and she did. She'd heard something about the cord that was attached to the baby, so she got some string and tied it round the cord, and then guessed about where to cut it. I was no help there. I was absolutely terrified. When I looked at Jimmy, I fell in love. He seemed to look right through me as if to say, 'What are you doing, you silly girl?'"

"Gosh! I bet it was messy."

"Oh, yes. My friend was marvelous, though, and let me hold Jimmy while she cleaned up. She became a nurse when she left school, and I believe she made a good one, bless her! He was a lovely baby. His little hands and toes with nails. I was fascinated. His hair was a mop of curls. He was perfect, or I thought so anyway. It broke my heart when I had to leave him."

"So why did you leave Jimmy in the porch at Gran's house? Weren't you afraid of him getting cold? The floor's tiled, isn't it?"

"I didn't leave him on the bare tiles. My friend gave me a few old newspapers, so I placed them underneath him, put a towel on the top of them, and wrapped him in another towel to keep him warm."

"Didn't your parents wonder where their towels had gone?"

"Don't tell anyone, but I took them off somebody's washing line when they weren't looking."

"What if Gran hadn't wanted him?"

"That never crossed my mind."

"Why Gran? Why did you choose her porch?"

"I knew her. I knew she was a lovely lady, and she was always so nice with us children. Gran would give us sweets, and she always had patience with us and listened to what we had to say. She was never one for complaining about the children playing and making a noise. As she didn't have any children of her own, I thought she would make a perfect mother for my son, and I would see him growing up. Was I bad? What do you think?"

"I think you've had a bad time, but it's over now, and I'm sure Jimmy would be really pleased to find that you're his mam. After all, he appears to think a lot about you."

"No, don't tell him. He might never want to see me again, and I'd hate that. I love him so much, and he's made a lovely man."

"I'll agree with you there. What happened to his dad?"

"He married and went to live in Australia. I went to watch him get married and thought, I know something you don't, when I looked at his bride. I didn't say anything, though. I couldn't do that to him."

"Have you lost touch with him now?"

Sue nodded. "Many years ago. I could never find him now. That song, 'It Had to be You,' was the song he used to sing to me when we were together. He wasn't very good at singing, but it meant a lot to me at the time. I thought he was wonderful."

"Does Jimmy look like his dad?"

"Yes, he has dark wavy hair like him, and his dad was good-looking, too."

Shirley leaned over to Sue and gave her a hug. "You're a very special lady. Are you going to tell Jimmy?"

"I can't."

"I wish you would. I'll let you go in there with him on your own if you want."

"I don't know. What do you think?"

"It's up to you."

Sue hesitated, and at that minute, they heard Jimmy shout.

"Eh, Sue, come here a minute."

Sue looked at Shirley. "I suppose I should. Wish me luck." The door clicked behind her.

Shirley could hear them talking, but not what they were saying. She finished washing and drying the pots and tidied up. They were still talking, so she sat on one of the chairs and waited, but not for long.

The kitchen door burst open and Jimmy stood there with a surprised look on his face. "She told you?"

"Yes, Jimmy, she told me."

"Isn't that wonderful? I have a mam, after all. Pity about my dad, though. Still, I'm not grumbling. At least I know where I belong now. I actually belong...and that's wonderful." Jimmy grabbed hold of Shirley and danced round with her in his arms. Sue came in and stood laughing. When Jimmy finally settled down, they went back in the front room.

"I vaguely remember you, Sue, when I was a little boy. I remember you taking me on the swings somewhere."

"In the park. I took you in the park."

"You were always there for me from as far back as I can remember."

"Of course, I'm your mam."

Jimmy left Shirley's side and went over to Sue and held her. "What a shame Gran never knew, or did she? I wonder . . ."

"I don't know, but I couldn't tell her. I felt as if I'd cheated her all those years."

"No, she wouldn't have thought that. She told me many times that she was lucky keeping me, and she blessed the day she found me, as I gave her a lot of pleasure."

"Really?"

"Yes, Mam." Sue screamed with delight at those words before she shed tears. "And now, when it's the right time, I can ask my favourite girl to marry me," Jimmy said as he looked at Shirley.

"Why not before now, son?"

Jimmy grinned at Sue. "Because now I know who I am."

Chapter 25

Jonathon still had problems with Michèle. She didn't want to go out any-more and would sit inside the house listening to the wireless, even on a sunny day. When the accumulator was ready for changing, he would go and get it done, and she would wait impatiently for him to replace it.

The shopping, she was quite happy to let Jonathon do. He tried to coax her into going with him, but she declined. There was always an excuse—Jan wasn't very well, or she had a headache—so he would take Jan with him. He blamed her indifference on the weight of the shopping at first, but underneath, he knew there was something else.

"Do you fancy a trip to the countryside this weekend?" Jonathon asked her one Friday.

"No, there's a programme on the wireless I don't want to miss."

"I thought it would make a nice change. We could walk over the brushes or go to Hartshead Pike and then call at a farm for a glass of fresh milk. I think Jan would enjoy it."

"No, I don't fancy it, Jonathon."

"Oh, Michèle, why don't you tell me what's wrong?" Jonathon pleaded.

"Nothing's wrong." That was always her answer.

"But poor Jan never gets taken out anymore."

"He's fine."

Jonathon worried about Michèle. She was still bursting into tears too easily. Why couldn't he get to the bottom of it all? She kept insisting that everything was okay, and even poor Jan was bewildered, but Jonathon knew there was something wrong. He worried about her feelings for him and hoped she wasn't having a change of heart. When he met her in France, she was full of life and energy. Now she was a shell of the woman he knew. Could it be because she became a mother…or a prisoner?

Jonathon went home from work at every opportunity. If he went out for cakes, he slipped home. If it was an emergency order, he slipped home. Any excuse he would go home and check on Michèle.

"Jonathon, you're home again, how lovely," Michèle would exclaim sometimes.

"Just checking that everything's all right."

"It's fine."

"And Jan? Is he okay?"

Michèle would frown as she answered him. "Jan's fine, too."

Jonathon still wasn't happy, because sometimes she would greet him in tears.

One day he insisted that he take them both out and took them to Bell Vue for the day. They prepared sandwiches and a flask before they went. Once Michèle was away from the house, she changed and became more herself. They had never been before, and Jan was thrilled to see the animals. They laughed at the monkeys, and Jonathon said how familiar they looked, comparing them with people he knew, especially one that turned its back on them—they noticed it had a Technicolor bottom. Jonathon said it looked like Voidt. Michèle thought that was really funny and laughed her loudest. At first, Jan was afraid of the lions and the way they roared, but Jonathon had to admit that they were frightening.

They ate their sandwiches on the grass and took their time to empty the flask, and then walked around the fairground. Putting Jan on one of the roundabouts frightened him at first until they began to wave at him every time he came round. He would wave back and laugh and didn't want to come off it when the ride was over.

§ § § § §

It was getting close to Christmas, and Jonathon came home with a Christmas tree.

"Oh, Jonathon, it's a lovely tree." Michèle's eyes lit up with the sight.

Jan was excited, and Jonathon and Michèle began to decorate it. Jonathon had been given three light bulbs painted red, blue, and green from his dad that were from when he was younger. Christmas tree lights were hard to get hold of, so he placed the bulbs towards the middle of the tree. They had only three glass balls, so after placing them on the tree, they dotted cotton wool about to fill it up. It looked full and pretty, and Jan clapped his hands with glee. It felt good to see Michèle happy, too.

The next time he went home unexpectedly, he passed Voidt coming out of the entry into the street and wondered if he had visited Michèle. When he opened the door with his key, he found Michèle hiding under the table with Jan.

"What on earth are you doing there?" Jonathon asked with surprise.

Michèle crawled out from beneath the table and stood on her feet. "I'm sorry, Jonathon."

"What the hell is going on?"

"That naughty man came, Daddy, and Mummy was fwightened, but shhh! Don't tell anyone, it's a secwet."

"Michèle, an explanation, please?"

"Oh, Jonathon." Her eyes filled with tears.

"I want to know what's going on, for God's sake."

"I don't want to tell you."

Jonathon watched the tears running down her cheeks, but hardened himself. She had to tell him the truth before he went off his mind.

"I think it's about time you did, don't you?"

"All right, you asked for it, but it's against my better judgment. You won't love me anymore if I tell you. I know you won't."

"Oh, yes, I will."

Michèle gave him a doubtful look. "I don't think you will."

"I'm sure I will. Tell me now," Jonathon insisted.

Michèle broke down in tears. "That man," she choked back a sob. "He was in the Gestapo."

"What man?"

"Voidt."

Jonathon sucked in his breath. "In the camp where you were?"

"Yes."

Jonathon was taken aback. He wasn't expecting that. "And…there must be more."

Michèle burst out crying again. "I can't tell you."

Jonathon took her head in his hands and stared straight into her eyes. "Oh, yes, you can…everything…now."

"I hated it, Jonathon, I hated it. He was brutal, and Jan brought him home regularly to use me as a sex object."

"Only him?" She looked as if she was holding something back still, as her eyes wouldn't meet his. "Or were there more?"

"There were more men, but he was the most wicked and the most regular visitor."

"You don't need to tell me anymore if you don't wish to. I think I've heard enough."

"You mean it?"

"Yes. It would only upset me. What happened in the camp is over. You must forget it, because it will never happen again, and it wasn't your fault."

"But he's expecting to carry on with the abuse."

That shocked Jonathon. "He's what?"

"I'm sorry, Jonathon, but that's why he came round. He said that if I refuse, he will tell everyone what a whore I am."

"And you refused, I hope?"

"I made the excuse that I couldn't with Jan around, so he told me he would be back when Jan started school. He asked me when he would be starting school, and I had to tell him he was starting in September, so he said he would wait until then."

"So, why did I keep seeing him around here?"

"He pestered me and kept reminding me how long I had to go."

"And would you go through with it in September?"

"I've been out of my mind with worry. My mind has been full of ways I could get out of it. I even contemplated suicide. I didn't want to hurt you and Jan."

Jonathon rolled up his sleeves. "I'm not a fighting man, and I hate violence, but sometimes…"

"No, Jonathon. He's not worth it. He's a vicious man, and I don't want you to get hurt."

"He's a coward. I've come across men like that before, especially in the war. He doesn't know what vicious is, but he soon will."

As he left the house, he heard Michèle trying to call him back, but he ignored her. He had a mission to complete, and nothing was going to stop him.

§ § § § §

Jonathon walked to the registrar's house and banged the doorknocker loudly. There was no answer, so he walked round to the back garden. He couldn't see the man, but there was a shed, and Jonathon looked in there. Just before he closed the door, he heard a noise. Going over to a pile of sacks behind an old door that was propped up at the back, he found Voidt hiding underneath. Grabbing him by the collar, he pulled him to his feet and dragged him outside.

"You grubby little coward," he said before he thumped him in the face. Jonathon heard a crack, and Voidt's nose exploded. "Don't you dare go and see my wife and threaten her. She isn't your prisoner any more, and you have me to deal with now."

"Please don't kill me…p-p-please," the man stuttered.

"Kill you! I'd rather give you a bit of the treatment you gave out to her, but I'm not in your league. Killing you isn't good enough, though." As he said it, Jonathon thumped him again and again. Voidt tried very hard to get away, but there was no way Jonathon was going to let him.

"Stop right there," someone called.

Jonathon kept hold of the collar of Voidt's jacket and looked round. There was a policeman walking towards him, but he didn't lose his hold on Voidt.

"I think I know what you intend to do…but don't, that's against the law."

Jonathon's knuckles were red with blood, and it wasn't his. "How did you know I was here? As if I didn't know."

"It was your wife. She was worried."

Jonathon looked at the registrar and found him smirking, but the policeman also had noticed it.

"You can wipe that sickly smile off your face. His wife was worried about *him*, not you." The policeman took a close look into Voidt's face, and then turned to Jonathon. "I gather he fell?"

"No…" Then Jonathon noticed the look the policeman was giving him. "Yes, he fell."

"We have a prison cell that has your name on it, sunshine. Come on. I think someone has been looking for you. The policeman took hold of Voidt.

Jonathon left them both in the garden while the policeman went through his routine. He couldn't wait to go home to Michèle and hold her. His wife had been through so much, but no way would he allow some sniffling German escapee upset her anymore. Now it was all over, and he was eager to tell her she could put it all behind her. When he turned the key to go inside the house, he could hear Michèle crying.

"Oh, Jonathon!" Michèle cried. "I was so afraid that he would hurt you. I told the police."

"I know."

"Have you seen the police?"

"Yes. The scoundrel is now in the hands of the law."

Michèle sobbed. "Did he hurt you?"

"No."

"Where has all the blood come from? What happened?"

"I left my mark, so let's just say that he won't be forgetting me for a long time."

"Honestly, Jonathon. What will happen now?"

"That's for the courts to decide. All I know is his days of pestering you are over, my love."

"Oh, Jonathon." Michèle wrapped her arms around him and held him tight.

"I think we shall start hunting for a house. We'll get you away from here and all its bad memories and make a fresh start."

"Can we afford it?"

"It doesn't matter; we'll do it. Go into debt, if necessary."

"I don't think that would be very wise, Jonathon."

"I don't care. Maybe my mam and dad can lend me the deposit."

Michèle covered his mouth with two fingers. "No, Jons."

"Don't you want to move?"

"Eventually, but not until we can afford it. When Jan starts school, I can work part-time, and we can put a little more money away for the deposit, but until then, we'll stay here."

Jonathon hugged her. "Are you sure?"

"I'm sure."

"I thought you would feel better away from here, where you'd have your own space, and a garden where you can grow a few flowers if you want."

"And potatoes and vegetables for you. I know, it's your dream…and it will happen soon enough."

"Well, at least we can make plans now."

Just then Jan came over to them. He must have thought he was missing something, as he placed his arms around both of them as far as they would go and clutched them, and both Michèle and Jonathon laughed.

"Happy, my *peu sorcière?*" Jonathon asked as he put his arms around them both.

"Happy. *Je t'aime,* Jonathon."

Jonathon noticed the tears in her eyes and dropped his hand from around Jan to wipe them away with his fingers.

Michèle looked at him. "Are you crying, too?" and she smiled as she used her fingers to wipe his tears away. "My hero."

"Don't be silly," Jonathon sniffled. "Heroes don't cry."

~THE END~

I DIDN'T UNDERSTAND

When I was young, active, free.

Didn't have much sympathy

for old folk with their aches and pains,

moans and groans, and their complains.

The way they walked so slowly, I

would hurry past in a blink of eye,

and wonder why they walked so slow,

when they had legs why wouldn't they "go"?

I didn't understand.

And in my teens I would listen to

the way things were before I grew.

Couldn't grasp how things had changed.

In their day it sounded strange.

No employment, money, fun,

and working until day was done.

I couldn't see them young at all

now they were bent and I stood tall.

I didn't understand.

They talked about the war that raged,

and Hitler with his cruel ways.

Air raid shelters to share their fears

with friends they knew, and shedding tears

for men who fought, but never returned.

Mums, dads, and everyone yearned

for things to be as once they were,

before nightmares that would often recur.

I didn't understand.

Now the years have travelled fast

I think about my misused past,

and moan and groan of how I feel,

youth of today, the weather's ordeal,

food I eat and films I've seen,

the government, the hospital scene.

With MRSA and something new,

How can we change it? What can we do?

Then there's contamination of our air.

Does anyone, anywhere really care?

Don't they understand?

—Denise Buckley

Lightning Source UK Ltd.
Milton Keynes UK
UKOW050001150713

213792UK00001B/7/P